SUPERHEAT

A Daniel Serrano Robles Crime Thriller

of Deception & Violence

by M.B.Wood

This novel – Superheat – is a work of fiction. Names, characters and incidents are the product of the author's imagination or are used fictitiously. Any resemblance to actual events, locales, or persons, living or dead, is entirely coincidental.

FAUCETT Publishing L.L.C.

Printed in the United States of America

Other Works Available from M.B.Wood
available at Amazon.com

Hunted

Blowout

Trash

Please visit my website and drop by to say hello. I love to
hear from my readers:

www.malcolm-wood.com

Chapter 1

Las Vegas, August 9, 1969.

A fist pounded deep into O'Brien's guts and drove the air from his lungs. Gasping, he staggered into the wall of the office. A blue mist filled his vision. The vertical stripes on the silk wallpaper seemed to sway like tall grass in the wind.

The man with arms bigger than most people's thighs picked him up off his feet by his coat lapels with no apparent effort and slammed him against the wall. "Don't ever be late with your vig." The man's raspy voice was flavored with garlic, whiskey and cigarette smoke. The man relaxed his grip.

As O'Brien sagged, the man's knee slammed into O'Brien's groin. A bright flash of pain dimmed his world. He collapsed to the floor, all strength gone from his legs. He tried to catch his breath as he rolled onto his side. The carpeting felt rough against his face as his chin slid on its pile.

The man's foot slammed into O'Brien's stomach.

He gasped. The man kicked him, higher, in the ribs. O'Brien's vision faded as the blue mist intensified.

Someone grabbed him by his hair and dragged him to his feet.

"You fuckin' chump," a voice said. "Don't ever say you can't pay. This is nothing to what you'll get if you don't cough up. Understand?"

O'Brien tried to nod as the world spun about him. For the first time in a long, long time, he was afraid, very afraid.

"I can't hear you!"

A fist slammed into his ribs again. These people were doing to him what he'd done to others. He'd always assumed his size and strength made him immune to this type of treatment. At six feet and two hundred twenty pounds of lean muscle, it'd been true once. "Yes," he gasped.

"Yes, what, asshole?"

The man grabbed his shirt under his throat and twisted, lifting him upwards. He couldn't breathe. The world began to spin and fade.

"Joey, let him go. He can't talk like that." It was the smaller man who spoke in a quiet voice filled with East Coast precision, hard and polished, steely and without mercy.

"I oughta kick the shit outa this asshole for sayin' he might pay us back. Who the fuck he think he is?"

The quiet voice spoke again. "If he doesn't pay, then you take care of him, capisce?" His words tapped out like a delicate hammer on hot steel. "Mr. O'Brien, I can reach out and touch you, anywhere. Every Friday you will give two hundred dollars to my man in Akron until you repay the entire two grand, capisce?"

O'Brien looked up at the withered, almost scrawny man in the gray silk suit who had spoken. His mouth was thin, without lips, snake-like. His pallor was pasty, lifeless. The man leaned forward in the over-stuffed burgundy leather chair, his manicured hands white on the wide mahogany desk.

O'Brien caught a breath. "Who's that?"

"He'll contact you next week, at your home." The man in the silk suit tossed O'Brien's wallet toward him. It landed at his feet. "If you run, we'll find you. We know enough about you to get you, no matter where you go." He nodded toward the big man. "Get him out of here." He waved his hand as though he were shooing a fly.

Joey grabbed O'Brien by the arm and twisted it into a lock that would have been a credit to any police officer. He pushed O'Brien out into the hallway and marched him down to the end of a corridor. Joey kicked open a heavy metal door with a loud bang. They entered a trash-strewn alleyway between towering walls of pink stucco lined with large blue rubbish containers. It was the service road behind the casino.

"The boss didn't say it, but I will," Joey said. "You

don't pay, I put your pieces in one of those." He jerked his thumb toward a dumpster overflowing with trash. "Understand?"

O'Brien winced from the movement. "I got you."

"Now get the fuck out of here." Joey threw O'Brien to the ground. The door shut with a loud metallic clang that echoed off the tall walls. He was alone.

O'Brien crawled onto his knees and vomited until nothing more came up. He staggered toward the street, every step an effort. He hurt all over. He had no money, only an airline ticket to get home.

#

At forty-four years of age, Patrick O'Brien, chief of security at Schirmerling Tire & Rubber in Akron, Ohio, found his luck had finally run out in Las Vegas. He'd lost all of his money at the casino's tables. He wished he'd quit last month, when he got cleaned out. But no, he'd felt sure he could win back his losses. As a regular, he borrowed two grand worth of chips from the casino.

Maybe it was having the blonde babe on his arm, the one who kept whispering things she'd do to him later; maybe it distracted him. It was all gone, including the hooker.

After the casino cut him off, men escorted him to a back office to "solve his credit problem." The man who bought his casino debt was small and was immaculately dressed. He acted as though it was a regular business transaction. The other man was very large, bulging out of his blue pinstriped polyester suit.

It was almost like being in a bank, providing information for a loan application, including lots of details about his home, job, and relatives. Even the office, with its silk wallpaper and mahogany furniture, reminded O'Brien of the offices at the bank he used in Akron.

As soon as he signed the "loan document," the smaller man's attitude changed. "You gotta stay current with the interest, the vigorish, or we call the loan. The vig's two hundred bucks every Friday, capisce?"

"That's a lot of interest," O'Brien said. "I might have trouble paying that amount. Can't you do better than that?"

"Joey," said the smaller man. "Straighten him out."

That's when the pain began.

#

After O'Brien landed at Cleveland Hopkins Airport, he called Blodgett, one of his security staff at Schirmerling, to come and pick him up. The drive to Akron seemed long.

The next day, after a soak in a bathtub with Epsom salts, he went over his finances. Between alimony payments and the vig, he had very little money left. He was in deep shit. He needed to make a score, a big one, to get this monkey off his back. He had to find a way to get some dough, and quick.

Chapter 2

August 11, 1969.

A staccato bang shook the dusty red brick walls of the power plant. The banshee scream of superheated steam followed, drowning the rumble of machinery. Overhead pipes rattled, releasing a cloud of gray dust. Brown dust billowed up from the turbines.

Daniel Serrano Robles ran toward the sound of the wild steam, climbing the steel-grate steps two at a time to reach the mezzanine. Steam billowed out of the door to the manifold room, turning the glare of the mercury vapor lamps into rainbow-colored halos.

Daniel slid to a stop, looking for the main shut-off valve, searching his memory. *Nothing in this damn plant is logical. It's cobbled together with junk and cheap substitutions.*

This assignment in Monterrey, Mexico, had come about because he was an engineer who spoke Spanish. The owners needed a certified engineer's report verifying the plant's capacity and operational safety to support its sale price. Luck had run out on the plant's owners, or perhaps it was too much neglect over too much time. After a week, Daniel came to the conclusion that the plant needed a major rebuild or abandonment.

Ah, got it, Daniel thought. As he cranked the main steam line's valve shut, rust splintered off its stem, a testimony to its infrequent use. The high-pitched scream of steam moving at near supersonic speed sighed into silence, yielding to the animal-like whimpers of human suffering.

Oh, God, no, Daniel thought. *Someone's in there.* As the fog thinned, he entered the manifold room. A thin jet of steam still whispered from a rusty rosette of jagged metal, the remnants of the burst pipe. A clump lay on the floor, unmoving, mewling like an exhausted cat. It was the floor sweeper, the old man with an ever-present smile and cheerful greetings.

Daniel gently touched the man on his shoulder. "Por favor, digame." Please, speak to me.

The man's moans faded. He whispered, "Ayudame, señor."

Help you? Daniel thought. *How?* The man's face had the red flush of a boiled lobster, and his bare feet under the ragged leather sandals were the same brilliant hue. *You poor soul, you've been cooked.* With care, he picked up the man and staggered down the stairs into cooler air. The distance to the infirmary was twice, no, ten times the distance he remembered, and the man's weight seemed to grow steadily. Silent staring faces watched his progress.

Daniel backed through swinging double doors and placed the man on a table. "¡Auxilio!" he called for help.

A heavy-set woman, bulging bosom tightly restrained by a stained white uniform, plodded into the room, her jaw methodically chewing. As her eyes caught the injured man, they dilated like those of a frightened cat and her mouth froze. She leaned over the man's motionless body and touched his wrist, checking his pulse. "No puedo ayudarlo," she said. I can't help him.

"Por qué no?" Daniel asked. Why not?

"Murió," she said. He's dead.

#

Daniel lugged his suitcase through the door to his apartment, his left hand full of mail. He'd just finished two back-to-back foreign assignments and upon his return to the home office of Matlock Engineering in Chicago, his manager had picked a fight with him. The manager had insisted Daniel write his report about the steam line break as if it were an unavoidable accident. The manager made it clear consulting engineers did nothing to 'damage' their clients. The manager insisted Daniel not write reports that implied negligence had caused the death of an unimportant worker.

Daniel's personal code of ethics, as well as being a registered professional engineer, conflicted with that order. When he tried to explain his views, his manager shouted him down. That incident and the manager's comment about Hispanics not understanding good business practices, confirmed to Daniel his days with Matlock were numbered.

The apartment smelled musty from being closed up during his absence of almost two months. After opening the windows, he turned to the mail he'd picked up at the post office and started sorting it. He had to get his overdue bills paid prior to calling Lisa.

She'd come into his life about six months earlier, lighting up his lonely existence. She'd introduced him to nightclubs, fine restaurants and places to go, something he'd been too insecure previously to do on his own. She'd made him realize there was nothing wrong with being thin and having a long face dominated by a big nose. And she didn't care that he was born in Mexico City. He started to think of her as 'The One' with whom he would settle down.

He shuffled through the letters, flicking most into the waste paper basket. A mauve envelope froze his hand. He recognized it as one from Lisa, like those intimate notes she sent. His heart beat faster. *How sweet of her, a little something to welcome me home.* He sniffed the envelope, but her personal scent was absent. The image of her presence filled his mind. The memory of her musky perfume, the warmth of her touch, and the way she aroused him, all came surging back.

He sliced open the envelope and pulled out a single sheet of mauve paper. He unfolded it and began to read.

Daniel, I've met someone else who can be with me and doesn't run off to distant places doing who knows what. You didn't even call or write me while you were gone, leaving me by myself, all alone. I've found that someone who cares about me, who makes me happy. I know you'll try to call me. Don't bother, it won't work. Lisa.

He'd tried a dozen times to call her from Mexico, but the combination of a third world telephone system and timing had frustrated his efforts. He also knew better than to mail letters in Mexico. He'd hoped she'd understand.

10

Daniel's guts lurched. *Oh, no, Lisa, please don't.* He grabbed the phone and dialed her number. After several rings, a voice answered. For an instant his heart soared.

"The number you have reached is not a working number. Please try again, or dial an operator."

Daniel called an operator and learned Lisa had changed her number to one that was unlisted. A wave of anger and fear swept over him. First Matlock and now Lisa. He opened a Stroh's beer and eased into the armchair and reread her letter several times. The words tattooed an indelible image in his mind. His heart grew heavier. *Has my life hit a new low? How can things get any worse?*

#

The next day, Daniel dialed her office, only to have the PBX operator say, "Miss Lisa Kozlowski gave express instructions that calls from you will not be accepted."

"But, she's my..." He heard the phone click and the line go dead. "Damn it." He slammed the phone back onto its receiver. The weight in his chest grew larger, and the lump in his throat threatened to choke him. *She's my love... My everything.* The image of her filled his mind--her long blond hair, the smoothness of her pale skin, her voluptuous shape and her quick wit.

He'd met Lisa while at a downtown hotel for a legal seminar. They had literally bumped into each other. After mutual apologies, she'd asked him if he would keep her company while at the seminar's lunch. He'd hesitated for a moment, then agreed.

He now remembered she dumped her boyfriend for him. It had seemed unimportant at the time, for Lisa introduced him to a life he had never before experienced. They became lovers, and that's when he realized she was quite sophisticated. She taught him how to make love to a woman, how to use his hands and tongue in places that brought her to a moaning ecstasy. She also showed him how to extend the length of their lovemaking, opening new vistas of pleasure he had never before experienced.

Now she's gone. He stared at the work lying in front of him, not seeing it. *No, she doesn't want me anymore, because she's found someone new. It's not the first time she's done this. Dear God, let it not be this way. Please. I want her. I need her.*

It's this stupid job, here at Matlock that kept me away from her. Yet he knew if she really were the 'One,' a couple of months apart would not have made her love die so quickly. *If she would only give me another chance . . .*

#

Daniel pushed away the bowl of cereal. He couldn't eat. He felt as though he'd been in a battle and lost. Yesterday, he tried to get into Lisa's high-rise apartment building. The burly doorkeeper threatened to call the police, saying he'd been warned to watch for him. It was as though she had developed a system to keep him at bay.

His manager at Matlock had grown increasingly hostile. Daniel looked up at the clock. *I should go or I'll be late.* He hated the thought of going to work. He felt drained, defeated.

He slipped on a coat and headed for the bus stop. *Maybe it's time to call that headhunter. He says there's a position at Schirmerling Tire & Rubber in Akron, Ohio, a nice, respectable company. It's time for a change, a time for something better. And Akron is near Kent, where Hector, my brother lives. Yes, it's time.*

Chapter 3

August 18, 1969.

O'Brien forced a smile. "Where d'you keep your
inventory of chemicals and the record of those who used
them?" He sniffed. Over the weekend, he'd read a police
bulletin that listed the chemicals used to make illegal drugs.
It'd given him an idea.The chemical storeroom of STR's
Research Center had an acrid aroma, but not as strong as the
harsh stink of the tire curing department.

Beckham, the stockroom clerk, cigarette dangling
from his lip, glanced up over his black-rimmed glasses.
"Who're you?"

"Captain O'Brien. Chief of STR security. I need to
check your records." He showed his I.D. "It's a security
issue."

Beckham looked back and forth between the I.D. tag
and O'Brien. "Everything's in those files." He pointed at a
filing cabinet squeezed into a gap between the shelves that
ran from floor to ceiling filled with amber jars of many
different sizes. Next to it was a battered gray metal desk with
an in basket overflowing with paper. The yellow linoleum
tiles on the floor had begun to curl and the faded green walls
had the pale brown pallor that came from a long history with
nicotine.

"Every Friday, I go to the computer center. I put the
transactions onto punch cards so I can enter them into the
IBM 360. That's STR's main computer." He enunciated
every word clearly, implying it was a special skill and a real
privilege to use the computer. "I keep a temporary running
record in the card file over there." He pointed to three card
file boxes. "They're listed by chemical name, manufacturer,
and user."

"Show me." O'Brien forced another smile.

After Beckham showed him how the system worked,
O'Brien asked, "So, how d'you know when to reorder?"

Beckham explained in detail how he reordered the logged-in chemicals once a week. "It's verified once a year with an audit," he said. "'Cept every year, some chemicals come up short. There're people who come in when I'm gone and don't bother to sign out what they took. Lazy bastards." He lit another cigarette and walked O'Brien through the system.

O'Brien settled down at the battered desk and began to look through the files. He waited for Beckham to get busy. *C'mon, hurry up*, he thought. Once Beckham was occupied, O'Brien pulled out the list of chemicals from the advisory and began checking in the card files. It didn't take long to locate them.

He saw a Zach Rogan had taken out three kilograms of phenyl acetone over the last three months, which was listed in the police bulletin as one of many precursors for making methamphetamine. *Maybe*, he thought, *the problem of how to make real money has just solved itself.*

#

Zach Rogan hurried down to the company parking lot. He was ready for a beer or two and to put his feet up.

Flags hung limply from the poles lining the front of the sprawling three-story tan brick building that was STR's Research center. The concrete walkway leading to the asphalt parking lot amid neat landscaping was deserted. Heat from a late August sun shimmered off the blacktop parking lot. He wondered if the latest issue of Playboy had arrived.

"Yo, Rogan." A gruff voice shook him from his fantasy of what the new issue might contain. A big hand clamped on his arm and squeezed hard.

"Hey, man, that hurts." Rogan saw a tough-looking man dressed in a white shirt with a black tie and tan slacks. He had the tall, blocky build that shouted muscles. His face was thin with a well-etched frown and he had a shock of blond hair shot with gray. Rogan had seem him somewhere before.

Rogan tried to pull loose, but the grip tightened.

"Like, what d'you want, man?"

"Zach Rogan, right?" The man's eyebrows rose.

Rogan glance around quickly. If this was trouble, no one was nearby. "Yeah, that's me. Who're you?"

"Good, let's get something cold to drink. I've been waiting for you." He released Rogan's arm. "We've got some business to discuss. The business of you using phenyl acetone to make speed." The man nodded toward Rogan's shiny new black '69 Chevy Impala hardtop. "We'll take your car."

Is he a cop? Rogan felt a chill of fear. "I don't know anything about speed." The man's size made him nervous. "I use that chemical to make blocked curing agents for polyurethanes--"

"Yeah, yeah, right. Open the passenger's side first, then get in and drive. Go to the Big Boy Drive-In that's in Goodyear Heights. Y'know the place?" The man had maneuvered himself between Rogan and his car.

"I ain't going anywhere with you--"

"Don't be a dumb ass. I've got enough evidence to put you in the slammer for twenty years for making illegal drugs. I'm giving you a choice of jail or working with me." The man's voice was louder, harder. His eyes narrowed and his jaw protruded. "Get moving. And turn on the damn AC."

Rogan eyed the man and decided that running probably wouldn't work. There was something menacing about him. "Okay, I'll talk to you, but I don't know shit about any drugs. You got the wrong dude, man."

The man smiled.

A tremor of fear rippled through Rogan. The man's smile made him think of a cat about to pounce on a mouse.

"You took three kilos of phenyl acetone over the past three months. If you don't cooperate, I'll make sure the cops know everything about what you've taken--stuff you used to make drugs, got it?" The man smiled again with even more menace as he reached into his shirt pocket and pulled out a slip of paper. "You use all of this to make your blocked whatever? Three kilos' worth? I don't think so."

Oh, shit, thought Rogan, *it does look like a receipt from the chemical stockroom.* "Er, I guess we can talk."

"Good. Get in and drive." The man got into the front passenger seat. "Don't try anything stupid, either."

#

Over the next hour, Rogan learned O'Brien was the head of STR's security and he did have copies of the chemical records. However, it soon became obvious O'Brien wanted to move in on his drug making rather than put him in jail. "So, why should I cut you in?"

"I can get the chemicals without leaving a trail," O'Brien said. "I have access to STR facilities at any hour of the day, which brings up another thing. I can set you up in a lab that no one will ever find. No sense in getting caught."

Rogan had lived in constant fear someone who really knew chemical synthesis would quickly realize his story about making blocked curing agents for urethane polymers was bullshit. "You have some other place in mind?"

O'Brien nodded. "There's a room in the boiler house. A long time ago the security department used it. I can make it empty and secure. It has a bathroom and no windows."

"For real?" Rogan needed running water to cool the condenser and to run the vacuum evaporator. He thought about where it was located and shook his head. "I'd stand out like a sore thumb going in and out of the boiler house."

"Not if you wear company overalls. They make you invisible, especially evenings and weekends," O'Brien said.

"Yeah? Tell me how you think this is gonna work."

Chapter 4

October 12, 1969.

"So, the ether rinse is the last step?" O'Brien asked.
Two folding tables covered with lab glassware
crowded the bathroom of the former boiler house security
office. Water rushed continually down the drain of the sink,
barely audible against the constant rumble of the boiler
house machinery. Rubber hoses ran from an aspirator in the
sink to a glass-fronted vacuum box. The shelves in the
vacuum box held Petri dishes heaped high with a white
powder.

"The last step is vacuum drying. The rinse is the last
operation with a chemical." Rogan's tone of voice implied it
was a question only a dense student would ask.

"That gets it clean?" O'Brien made his eyebrows rise.
The kid's attitude made him want to punch his lights out.

"Right." Rogan nodded. "That's the final step to
making pure white crystal meth. This is the real deal-Neal.
Kick-ass speed." Rogan had said several times how proud he
was of the one-step hydrogenation process he'd perfected.
"You gotta try this. It's really boss. You'll be up doin' it all
night long."

"Yeah, right." O'Brien ran his eyes over the lab
setup. He was confident his notes fully covered the process.
"Maybe later. Look, we've got to move this batch. I need to
see some bread, understand? Like this is for real, get me?"

"I can dig it. This'll be dry by tomorrow. Then we
can package it up and ship it out. I'll call my contacts in San
Francisco to let them know I've got more ready."

"Why don't we get some chow while you explain
how it works?" O'Brien pointed toward the door.

"Sure. Let's grab some Chinese and go to my place."
Rogan licked his lips as though he could already taste it.

"Okay." O'Brien didn't care much for Chinese food,
but because Rogan loved it, he went along with his wishes.
He had to convince the kid they were partners. He needed

money. The damn vig was eating him alive.

#

The idea that any of the money went to Rogan, a longhaired asshole, was driving O'Brien crazy. In the last month Rogan had shipped out six one-pound lots and received six thousand dollars, of which, O'Brien got one half. With the debt gone, the extra thousand bucks were burning a hole in his pocket. He dropped in on Rogan at his apartment. It was time.

"So, Rogan, d'you have any customers other than this Fats guy in San Francisco?"

A small mirror with a trace of white powder sat in front of Rogan. From the stereo came Jim Morrison's mournful voice singing, "The Summer's Almost Gone." The shades were closed and the lights turned down low.

Rogan belched and shook his head. "Naw. It's just Fats. I don't want a buncha speed freaks bugging me all the time. He knows the scene." His face lit up like a little kid with a new toy. "Hey, I've been talking to a travel agent about going to Club Med in Jamaica. It's where all the chicks go."

"When d'you plan to go?"

"Mebbe in December. I figure that's the best time to go and score some pussy."

"I see." O'Brien nodded his head. *Dumb shit*, he thought, *who'd want to get it on with a scrawny, pimple-faced, dumb ass like him?* "Say, when you go on vacation, I can keep making meth. That way you'll have money waiting when you get back."

"Playboy says a lot of women go to Club Med just dying to get laid." Rogan's eyes lit up. "Yeah, and with a little helper," he nodded towards the mirror with the white powder, "I can ball all night long. Maybe even make it with two chicks in the same night."

O'Brien glanced at his watch. "Okay, cock hound, time to go to work. I got another batch of chemicals at the lab. Let's go." He forced his voice to remain low and calm.

18

He rose and headed toward the door.

"Aw, man, do we hafta go now? It's like, late, man."

O'Brien nodded. *I have to stay on track*, he thought. *No screw-ups.* "Less chance of anyone seeing us. If you want to go to Club Med and get laid, you're gonna need money. Let's go." As usual, they put on the blue overalls like those used by maintenance workers.

#

O'Brien steered his company car, a Ford Fairlane sedan, through the gate to STR's plant on Schirmerling Avenue. He parked in the shadows behind the boiler house. He waited five minutes without seeing anyone. "Okay, let's do it." They walked into the boiler house to the laboratory. He unlocked the door, and they went in.

Rogan leaned over the lab table and frowned. "Like, where's the phenyl acetone, man?" He picked through the amber colored jars, examining each label. "I don't see any here . . ."

O'Brien slipped the garrote out of his back pocket, stepped behind Rogan and raised the garrote. He looped the cord around Rogan's neck, crossed it and pulled hard.

Rogan jerked and struggled, fingers clawing at his neck.

O'Brien pulled the garrote tighter. He leaned backwards, lifting Rogan off his feet. He maintained tension on the garrote until Rogan went limp and slumped to the floor. He emptied his pockets.

O'Brien put on an old baseball cap and jammed it low over his eyes. He stepped out into the hallway and got the dolly with the steel drum, which he'd put at the end of the corridor. Once back inside the lab, he put Rogan's body into the drum and slipped its lid back on. He checked the corridor. No one. He wheeled the drum out of the lab and locked the door.

O'Brien took the drum down to the furnace room. He opened the inspection gate into the bowels of the combustion chamber. The fresh influx of air caused the flames to roar forth from the bed of red-hot coals. It was like a glimpse of hell. After checking to make sure no one was within sight, he raised the barrel and slid Rogan's body into the furnace. He watched the flames for a few seconds before tossing in the garrote and slamming the gate shut. In the distance, a steam whistle blew, marking the midnight shift change. *Right on time*, he thought.

If anyone had been watching outside, they might have noticed a flurry of black smoke emerging from the chimney of number three boiler.

No one did.

Chapter 5

September 15, 1969.

Daniel Robles sat on the edge of the couch in the anteroom to the office of Mr. Ben Hodges, the Production Plant Manager of Schirmerling Tire and Rubber Company. The office had wood-paneled walls, two couches, and a coffee table littered with three-month old trade magazines. *My first day on the job*, he thought. *Orientation should be the first item.*

"Mr. Robles?" A middle-aged woman with bleached-blond hair peered over half-frame glasses, her pencil-thin eyebrows raised. She wore bright red lipstick and a tight floral print dress that had been stylish in the fifties. It squeezed her ample bosom upward and outward, offering a glimpse of her generous cleavage. She also pronounced Robles as Ro-bulls, but he was used to that. It seemed most Anglos didn't know his last name was pronounced Robe-lace. "Mr. Hodges will see you in five minutes."

"Thank you." Daniel's mind went to the five years he'd spent with Matlock Corporation. It had been a steady stream of consulting assignments in different cities, primarily to petroleum and power companies. The pay had been good, which he used to pay off his college loans, but there always had been an undercurrent of slurs based upon his Hispanic background. He hoped that Schirmerling meant freedom from insults and living out of a suitcase. And, he wanted no more ruined relationships. He thought he'd found a woman he could love in Lisa. Her loss still hung heavy on his heart.

Daniel had a master's degree in chemical engineering from Case Institute of Technology and five years' experience in power generation systems and combustion. He also wanted to live in Kent and be near his brother, Hector, who had helped put Daniel through school after both their parents had died in an auto accident. He longed to live a normal life, perhaps even get married and raise a family. At twenty-nine, he was ready. During the interview, personnel had hinted that this job could even lead to upper management.

The receptionist crooked her finger.

"Yes?" Daniel quickly rose to his feet.

"Mr. Hodges will see you now." The receptionist opened the mahogany door, which led into a large corner office.

Ben Hodges' hair was white and brush cut, his head level with the top of the leather high-back chair. He had chubby cheeks and a red face. He sat behind an eight-foot wide cherry desk with a matching credenza. A certificate on the wall attested to the honorable service of Lieutenant Benjamin Disraeli Hodges, U.S. Marine Corp. A leather couch, a coffee table, and a TV were the only other pieces of furniture in the room.

A single sheet of paper occupied Hodges' gleaming desk. "Welcome to STR, Robles, I'm Ben Hodges, plant manager. Your resume says you've worked on boilers; is that right?" He pronounced Daniel's name as though it rhymed with nobles.

Daniel took a quick breath. *What, no pleasantries or small talk?* he thought. "Yes, sir, I've worked on combustion systems for power plants, refineries and incinerators, optimizing efficiencies, and improving safe operation--"

"Good, you have experience," Hodges said. "We need to improve efficiencies in our utility boilers that provide superheated steam for curing tires. The operators have reported leaks in the system."

Hodges swiveled in his chair and retrieved a sheet of paper from a filing cabinet behind his desk. "This is a memo from the boiler house foreman that describes the problem. Your assignment is to inspect the system, establish what needs to be done, and prepare an AFE—an Authorization for Expenditure, for next year's budget. The deadline is December 15; however, I want progress reports on my desk every Monday morning. Miss Krieger, my secretary, will brief you on their requirements. That'll be all."

"Mr. Hodges, what's the problem with the steam system?"

"Grabowski in the boiler house will give you the lay of the land." A brief frown crossed Hodges's florid face. "I expect your first report next Monday. Dismissed."

#

The low rumbling vibration from the furnace draft induction fans filled the building and steam hissed continually. Four-inch diameter steel pipes snaked down from the ceiling to connect with a row of wheel and lever operated valves mounted on the wall. The manifold room was about one hundred feet long and sixty feet wide. It was dim and had the wet cardboard smell that came from steam leaks. Heat from the nearby superheaters made it feel like a trip into a tropical night. Heavy steel support beams rose from floor to the ceiling. Dust-coated items that had been stored and forgotten lay scattered around. A massive, sliding steel fire door opened onto the second-floor mezzanine of the boiler house. At the rear of the manifold room, a red exit sign glowed dimly over a rarely used door.

"So, old Iron Butt sent you over to figure out what needs to be done?" Grabowski, the boiler house foreman, was a short, stocky man whose substantial beer belly filled out his blue coveralls. He wiped sweat from his brow.

"Iron Butt?" Daniel let a trace of a smile show. He could almost guess what was coming.

"Yeah, plant manager Hodges tries to run the place like the military. He was in the Marines for six years and liked how they ran the outfit. Here, he acts like we're a part of his command. The union's always on his case 'cause he's such a hard ass. That's why you've got this job."

Daniel chuckled and let his smile widen.

Grabowski nodded. "Money's tight around STR. Old Iron Butt's always looking for ways to cut costs. He's the type that would squeeze a nickel and make the buffalo fart."

Daniel noticed that some of the lines needed insulation replaced. What looked like steam return lines had leaks from their joints and flanges. *This place hasn't seen real maintenance in years. It's going to take a lot of work to get it back in shape. It probably needs a shutdown to get it fixed.* "When was the last turn-around?"

Grabowski's eyebrows rose. "Turn-around? What's that?"

Daniel spoke loudly to be heard over the background noise. "It's a term for a shutdown to make major repairs."

"We can't shut down the utility boilers." Grabowski shook his head. "We've got to keep the steam flowing so the plant can keep up production. We make tires twenty-four hours a day."

"I see." *That will make things more difficult*, Daniel thought. "So, how do you isolate defective steam lines?"

"We put in shunts to bypass the sections that we work on." Grabowski pointed to a pipe that protruded at right angles from one of the overhead steam lines and dropped to waist level and ended with a large lever-operated valve. "We hook up a flexible hose to a main line tap and shunt the steam around the area we're working on." He pointed at a lever-operated valve. "Open that valve, and you've got six-hundred-degree superheated steam flowing at two hundred and fifty pounds per square inch. Be damn careful around it. It can kill you in an instant."

Daniel nodded. "Right. I've worked with high-pressure steam in power plants. Dangerous stuff. I don't see any safety plates on the steam taps, nor do the lever-operated valves have safety locks." That worried Daniel, for it violated most of the standard safety recommendations for steam boiler operations.

Grabowski's eyes widened as he nodded approval.

It was worse than Daniel had expected. The entire return side of the system needed an overhaul. It was a victim of long-term deferred maintenance. *I'll need to check every line in the building to make sure that there's nothing else outside the manifold area that's about to break. This'll take time.*

Daniel began a methodical inventory of the entire system, listing each valve, flange and union according to its condition. He intended to do a first-class job on this. He wanted to start off on the right foot in his new position.

Chapter 6

Daniel looked around the apartment.

It was the furnished upstairs of an old frame house on West Main Street in Kent that pre-dated the Great Depression. Its bedroom was quiet, facing away from the street, next to a bathroom with an old-fashioned iron tub and yellow plastic shower curtains. The large living room overlooked the street and had worn carpeting and faded drapes. The tiny kitchen would have been at home in a boat. The rent was cheap, which fit in with his plans to save money to buy a house. The apartment also came with a garage where he kept his eight-year old Ford Econoline van and stored his unused items. The apartment was ten minutes from his brother, Hector, who lived in Twin Lakes, just north of Kent.

Okay, he thought, this'll do as my home for a while.

#

Daniel glanced at his watch. Better get a move on. I promised Hector I'd be there by six and join him for supper.

The drive from the apartment, first through the side streets in Kent and then north on Route 43, brought back memories. He pulled into the driveway and stopped. He noted that Hector's home, a white center-hall colonial, had peeling paint. Yeah, that's just like my brother, more concerned about politics than paint.

"Daniel, good to see you. C'mon, let's have a drink." Hector steered Daniel through the house and out back to the patio. "I opened a nice burgundy, just for you."

Daniel noticed that Hector had put on some weight and was beginning to have a bit of a belly. There were more lines in his face and there was a trace of gray in his black hair. Still, he had the patrician look with a long nose and an angular face. It was obvious that his enjoyment of fine wines had grown.

Oh, boy, Daniel thought. A running start on the wine

before dinner. He knew that his brother liked to eat and drink well. "Don't forget I start work early tomorrow..."

"Eh, we can take our time. My first class isn't until eleven tomorrow morning." Hector poured a generous glass of the ruby red wine. "To your health, little brother."

"And yours." Daniel sipped on the wine. "This is pretty good, what is it?" He put the glass down, with a mental promise to go easy on the wine. After all, tomorrow was a workday.

"It's a Vosne Romanee." Hector went on to extol the wine's pedigree for several minutes. "But that's not important. Tell me all about your new job."

"Well, it's with Schirmerling..." Daniel went on to explain the position and what it entailed.

Dinner started about eight-thirty and lasted until almost ten. Daniel tried to resist, but Hector insisted that he try a glass of each of the three bottles that were open. Daniel realized that his brother was really glad to see him, but made a mental note to only visit on the weekends when he had enough time to recover from Hector's largesse.

It was almost midnight before Daniel left. He drove carefully back to his apartment. He knew from his current buzz, morning would come way too soon. He also realized he had made the correct decision to live by himself rather than take up Hector's suggestion he move in with him. His career and liver would last longer by living alone.

#

Daniel steered his van down the gravel driveway, splashing through the potholes. He pulled up in front of a barn that had been painted rust-red some time in its distant history. A peeling green sign read, 'Garrison's Riding Stables, Horses boarded, Grooming.' In small print were the words, 'Riding Instruction.' Those were the words that had caught his attention while driving on the south side of Ravenna.

"Yes, Mr. Garrison, I'm interested in learning how to ride." Daniel had always wanted to ride horses and the sign by the road had triggered an impulse to turn in and ask. He eyed the silver-haired man who carried a substantial beer-belly above a set of jean-covered legs that bowed out at the knees.

"You ever ride before?" Garrison tipped his stained baseball cap back, revealing a baldhead covered with beads of perspiration. The warm, earthy aroma of fresh horse droppings filled the air. The inside of the barn was lit by bare bulbs dangling from a spider inhabited ceiling and decorated with fly specks. It was warm in contrast with the gray, sullen autumn day outside.

"No, I haven't." Daniel said.

"Well, I do have an old mare that'd be good to start on. She's got a nice disposition and won't do anything unexpected." Garrison leaned against the barn's doorframe. "We give instruction only on evenings and weekends. My instructor is part-time. Is that okay with you?" He pointed to a sign, which showed the rates for rental and instruction. "And that's what we charge."

To Daniel, the price seemed quite low compared to those he'd enquired about while working in Chicago. "I work full-time, so those hours are fine for me."

"Okay, let me introduce you to Carol, she's our riding instructor. She's in the barn." Garrison led the way deeper into the barn.

Daniel followed, stepping carefully on the few patches of straw to avoid the horse droppings.

At the end of the barn was a woman who was in her early twenties. She was about five feet five, with long blonde hair tied in a ponytail. She wore a loose-fitting sweatshirt and her form-fitting jeans emphasized shapely hips. She was busy shoveling horse droppings into a wheelbarrow.

"Carol." Garrison gestured toward Daniel. "This here gentleman's interested in riding lessons." As Carol straightened up and shook her ponytail back over her shoulder, Garrison turned back to Daniel. "What did you say your name was?"

"Hello, I'm Daniel Robles." He extended his hand.

Carol leaned the shovel against the wall, glanced at her palm, shook her head and withdrew her hand. "Hi, I'm Carol Meadows." She asked him the same questions that Garrison had. "I start everyone with the basics. You get on a horse right away and practice in the paddock. Once you learn how to control the horse, we go out on the trail."

"Where's that?" Daniel hadn't seen any sign of parks in the area.

Carol pointed out of the back of the barn towards a patch of woods beyond the fenced in area. "It goes through those woods and then down by the river. It's a couple of miles. It's a nice length for practice."

"Sounds good to me. When can we start?" Daniel was glad Carol would give the lessons. She was a lot easier on the eyes than Mr. Garrison.

"Let me check. I've got a student coming in tonight." She squinted her eyes as she looked at a calendar advertising animal foods. "I can fit you in on Tuesdays and Thursdays, at six, and Saturday mornings at nine. No lessons on Friday night. How's that for you?"

Daniel realized that schedule would work. "Sure. Tuesdays and Saturdays are good for me. Let's try that and see how it works out."

Carol eyed him up and down. "D'you have riding boots?"

"No, do I need them?"

Carol pursed her lips. "You don't <u>have</u> to wear boots, however, if a horse cow-kicks you, you'll be sorry you don't have them. Boots will also give you a better purchase in the stirrups." She looked away for a moment. "They don't have to be expensive. Even the local K-Mart carries cowboy boots these days and they'll work fine for riding."

"I understand. Okay, next Tuesday at six, right?"

"Yes. When you show up, pay Mr. Garrison before you come out to the barn. That's his rule."

#

After two riding sessions, Daniel began to enjoy Carol's friendly, down-to-earth nature. She didn't seem to have the pretensions of the coeds he'd met in the bars at Kent. He liked her quick smile and easy demeanor, and she was quite pretty.

On the third week of instructions, Daniel learned she was also a bookkeeper at Rick Box Honda, which was just down the street from his apartment. It was toward the end of that lesson when she gave him a bit of advice. "Sit up straight. Good posture is less tiring."

"Okay." As Daniel straightened up, he had a feeling of being a 'hidalgo,' a gentleman, a step up in the world. He liked the fact, he really belonged on a horse, and had this image only nobility rode horses. His view from the saddle gave him confidence to muster up the courage to ask, "Would you like to catch a show Friday evening?" He swiveled in the saddle to look at her.

"This Friday? Sure." Carol nodded. A trace of a smile flickered across her lips.

"There's a flick playing in Kent, 'Butch Cassidy and the Sundance Kid.' It got good reviews." Daniel took encouragement from her smile as if she were pleased that he'd asked her. "We could eat at Lujans before the show." Lujans was a burger joint frequented by college students.

"Yes, that'd be nice." She urged her horse forward and called back. "I can be ready by six-thirty."

"Great." Daniel felt a surge of excitement at the idea of actually going out with her. He slowed his horse as they approached the barn, came to a complete halt and dismounted. "Where can I pick you up?"

Carol held her horse's halter while stroking its nose. "I live in Ravenna, with my mother." She gave him directions as she maneuvered the horse into a stall.

As Daniel handed the bridle to Carol, she grasped his jacket and pulled him close. She gave him a quick kiss. "See you Friday." As she turned away, a smile flickered over her face.

His heart began to pound harder. The kiss had been completely unexpected. And her smile spoke volumes. He liked its implication.

#

Friday evening, as they ate at Lujans, Daniel learned Carol's father had walked out on her mother when she was a baby. He found it quite believable when Carol told him she'd been the runner-up for Homecoming Queen at Ravenna High School. Time flew during the meal and they had to rush to the cinema to catch the movie's start.

After the movie, Daniel took Carol home. On the doorstep, he attempted to kiss her on the cheek, but she put her hands on both sides of his face and brought her lips to his. Her body molded itself to his and her tongue entered his mouth. He felt an instantaneous arousal.

As they parted, Carol whispered, "Next time, let's spend time together, some place private. Your place, maybe." She smiled and turned the key in the door, opened it and said loudly, "Goodnight." She disappeared inside.

Daniel's arousal lasted all the way home.

#

Daniel stared at the flow diagram. There were red marks all over the drawing, indicating the lines he believed needed replacement. So far, he realized, *I've done only a preliminary inspection. I haven't tested the pressure regulators, valves, nor surveyed the combustion chamber walls.*

The three-ring binder of notes had steadily grown. Daniel consulted the Thomas Register several times to locate manufacturers who still made equipment that would fit the boilers. *This is going to be expensive, and I still haven't got quotes back on some of the parts needed.* He'd held off putting down any kind of cost estimate after Hodges complained about his first progress report. When he'd stated that the numbers he gave Hodges were a ballpark number, Hodges had said they were 'unacceptable.' *Well, if what he wants is an exact number, he's gonna get it.*

31

Man, he thought, *it's going to take months to fix these boilers*. Plus, he'd joined a waste minimization committee to figure out ways to save money for STR. He realized STR's glossy public image was far different than the gritty reality of seeing what the company was really like from the inside.

#

Carol rolled over and yawned.

Daniel sighed. They'd made love twice the previous night and upon waking, had sated each other thoroughly. *She's wonderful*, he thought, *so spontaneous and so sensual. I think I'm in love*.

They'd become lovers on their third date. Sometimes Carol would drop by his apartment after work to steal a few intimate moments before going home. Often, their dates were evenings in bed, yet Carol always seemed to want more. Last night, they'd fallen asleep after an overdose of sex and champagne, after celebrating the arrival of the New Year.

Carol sat upright and stared at the alarm clock. "That can't be right," she said. "It can't be seven-thirty."

"Yep," said Daniel. "Seven-thirty, New Year's day. Happy New Year, sweetheart."

"Oh, my God." Carol jumped out of bed and ran for the bathroom. "My mom's going to kill me." The shower burst into life and a few moments later, its curtain rustled.

Daniel went into the bathroom and stepped into the shower. He put his arms around a wet and soapy Carol, reaching for her breasts. Her hands slapped his down.

"Not now," she said, "I'm in trouble. You know my mom doesn't allow me out overnight without a very good reason. She knows I went out with you last night. Her rule is I have to be home no later than two am."

"But, Carol, you're over twenty-one, and it was New Year's Eve--"

"You don't understand, do you? She doesn't trust men. She doesn't like me going out with guys, any guy. She hates men because my father abandoned us. I've got to get

32

home. I've got to figure out an excuse, or she'll kill me."
#
Daniel opened the door of his apartment. Carol stood silent, nose red and bags under her eyes. "What happened?" He hadn't heard from her since yesterday, yet had been afraid to call her at home.

Carol sniffled. "My mom and I had a fight." Tears began to fill her eyes. "It was horrible. She called me a slut; she said I was acting like a tramp. She said she was trying to prevent me from making the same mistake she did, of letting a man take advantage of me. When I said I was going to see you again, she threw me out. Now I have no place to stay. I don't know what I'm going to do." She blew her nose and put her head in her hands.

"Wow, Carol, I'm sorry. I didn't know she felt that way--"

"Well, you should have." Carol blew her nose again and looked at her fingers as though consulting an oracle. She glanced sideways at him. "I'm sorry, I shouldn't have said that." She sniffled again. "But she did throw me out. I don't have any place to live. I don't know what I'm going to do."

Daniel took a deep breath. "You could stay with me." He bit his lip as soon as he uttered those words for that implied more than just shelter. That meant they would be together every night. It both excited him and filled him with apprehension. Do I know what I'm getting in to?

Carol cocked her head at him, red-eyed and makeup smeared. "I can? Really?"

Daniel nodded. "You mean a lot to me. I haven't felt this way about anyone before. We get along and like a lot of the same things. I'm not messy and I know you're tidy, so we should be compatible as roommates." He felt a little awkward saying that, as if he had to convince himself of the wisdom of this commitment, when in reality, he felt immediate arousal at the thought. He had never lived with a woman before. This was a step he'd never before taken. It scared him. It also excited him with its implications of intimacy.

Carol stepped close to Daniel. She put her arms around him and kissed him. "We're also compatible as bed mates." She ran her hand down his front. "Why don't we make sure that's still true?"

Chapter 7

January, 1970.

Daniel examined the trace of the ultrasonic test on the wall thickness of the boiler's superheaters. It didn't look right. He leaned back in the old wood chair in the boiler operations office and rubbed his chin.

He'd quietly took over a dusty, seldom used room that had been the boiler engineering department's office. It was near an infrequently used rear entrance to the utility boiler house. A pair of battered file cabinets kept company with two tall bookshelves that held a collection of three-ring binders that were the boiler manuals, plus an accumulation of out-of-date catalogs.

Daniel leafed through one of the operations' manuals until he found the specification. He ran the calculations. He didn't like the results, so he repeated them being doubly careful. *Uh-oh, the superheater's wall thickness on number three is borderline for safe operation. Hodges isn't going to like this.*

It only took a few minutes reviewing the manual to realize the boilers would have to be shut down sooner or later to replace the superheaters. Probably should be sooner. To get this job done in two weeks, they'd have to work around the clock. He figured Hodges would like that even less.

After Daniel made copies of the ultrasonic trace, he placed the originals, along with his signed and dated calculations, in a pocket of one of the boiler operation manuals. He knew it was good practice to put items concerning safety with the operation manuals. Not that it would do much good, for he'd found the operators never used the manuals and no one else ever touched them. He returned the manuals to the bookshelf. He saw no reason to take them to his office in the research center, for he did most of this work in this office.

#

Daniel prepared a memo on the boilers and manifold system, which was only one page long. He attached eighteen pages of calculations, test data, quotes, catalog clips and copies of the ultrasonic traces. *I wonder when would be the best time to give this to Hodges? Probably late on Friday. Then he'll have the entire weekend to cool-off after seeing the estimated cost of repair and reviewing the notes. It'll also give him time to read all of the supporting data and see the logic of my estimate.* He'd also included an estimate of the cost to bring the boilers into compliance with the Clean Air Act, which would soon come into effect. There was no estimate to replace the superheaters, since he'd only just sent the vendors a request for a proposal to rebuild them. However, he knew it would be a substantial amount, perhaps as much as a million dollars. Hodges definitely won't be happy at that news.

Daniel knew his mid-January submission for the report was late, but the vendors had been slow to respond to his requests. Hodges' comment that the ballpark cost estimate was unacceptable had stuck with him. Well, this estimate is fully documented, definitely not a ballpark number. Several vendors had complained to him that STR would order parts and then take months to pay. He couldn't control that. It didn't make him feel better about his new employer.

Now, Daniel thought, *I've got to get the procedure for using scrap rubber as boiler fuel prepared for the Waste Minimization Committee.* That offered the potential to save some real money. *Maybe it will get me a little recognition. After all, it is one of my areas of expertise. Maybe even enough to pay for the boiler repairs. Maybe not.*

Daniel closed the door to his office and began to assemble the data on tire burn rates, temperature profiles and estimates of cost savings. He knew it would keep him busy for several days, just in time for Hodges to digest the memo.

#

"Robles. This estimate is completely unacceptable." Hodges' round face was bright red as he rose to his feet, all five feet eight inches. He reminded Daniel of angry bantam cock about to enter battle. "STR expects deadlines to be met as well as better work than this."

"Mr. Hodges, I don't understand what you mean. That estimate has quotes and solid estimates. It's as good as it gets. Isn't that what you wanted me to do?"

"Robles, you're either stupid or ignorant. I clearly told you the cost estimate was unacceptable. Only a dolt would fail to understand it was the magnitude of the puffed-up cost that needed paring. How can STR make any profit if it has to spend a fortune to make unnecessary repairs on boilers that work perfectly well?" Hodges leaned forward over his polished desk. "Well?"

"Sir." Daniel was at a loss as what to say. He struggled to find the words. He felt like he had just stepped onto a sheet of wet ice. He'd never encountered a client that set the price of repairing something obviously in need of maintenance prior to examination. Only fools did that. "I examined the boilers carefully. If you will note, there are safety concerns-"

"That's another thing you've got to learn." Hodges stabbed his finger toward Daniel. "Never put anything into writing that the union can twist and use against STR." He sat down heavily and let out a deep breath. "This memo needs to be revised to STR standards. You'd better get attuned to management's thinking and understand STR's priorities. You need to get the 'right' attitude so you don't write any more dumb ass memos like this one." He tore the memo in half and deposited it in the waste paper bucket under the credenza.

"Yes, sir." Daniel couldn't think of anything to say.

"You need to spend some time with management to get the proper company orientation, and soon. Like this week."

"Yes, sir," Daniel said. *Oh, shit, I'm righteously*

screwed. What's this orientation? I haven't seen anything posted on the announcement boards. "When is it?"

Hodges nose flared. "The Vulcan club meets this Friday evening at seven-thirty at the Tangiers Restaurant. Be there." He stared again at the memo. "Oh, yes, and dress properly. Something decent. And get a haircut, too."

Daniel repressed a smile. *Dress properly? The dress standards at STR are, well,* he thought, *sloppy when compared to those required for consultants.* And after his wardrobe makeover at Lisa's behest, he knew that he could dress with the best. He still had a couple of those suits and he knew his dress standards were equal to the best of STRs. *Haircut? Maybe, maybe not.* Carol liked his hair long. And he liked to please her, for when he did, she pleased him in ways he really liked.

Chapter 8

A blast of warm air with hints of garlic, spices and grilled meat greeted Daniel as he stepped into the Tangiers Restaurant. Draped fabrics and brass decorations emphasized its Middle Eastern theme. *Wow,* he thought, *looks sort of exotic.* At eight o'clock in the evening, there was a steady chatter of conversation amid a constant clatter of dishes. Waiters and bus boys in ruffled white shirts and black pants rushed back and forth carrying trays of food and empty dishes.

"Yes, sir, may I help you?" asked a man wearing a tuxedo, pursed lips and elevated nose.

"The STR meeting?" Daniel said.

"STR?" The tuxedo-clad man looked up after consulting a list, frowning. "I don't have anything by that name."

"Er, try the Vulcan Club."

"Ah, yes." The tuxedo-clad man smiled like he'd recognized an old friend. "Please, check your coat." The man gestured toward a closet with a half-door, where a buxom woman wearing a small turban leaned over its counter. Daniel gave his coat to the hatcheck woman who handed Daniel a numbered plastic tab.

The tuxedo-clad man sniffed. "Come right this way, please." He led Daniel down a corridor and into a private room decorated with pictures of mosques and other Arabian scenes. At one side, a bartender in white shirt with a black bow tie served drinks to a group of middle-aged men wearing similar navy blue suits that had the polyester shine of extensive usage.

"Robles. How come you're late?" Hodges florid face was even more flushed than usual. "What're you drinking?"

"I went home to shower and dress suitably," Daniel said. "I live on the other side of town." He smiled. "Scotch." *And,* he thought, *I wanted to be fashionably late, to avoid as much of this as possible.* "Sorry," he said quite insincerely.

Hodges steered Daniel to a group of balding, middle-aged men, who, at close inspection, who wore rumpled clothing in need of cleaning and pressing as well as replacement. After just a half-hour, Daniel realized that their only topic of conversation was complaints about government taxes, regulations and reporting requirements. Not only were they complaining about them, but they were also discussing ways and means to get around them. Some of the methods were legal and some were not.

Daniel felt a nudge in his ribs. It was Hodges who had a grin on his face.

"This's the STR team," Hodges said. "It has the right attitude on how to get the job done. Now, I want you to soak this up and come back to work with a new and improved attitude. One of doing things the right way to make STR successful."

"I see." Daniel had come to the conclusion that these guys were figuring out ways to circumvent the law. *I'm a professional engineer and if I get caught doing this crap, I'd lose my certification. Then what would I do for a living?* At that moment, he made up his mind. "Excuse me," he said, "I need to step out for a moment."

"Don't be long," Hodges said, "we've got a topless belly dancer for entertainment." As he grinned, he licked his lips. "She'll be on in a minute. She's got quite a pair and really knows how to move them." His eyes left Daniel and alighted on something across the room. "Excuse me."

Right, Daniel thought as he left the room, *just what I need to see.* He picked up his coat from the hatcheck girl who made an effort to display her copious cleavage. He put a couple of quarters in the tip jar and left. He knew Carol would be glad to see him come home early.

#

"Grabowski, open this door." Daniel had traced a steam line that disappeared behind a wall. He'd thrown himself into his work and avoided Hodges as much as possible.

Grabowski struggled with a ring of keys, trying one after another. "I don't think I have one for this lock," he said. "This used to be a cop station."

"Cop station?" Daniel said. The door had an opening that was at one time a window, but was now sealed with a metal sheet. He examined the lock. It was a substantial Yale lock surrounded with a stainless steel plat, which looked new.

"Plant security. It was a substation during the Second World War." Grabowski shrugged. "It was to prevent sabotage."

"So, open it."

"How?"

"I don't care. Anyway you like."

"Anyway?"

"I'm sure you know how to open it." Daniel was in no mood to screw around with a door that should not be locked.

Grabowski raised his eyebrows, smiled and left.

Grabowski returned with a cart carrying several toolboxes. After several tries, he picked up an electric drill. "This's gonna ruin the lock." He looked up at Daniel and shrugged.

"That'll cost less than the time we've wasted trying to get in," Daniel said. "Do it."

Five minutes later, the door swung open and Daniel stepped inside. He traced the pipe across the ceiling and noted that it took a right-angle turn. So that's why I couldn't follow it.

Water running in the sink of the bathroom caught his attention. It had hoses connected to a small oven-like box, which he recognized as a vacuum oven. There were jars of chemicals in amber glass bottles and laboratory glassware assembled on tables. He knew from his chemistry courses that this equipment was used in chemical synthesis. "Who's responsible for this room?" he asked. "Who's working here?"

"Dunno," Grabowski said, "it's still listed under Plant Security, but they never use it. We don't either."

"Well, somebody's using it now." Daniel read the labels of the chemical jars on the table. *I didn't use any of these when I took organic chemistry,* he thought. *Certainly aren't anything used to make polymers.* He made a list of the chemicals. *I'd better check to see what they're used for.*

\#

Daniel made a quick call to the facilities administrator of the Research Center to find out if any researchers were using any rooms in the boiler house.

"There aren't any personnel working off-site, nor any in other buildings in Akron," the administrator said. "We actually have surplus space in the Research building," he added. "There have been reductions in staff due to cost-cutting efforts. It's really been quite sad. The company has seen better days."

"Thank you," Daniel said. *Next step,* he thought, *is to check out what can be made with these chemicals.* He headed for the Research Center's library. Within an hour, he realized that the phenylacetone and methylamine he'd seen in the boiler house could be used to make methamphetamine, or speed. *Holy cow. Someone has a clandestine drug lab,* he thought, *or at least it looks like it. And there's that vacuum oven that has chemicals drying. There may be drugs in there.*

Daniel returned to his office and called Plant Security. "Let me speak to Captain O'Brien..." He waited a few moments until a gruff voice spoke in his ear.

"O'Brien here. What d'you want?"

"This is Robles, plant engineering. While tracing a steam line, I had to drill open a lock in a door in the boiler house to get in. Once inside that room, I came across what looks like a clandestine drug lab."

"Where in the boiler house?"

Daniel gave him the details.

"Okay, I'll take care of it." O'Brien hung up the phone.

#

A week later, while tracing another steam line, Daniel saw the door to the room containing the secret laboratory, had a new lock with a thick steel guard plate, plus a big padlock. He put his ear to the door and heard the sound of water rushing. It sounded just like the vacuum aspirator of the drug lab. *What the hell?* Daniel wondered if O'Brien had called in the police.

"Hello, Grabowski?" Daniel spoke into the phone. "That room in the boiler house... yeah, that one. Did the police come by and examine it. They didn't? Okay, that room, can you seal it up?" he asked. "That's right, make it secure, real secure."

He had already reached the opinion that most of the plant security officers were just for show. After the Vulcan Club episode, he didn't trust management to do the right thing. As for O'Brien, well, he might just be cut from the same cloth. He leaned back in his chair for a moment before he picked up the phone and called the Akron Police. He was shunted around to several officers before he heard, "Detective Grueden, can I help you?"

"Yes, I believe there's an unauthorized lab in the STR boiler house, which might be making drugs. Has anyone contacted you about it?" Daniel said. "I see. Yes, right, I've checked and none of the chemists are supposed to be working in this location. The chemicals in the lab are listed as precursors for making methamphetamine sulfate. Yes, I informed plant security a week ago. No, I didn't touch anything. Yes, I called you. Company management? I don't know. My name? I'd prefer not to say."

Chapter 9

Detective Jack Grueden of the Akron Police recalled that Zachary Rogan had been reported missing by both his employer, STR and his parents, who'd tried to call him several times to wish him 'happy birthday.' A week later, they'd called the department.

This doesn't make any sense, Grueden thought. He'd gotten involved when the report on the forensic sweep of Rogan's apartment had uncovered tiny amounts of methamphetamine in the carpeting. The lab had reported a small mirror had traces of the same drug, which suggested it had been used for snorting the drug. Grueden ordered a complete examination, which revealed nothing. No fingerprints, no address book, not even any trash. The place looked like a professional had cleaned it. Rogan's car was still parked outside, a brand-new '69 Chevy Impala, with nothing out of place. Records showed the car's title was clear, and the kid had paid cash for it. That made him check Rogan's financial records and discovered he had twenty-four hundred dollars in a savings account. That was a lot money for a kid making seven hundred dollars a month, especially with a new car, an expensive hi-fi stereo system and a huge stack of record albums.

Grueden suspected Rogan had been involved in dealing meth. However, at his work office there was no trace of drugs. None of the addresses in his office Rolodex led anywhere. It looked like it was going to be another unsolved disappearance where they suspected foul play, but could never solve. Now, a person at STR, who didn't want his identity revealed, called yesterday and said there might be an illegal drug lab in the STR boiler house. Was this connected to Rogan's disappearance? It was worth checking out.

"Was there a call back from O'Brien, at STR?" Grueden called across the room to the departmental secretary, Diana Mintz. She was twenty-one, blonde and hunting a husband. However, she was conscientious about her work, so he overlooked her flirtatious ways, which, thankfully, weren't aimed at him.

"No," Diana said. "I did talk to someone in his department again, who said he was out of the office." Grueden's department was in an open area with metal desks arranged in two rows of three. Diana sat behind a counter at the door.

"Okay, I'm going over there to take a look." Grueden reached for his raincoat. "See if Kincaid's available, and if he is, have him meet me at the motor pool."

"Sure thing, Detective," Diana said. "You have fun, now." She winked at a young uniformed officer as he came in through the door to the office.

"Yeah, right," Grueden said.

#

"Then where is O'Brien?" Grueden stabbed his finger onto the counter of the guard in the front of the STR Office of Plant Security. "I get a report of drug activity and your boss doesn't return my calls. I got a problem with that. If I got a problem, your boss's gonna have a bigger problem if I have to get a search warrant, understand?" It was time to do a little bluffing with this toy cop.

The office was brightly lit and professionally decorated. There were two new desks in front of a frosted glass walled office, which had O'Brien's name in large gilt letters on the closed door.

The round-faced, over-weight guard whose badge said 'Blodgett' swallowed hard. "Well, Captain O'Brien is out of town," he said. "He'll get back to you as soon as possible."

Grueden swore under his breath and looked away for a moment. "Okay, why don't you take me over to the boiler house and show me this alleged site of illegal activity?"

"Er, I don't know whether I can do that. I have to clear it with Captain O'Brien--"

"Look, if you want any future cooperation with the Akron Police, you'd better re-think that answer." Grueden's face felt hot. *What the fuck's going on?*

The security guard pursed his lips. "Well, I guess I could take you over there, but I can't let you touch anything until I've cleared it with Captain O'Brien and our legal department."

Grueden nodded. *Yeah, yeah. And if this's a meth lab, I'll get a search warrant so fast that it'll make you and STR's lawyers' heads spin.* He knew the local judges took a dim view of the recent wave of shootings and deaths linked to illegal drug usage, especially meth. With the mayor ranting to the news media about judges being soft on crime, judges had become more willing to authorize searches. In addition, they were supportive of his efforts, especially after he'd put a number of dealers in the slammer. "We'll go for a walk-by, okay?"

Grueden watched the guard buckle on his equipment belt, complete with its nightstick and forty-five automatic. As they stepped outside, a blast of cold air filled with snow hit him. *Damn February*, he thought, *coldest month of the year*. They walked through gray slush, past hulking buildings that bustled with activity into an open yard. Opposite was the boiler house, a three-story, cubical redbrick building with three tall brick chimneys.

Inside the boiler house, it was hot and humid, with a deep vibration from the fans and the continual hiss of steam. The security guard pointed to a pale green painted door. It had two steel bars across it, welded to the frame and the door.

"What the hell's this?" Grueden asked.

"I dunno," the security guard said. "It wasn't like this the last time I made my rounds through here."

"When was that?"

"Er, four days ago."

Grueden sniffed. It was a chemical smell similar to that which he'd noted at other drug-making locations. "Who's in charge of this building?"

"Er, Ted Grabowski is the foreman." The security

guard nodded his head. "Yes, Grabowski."

"Why don't we go see Mr. Grabowski?" Grueden said with elaborate politeness. *This guy*, he thought, *is a dumb shit.*

Grabowski leaned back in his chair and masticated a bite of his sandwich to completion, swallowed and silently belched. "Yeah, I sealed the door at Mr. Robles' request," he said. "He didn't want anyone messing around with it before the cops got here. He thought someone might take it into their head to clean it up." He swung forward and put his feet on the floor. "He's a good kid. Works hard. Knows his way around a boiler house. Best engineer I've seen around here in a while."

Grueden nodded. "I want to get in there, but he says I still need to have Captain O'Brien's okay." He looked at the security guard. "Let O'Brien know I want in tomorrow, okay?" He turned to Grabowski, "Can you check on that door from time to time? So that no one opens it?"

Grabowski took a sip of coffee. "Yeah, I suppose." He pursed his lips. "It'll take cutting equipment to open it. I'll make sure that our tools are locked up. That'd make it more difficult for someone to sneak in and pop it open."

Grueden reached out and shook Grabowski's hand. "Thanks, I appreciate that." He turned to the security guard. "Let's go." Grueden felt he'd made some progress. *Maybe there'll even be some information about the missing Rogan guy.*

#

"Right, your honor." Grueden nodded, while hunched over the phone at his desk. O'Brien hadn't returned his call, so he'd taken the next step. "I was there and could smell chemicals. They bore a strong resemblance to the ones that were at that drug house in South Akron. Yes, sir, that's what it says in my affidavit. Thank you, your honor, I appreciate your acting so quickly. Yes, I'll be meticulous with the evidence. Thank you."

Grueden replaced the phone gently. "Okay, we got

it." He looked up at the tall, muscular police officer who had a fringe of ginger hair sticking out from beneath his cap. "Notify Forensics to meet us at the motor pool. We have to swing by Judge Milano's offices to pick up the search warrant and subpoena. Then we'll go see what we can find at STR."

Chapter 10

February 16, 1970.

"Say that again." Barry 'Bull' Mansky yawned. As CEO of STR, he'd listened to accountants over the years, but he found the comments made by Larry Feinberg particularly hard to follow. Feinberg was the lead accountant from Dulhot, Askins and Kristol, also known as 'DAK', who were doing the audit for the 10K and the annual report. Three members of his audit team sat behind him, clones in dark blue suits. On the opposite side of the table, STR's accountants stared back, frowns in place.

STR's boardroom was a mix of pale beige silk wallpaper and mahogany paneling. Overstuffed red leather chairs surrounded the huge mahogany table that dominated the room. The floor-to-ceiling drapes were pulled back to reveal a view of the small, rectangular park-like setting that separated the main offices of STR from its research center. Dingy snow lined the open spaces and a sky the color of weathered lead hung low. "What was that about capital impairment?"

Feinberg cleared his throat and raised his eyebrows. In a high-pitched voice that grated upon Mansky's nerves, he began. "In the opinion of DAK, STR will suffer a significant capital impairment from write downs required under GAAP-_"

"Why?" Mansky knew those words implied serious problems. "Our operating revenues are up this year. Yeah, inflation did impact our margins, our profit's up, but not what it should be. What capital impairment?"

"STR must write down its investment in the rubber plantation in South Vietnam this year. That's a significant amount of money." As Feinberg droned on, he tapped his pencil against the columnar work papers neatly stacked before him on the highly polished table. "It's about eighty million dollars, which is the adjusted figure for realized revenues."

"Why this year?" Mansky rose and leaned his hands on the table. He was six feet tall and had been on the offensive line at Penn State. He worked out regularly and weighed two hundred and fifty pounds. He wasn't above using his physical presence to get his views across. "The outcome of that stupid war still isn't clear." His jaw jutted forward and the muscles in his arms bulged, showing through his fine cotton shirt.

Feinberg took a deep breath. "The problem is that none of STR's personnel remained in charge after the Viet Cong overran the rubber plantation." He tapped his pencil against the work papers again. "More importantly, STR hasn't realized any production or revenue for at least one full year."

"How the hell could we?" Mansky said.

Feinberg plowed on as though he hadn't heard the question. "Meanwhile, STR still has to make interest payments on its project financing facility, with nothing to principal, as called for in the loan documents. Consequently, by definition, it is non-performing. It is a real drain upon the company."

"Dammit, Feinberg, STR doesn't need take a loss this year." Mansky glowered across the table. "Can't you figure some way to continue its performing status for at least another year?" The room grew quiet enough to hear faint sounds of traffic from the street six stories below.

Feinberg shook his head slowly. "STR's plantation investment was a gamble from the very beginning. It's now apparent Michelin wouldn't have sold it if they thought the Viet Nam war was winnable. The French learned their lesson at Dien Bien Phu, so they must have decided to cut and run."

Mansky started to speak. "But--"

Feinberg raised his hands. "Yes, yes, I know all about the logic of needing a source of natural rubber to make aircraft tires and take advantage of the military build-up.

However, it's a drag on your financial statement. There's another consideration that requires STR take a charge-off this year."

"What's that?"

Feinberg picked up a sheet of paper. It was a letter from the lead bank of the project financing facility. "This is a reminder that the loan covenants require STR pledge other assets if the income stream from the facility fails to service its debt, including payments on principal."

"So?" Mansky said.

"The problem is that all STR assets are currently pledged to its revolving credit facility."

"Damn." Mansky straightened up and walked to the window. He knew that Wall Street would take a dim view of this. STR's stock price would take a dive. That would lower the value of his stock options and any chance of retiring soon. Plus, it'd weaken his position with the Board of Directors, which he didn't need. He faced the table and the many blank faces in dark blue suits sitting around it. "Okay, I guess we've got to do it. I want no announcements just yet. I want to see what my management team can do to reduce costs to boost cash flow in the coming year."

#

"Okay, what've you got for me?" Mansky leaned forward over his desk, and waited, hand extended for Jeremy Cooperthwaite to hand him the memo. Mansky's corner office was paneled in maple, with a large desk in the center, two couches, and a small round table with four chairs. Bookshelves lined one wall. An interior decorator had described its appearance to him as modern and forceful, to match the CEO's personality. He liked the description. It fit his self-image.

"It's like this," Cooperthwaite said. "We must cut our budget and eliminate all non-essential items, and postpone expenses. I've identified about one hundred million dollars of potential savings if we hold the line on hiring, cut maintenance in half, postpone all capital expenditures and ride our vendors for an additional ninety days." He handed the sheet to Mansky. "It's a one year hold on almost everything."

Cooperthwaite was good with numbers. With an MBA from Wharton and a fiercely competitive drive, at age thirty-two, he'd risen fast in STR to become Mansky's favorite financial analyst. He knew nothing about making tires or running a production facility, but he sure knew how to make the numbers sing.

Silence filled the office as Mansky scanned the list. He wanted—no--hungered to succeed in meeting the loan covenants and keep STR's stock price up. He had planned to retire early and cash in, because he had almost five million in stock options. He was also a realist. "Is this do-able?"

Cooperthwaite nodded slowly. "It's going to make every divisional VP and line manager scream bloody murder. Every one of them claims that there are only "must haves" in their budgets." A trace of a smile crept onto his face. "However, maintaining STR's image and stock price is paramount."

Mansky nodded in cadence with Cooperthwaite. "Okay, I'll sign the memo. Get it distributed ASAP."

"Yes, sir." Cooperthwaite left the office.

Mansky leaned back in his chair. *I hope this works for at least a year. I want to cash out before the shit really hits the fan.*

Chapter 11
February 17, 1970.

"Hello?" Daniel said into the phone and continued working. He was at his desk in his cramped office in the boiler house. The scratched metal desk was squeezed between two filing cabinets and bookshelves filled with catalogs and three-ring binders. "Yes, sir." He sat up straight. The wooden chair squeaked at his sudden movement. "I'll be right over."

Oh, boy, Daniel thought, *I wonder what old Iron Butt wants now?* He'd got into the habit of thinking of Hodges by the nickname used by the boiler house operators. Daniel had just finished writing up the procedure for burning scrap tires in the boilers, which was practical if properly controlled.

Daniel realized the boilers, which were designed to burn bituminous coal, could also burn rubber cleanly. That required controlling the fuel feed rate and the airflow to prevent the combustion zone from moving up into the superheaters. If that happened, it could increase steam pressures beyond safe limits. With the current condition of the superheaters, the operators would have to be extra careful. If the superheaters were pushed too hard, they could even possibly explode. The thought of that happening made Daniel shiver.

He'd figured out the optimum feed rate would cut coal usage by sixteen percent and save more than a million dollars per year. It was a discovery that made him feel proud. He was sure it was enough to merit management's attention, and perhaps even get a raise.

#

Daniel stood before Hodges' desk. It was like being called to the principal's office--except this principal sat behind an eight-foot wide cherry desk that had a matching credenza in an office ten times larger than his own. He hadn't been invited to sit down after he gave Hodges his report on using scrap rubber as fuel. He had the distinct impression that his words were falling upon deaf ears.

Hodges glowered at another memo that lay before him. "Robles. Why did you call the police about an alleged illegal activity without informing management?" He looked up, face redder than usual.

Oh, crap, Daniel thought. *How did he find out it was me?* "I called the plant security chief, O'Brien. I did it because it looked like something illegal was going on." He took a quick breath. "When plant security did nothing, I called the Akron police directly--"

"Captain O'Brien informs me you did not discuss this with his department prior to calling the police, thus jeopardizing our relations with the police. In addition, you besmirched STR's fine reputation in the community, implying it's the home of a bunch of hop-heads." Hodges sniffed as though something was rotten. "I'm placing an official reprimand in your personnel file for failing to follow chain of command."

"But sir, I did call plant security," Daniel said. "I'm a law-abiding person. I believe I did the right thing to call the police when I saw something illegal--"

"Robles, it's just another example of your headstrong attitude and lack of team spirit. You're a loose cannon, doing what you want without taking the whole picture into consideration." Hodges shook his head. "You only think of your own interests and concerns, and not those of the company. In a word, you don't take orders well."

"What?" Daniel found Hodges' comment hard to believe. He always strove to do his best. He wanted to establish roots back in this area and having a stable job was the first step. "Sir, I don't agree with you."

"I believe I gave you a direct order to revise your memo on the utility boiler to STR standards, is this not correct?"

"Yes, but--"

"You didn't, did you? You gave me an inflated cost estimate, puffed up beyond all reason with unnecessary items." Hodges raised his eyes, steely gray and hard. He'd clamped his jaw tight in a bulldog fashion. "And now you take it upon yourself to give STR a bad reputation."

"Mr. Hodges," Daniel said. "The boiler and manifold system need action now. I prepared an estimate for the cost of their repair. Safety considerations require their repair, and soon." He stopped when Hodges opened his mouth showing clenched teeth.

"That's your opinion," Hodges snapped. "Chairman Mansky has ordered that all unnecessary maintenance projects be halted for one year. It's my opinion that you've overstated the need for this repair--."

"Didn't you read my follow-up memo on the superheaters, particularly about number three?" Daniel interrupted Hodges. "They need replacing. The wall thickness is marginal."

"STR needs to cut costs." Hodges handed Daniel a copy of Mansky's memo. "In that, CEO Mansky gave a directive that applies to all employees of STR. It doesn't exclude one Daniel Robles, who seems to think his projects are more important than those of anyone else."

"I beg to differ--"

"Look, dammit, get in line, will you?" Hodges tapped his desk with his index finger. "I've tried to help you. I invited you to join the STR team, the Vulcan club, so you could learn the STR way and get the right attitude. You just don't seem to want to learn." He sat down in his chair. "Mansky's memo has gone to every manager within STR. That means this is policy, which even applies to Daniel Robles. Do you understand?"

"I believe this is a safety issue--"

"That's another thing," Hodges said quickly. "Don't ever put such things in writing. Communicate them verbally. I expect you to retract this memo and reissue it without the inflammatory crap about unsafe conditions."

"You hired me because I'm an engineer with knowledge about boilers and combustion. I have real experience in this area, yet you ignore my recommendations." Daniel shook his head. "I don't understand this at all."

"What don't you understand?" Hodges' jaw muscles flexed.

"You want me to gloss over unsafe conditions," Daniel said. "Another thing, I don't think I ought to be required to attend offsite meetings where the message is that I should learn how to violate laws, regulations and safety--"

"What did you say?" Hodges came to his feet, eyes bulging.

"You're pressuring me to ignore safety, violate the law--"

"How dare you say that? I've done no such thing, you insubordinate, snot-nosed kid!" Spittle flew from his mouth. "That's it, you're out of here. Pack up your stuff, now. You're fired."

#

Two uniformed and armed security guards in crisp, white shirts with gold-braided epaulets and peaked hats stood alongside Daniel as he emptied the contents of his desk into a cardboard box. He reached for the file drawer in his desk.

"No files, Mr. Robles," the older of the two guards said. "You'll have to leave your personal effects for inspection," he said. "You can pick them up later."

Daniel felt a surge of anger. "What? Going to check to see if I'm stealing STR's paperclips?"

"STR wants to make sure that you just get your personal possessions, and only your possessions." The guard's voice was flat, controlled. His face had the forced neutrality of someone who either didn't care or could hide his feelings. "Are they all in that box?"

Daniel looked at the box that contained four engineering texts, a slide rule, a CRC math handbook and miscellaneous pens, pencils and other engineering drawing equipment. "Yeah, that's about it. Let's get on with it."

"We have to escort you to personnel where you have to fill out the exit papers. When that's done, we come back here to pick up your personnel effects after they've been inspected."

As the afternoon went by, Daniel realized that the exit procedure was designed to humiliate those fired from STR by parading them through the organization, escorted by armed guards as though they were criminals. As he went into each room, conversation ceased and eyes followed him, eyes full of the unspoken accusation that he was a failure, and perhaps worse, a criminal, a Hispanic criminal. The only moment of relief came when he sat down with William Dieter in Human Resources.

Dieter explained that he'd just received two backdated reprimands to put in Daniel's personnel file. "I don't know what's going on, but Hodges has fired more people than anyone else in STR."

Daniel had met Dieter when he'd hired in, and later learned that Carol's mother's first husband was related to Dieter. They'd had a couple of beers after work. He'd found that Dieter was a straight shooter, who'd given him a few cautionary words about Hodges, but obviously not enough.

Dieter passed a card to him. "Look, give me a call from time to time and I'll let you know what I can."

Daniel examined the card. "What's this WATs number?"

Dieter sniffed. "That's an inward WATs or wide area telephone number. You can call me without charge from anywhere in the country. I usually give it out to kids I'm recruiting at colleges." He rose and walked to the door and paused. "Look, I don't like this any more than you do, but I've got no choice in the matter. Gimme a call."

"Okay, Dieter, thanks."

Dieter opened the door. The two security guards were outside, waiting to take him for his final walk through STR.

Chapter 12

February 17, 1970.

"Carol, can I see you for a minute?" George Schmidt called from his glassed-in cubicle that looked out on the showroom. It was cluttered with filing cabinets and sales awards covered the wall. Schmidt, sales manager for Rick Box Honda, was forty-five and married with three kids but acted as though he were single and in his twenties. At five feet nine inches and one hundred and eighty pounds, with thinning black hair well lubricated with Brylcream, he failed to convince anyone that he was God's gift to women, particularly Carol.

"Yes, Mr. Schmidt, what can I do for you?" Carol stood at the entrance to his office. She'd felt increasingly ill at ease in his presence, especially after she'd seen him talking to Eric Slazenger, who'd graduated from high school with her. They'd both been grinning while watching and obviously talking about her. She'd dated Eric's close friend, Jimmy Wentworth, and was sure Eric knew they'd been intimate. After that, Schmidt's eyes followed her all the time. When he looked at her, she felt as though he was seeing her naked.

Carol had dated widely in Ravenna High School and had gone all the way with two of the guys she'd dated because it kept their attention. By the time she graduated, she realized she had the reputation of being easy. She wished things had been different.

"C'mon in, Carol. Close the door." Schmidt pointed to a chair in front of his desk. "Please, take a seat." He leaned back and smiled. "You've been here five months, right?"

"Yes, Mr. Schmidt, that's correct." Carol was careful to be polite and say as little as possible. She folded her hands in her lap and kept her legs together.

"Rick Box Honda reviews new employees after six

59

months," Schmidt said. "If their performance is above grade, they get a raise." He leaned forward and raised his eyebrows. "A raise would be nice, wouldn't it?"

"Yes, Mr. Schmidt, it would." Carol felt a quick rush of excitement, for she could always use more money.

Schmidt frowned briefly. "Y'know, I haven't gotten a good feel for your talents, because we haven't spent much time together. Yet I'd like to recommend you for a raise, a big raise, 'cause I think you're a good kid."

"Thank you." She knew if it sounded too good to be true, it probably was. She suspected she knew where this was going.

"We oughta spend more time together." He looked around as though seeking inspiration. "Don't you think that would be a good idea?"

Carol nodded reluctantly.

"I tell you what, we could get to know each other much better if we both went to the Detroit Auto Show next week. Y'know, the big one held in Cobo Hall. You'd get to see all the new cars and the company would pick up the expenses. How does that sound to you?"

"Well, I really don't know, Mr. Schmidt." Carol didn't know how to tell him she didn't want to go to the show.

"We could drive up together. Do the show, eat at a nice restaurant, have a few drinks." Schmidt smiled as though he'd just sold a car loaded with every option. "Then afterward," he lowered his voice, "we'll go to my motel room and spend some time together. Y'know, so we could get to know each other better, a whole lot better." He winked and smiled. "Right?"

Carol felt a huge weight descend. "I, I have to think about that." From the leer on his face, she knew exactly what he had in mind. She desperately wanted to flee.

Schmidt picked up a sheet of paper and waved it. "Don't take too long thinking about it," he said. "I've got to turn in your performance appraisal next week, right after the

Auto Show. You'd want me in a good frame of mind, right? You do want a raise, don't you?" He leaned forward, eyebrows raised and nodded.

She forced herself to reply. "Yes."

"You want to keep your job, right?"

Carol heard a phone ring at her desk. "I have to answer that, Mr. Schmidt." She got up and left.

#

After meeting with Schmidt, Carol went home early from Rick Box Honda. She told the business manager she was sick. She felt nauseated and about to throw up. She felt trapped and wanted to flee. *Men*, she thought. *They only want one thing.* After a while, in the quiet of Daniel's apartment, the problem seemed distant and not so pressing.

Carol wandered around the apartment and stopped at the filing cabinet in which Daniel kept his records. Most of the files were on stupid engineering stuff about combustion and steam. At the back of the bottom drawer, she found a brown manila folder. *I wonder what's in here?* She thought. After she unsnapped the elastic band, she found that it was his tax returns, paid bills and statements from the bank. His checking account carried a balance of two hundred and fifty dollars. However, his savings account showed steady deposits of three hundred dollars a month since he'd opened it last October, plus a lump sum of two thousand three hundred dollars at its opening. *Twelve hundred dollars in four months? Hmm,* she thought, *he must earn a lot of money.* A minute later, she found his paycheck stubs and saw he earned eight hundred and fifty dollars a month. *Wow, that's more than twice my salary,* she thought. *And he's got over three thousand saved.*

Carol put everything back just as she had found it and once done, sat down with a cup of tea to think. *I like Daniel. Do I love him? Maybe. The fact he earns a lot of money doesn't hurt. He has more polish than any of the guys she'd known at Ravenna High School. He was the kind of guy who was easy to underestimate, like when he came to the stables, driving that old white Econoline van. At first I thought he was just a delivery guy.*

I could do a lot worse, she thought. *He's the best boyfriend I've ever had. When we have sex, he does things the other guys didn't do.* She remembered the first time they had mutual oral sex and remembered how much it'd turned her on. Her previous boyfriends had pushed her to perform oral sex on them, but they hadn't offered to do the same to her. Daniel was the first one who ever did it to her. Just the thought made her excited, for it satisfied her more than regular sex.

Yes, she thought, *I could do far worse. If we got married, mom would forgive me because he has a good job and takes care of me properly.* The more she thought about it, the more certain he was a good catch. *If we get married, then that slimy George Schmidt will leave me alone. Why, I might not even have to work at all, what with all the money that Daniel makes. Then I could go shopping every day.*

The downstairs door slammed shut. Carol glanced at her watch. Daniel came in without saying a word and stood still, arms slack at his side. "You're early," she said.

He bit his lower lip. "I've got some bad news."

"Oh," Carol said. "Nothing serious, I hope."

"I've just been fired."

Chapter 13

William Dieter had worked in the Human Resources department at STR for six years. With three other employees in Human Resources, it meant there were no real secrets. He found the work had both its ups and downs, but when he learned that Daniel Robles had been fired, it hit him hard.

He leaned back in his chair. He'd closed the door to his office, which was small but furnished with a new oak desk, matching guest chairs and a small couch. Along with matching credenza and files, it exuded the appearance that STR was a successful and perhaps even a generous organization. All very necessary, Dieter thought, if we're recruiting personnel, which we're not doing now.

Dieter had led the effort to find and recruit Daniel, luring him away from Matlock in Chicago. He'd thought he'd done a good job getting Daniel at a salary level within the budget and minimal moving expenses. He had the right profile to make a good employee: a graduate from a local university, relatives in the area and a solid work record of steadily increasing responsibility. He liked the guy.

It was only two months after Daniel was hired, Dieter learned he was dating Carol Meadows, who was related to his wife. Carol lived with her divorced mother. Carol's mother got by on what she made working at the local five-and-dime. She was vocal about how she distrusted -- no, hated men. Carol seemed okay, even if she'd dated the wrong guys in high school. He hoped things would work out between her and Daniel.

He'd called Daniel and mentioned his relationship to Carol and suggested lunch. They'd gone to lunch and talked about memories as students at Kent State. He learned Daniel's father had taught there and his brother was an associate professor of foreign languages. With that kind of background, Dieter had been sure Daniel would be successful in the STR organization with the potential to advance up the managerial ranks. *Lord only knows,* he thought, *STR needs some fresh talent in that area.*

Now Hodges has fired him. *For insubordination? That's crap,* Dieter thought. *It sounds more like a personality conflict, which should have been resolved, except Hodges never showed any flexibility. That's the third engineer he's fired in the past five years, all for the same reason. Now Hodges has sent over a bad performance review and a reprimand to put into Daniel's personnel file, both obviously backdated. Sometimes this job makes me feel like a real shit.*

Well, there's not much I can do for Daniel, he thought, *I need this job. Maybe I can put him in contact with a good headhunter, or even leads to other companies that might need a good engineer.* He felt betrayed about what had happened.

#

As Daniel climbed the stairs to his apartment, he recognized a tune from the Grateful Dead's album 'Anthem of the Sun' that was playing in the apartment below. He only knew his neighbors as nodding acquaintances. They had long hair, dressed weird and smoked dope. The aromatic smell of marijuana smoke lingered lightly in the dimly lit stairwell.

"You're early." Carol had on a pair of faded jeans with a worn band of embroidered ribbon at the bottom. She had on a burgundy cable-knit sweater that complimented her well-rounded form. She had her long blond hair gathered into a bun with a leather clasp.

He glanced at Carol, worried how to tell her. "I've got some bad news."

"Oh," Carol said. "Nothing serious, I hope."

"I've just been fired." Daniel felt a tightening in his chest. "Hodges said I was insubordinate, then he fired me." He shook his head. "I tried to do my best, but it wasn't good enough for him. I really don't understand it at all."

Carol stared at him silently.

Daniel hung up his coat. As he sat down on the couch, its springs protested with a metallic sound. He glanced at the TV, almost automatically. Images of soldiers jumping from helicopters appeared. Nixon's face filled the screen announcing the withdrawal of thirty-five thousand troops from Vietnam. *Crap*, he thought, *this stupid war won't end too soon.*

He got a Stroh's beer from the refrigerator. He felt bruised, almost tainted from the way people watched him as he'd been paraded through STR. "I thought I had friends there," he said. "Well, that just goes to show you."

"What're you going to do?"

"I guess I should look at it as an opportunity for a vacation." Daniel put his feet up on the coffee table and took a swallow of the Stroh's.

"If you don't have a job, what will we do for money?"

I should've known that Carol would ask that, Daniel thought. *Always worried about money.*

"I don't earn enough to support both of us." She consulted her fingers as though they were a crystal ball to the future.

Daniel took a deep breath. "Well, I have some money stashed away. It should be enough to pay the rent for a month or so. But I do need a job and soon."

"Oh, Daniel, no matter what happens, I'll stand by you." Carol knelt next to him and looked down, consulting her fingers again. Tears began to fill her eyes. Her lower lip protruded and began to quiver.

"What's wrong?" Daniel squeezed her shoulder gently. He was sure something else was bothering her.

She looked up. "Schmidt, the sales manager, wants me to go away on a dirty weekend with him. He wants me to go to the Detroit Auto Show and spend the night with him." A tear trickled down her cheek. She moved onto the couch next to him.

Daniel felt a mixture of anger and fear. *You bastard, he thought, trying to hustle my Carol.* He felt a surge of rage. He wanted to grab this asshole and punch his lights out. He took a deep breath to calm himself and he put his arms around her and stroked her hair.

"Carol," he said. "He can't do that. Why would he think you'd ever agree to something like that?"

"It's my performance review time." Carol sniffed. "If I go with him, he said I'd get a good review and a raise." Her eyes filled again with tears. "If I don't, I lose my job."

It is moments like this, Daniel thought, *that makes dropping out seem right. The goddamn establishment tries to fuck us one-way or the other—sometimes literally.* He stroked her hair. "Sweetheart, you don't have to go with him. There's no way that he's going to get away with this." He kissed her forehead and the idea of punching out the guy came back. *Maybe,* he thought, *but knew beating up the guy would bring in the cops.*

"I need the job--"

"There're other jobs, where you don't have to put out to keep them. Believe me, he's gone over the line." He rose, took her hand and led her to the kitchen table. "I'll make you some tea." He knew she liked to relax with a cup of orange spice herb tea.

#

Daniel took a swig of beer and the phone rang. It was his third beer, but he still felt the pain inside. Two weeks had gone by and he'd learned that he wasn't eligible for state unemployment benefits because he'd been discharged for cause. At least, that's what the report from STR had said. When he'd checked with Dieter in Personnel, he learned Hodges had insisted STR send in the report that stated Daniel had been an insubordinate employee, discharged 'for cause.'

"Yeah?" Daniel covered the mouthpiece and stage-whispered to Carol, "it's Fats, he's calling from San Francisco." He referred to his high-school buddy, Fielding A. Terzillo whose initials got him the nickname Fats. "He sends you a wet, sloppy kiss."

Daniel winked and went back to listening, dropping

in a "yeah" or a "sure" at appropriate spots in Fats's monologue about life on the West Coast. "Well, I don't have a job anymore," he said. "Yeah, right, come out to San Francisco. Drop everything and hit the road."

The conversation lasted almost a half-hour during which Fats offered--several times--to provide a place for them to stay in their time of troubles. Daniel related bits and pieces of the conversation to Carol.

Daniel hung up the phone. "Want to go to California?" He found the idea appealing. Maybe it was the beer. He tipped up the bottle and tried to coax another drop from it. It was already empty and the last one from the six-pack.

"California? Are you crazy? Here at least, I have a job."

"Yeah." He pursed his lips. "Do you like your job? Does it pay well? Do you like your boss?" They both knew that Carol could hardly stand working at the local Honda dealership. Schmidt had given her a bad performance review and no raise when she had refused to go on the Detroit trip. He'd also extended her probationary period for another six months and hinted if she didn't change her tune, he'd get her fired. The fact it was within walking distance and had flexible work hours, barely made up for the low pay and a manager who kept hinting that keeping her job depended upon her spreading her legs.

"The only thing keeping you at the dealership is my lack of a job," Daniel said. "I'm still paying the rent."

"Oh, so the fact I pay for the groceries and utilities means nothing?" Her anger was brief.

"Forget I said that. It was uncalled for. Fats says there's lots of work available. We should go." All through the late sixties, the economy had expanded--why would it change?

It was the first time he'd lived with a woman. He liked Carol's looks and had never experienced sex like this before. It had changed the way he looked at life. The last three months together had been wonderful. He enjoyed every moment with Carol and their sex life had been especially satisfying. They had sex every day, and on the weekends, several times a day. Their relationship had changed him, made him more tranquil. They'd clicked. So, why not run off together? Start a new life in the Promised Land. The Golden State was the future, right? "Do you wanna go to California?"

"If you want me, I'll go wherever you go." Carol looked down. "You know that, don't you?"

Chapter 14

March 1, 1970.

It took two weeks for Daniel to tidy up his affairs. He saw Carol got considerable satisfaction from leaving Rick Box Honda. Without putting anything in writing, she advised the business manager she was leaving due to the sales manager's sexual advances. A day later, after she sold her five-year-old Corvair for six hundred dollars, she told him, "I can use the money for my hope chest."

"Hope chest?" Daniel said.

Carol put her arms around him and laid her head on his chest. "It'll be for us, when we get married."

He felt a tremor in his heart. *Uh-oh. Why is she talking about marriage? I never said anything about getting married. Yeah, I like Carol, but marriage? I'm just not positive she's the one. There's still a lot I don't know about her.* "I don't have a job, so any decision about the future, getting married is premature." He stroked her hair.

"I wasn't talking about us getting married just now, but even if I was, you make it sound, well, I thought you felt differently about me, Daniel. I thought, you know, you felt the same way about me as I feel about you." Carol released him and looked up, eyes serious and her lower lip extended, the beginning of a pout.

"We're not going through Las Vegas." He winked and smiled. He hoped that would lighten the situation. "Look, neither of us has a job. We're moving to California where we'll be on our own."

"I'd do anything for you," she said. "Go anywhere with you. All I need to know is that you really care about me." Tears began to collect in her eyes. "I split from my mother for you."

"Will a ring make things any different from the way it is now?" For a moment, he wondered if he were doing the right thing by taking her with him. There were things that had begun to bother him; her quickness to tears as a means to get his attention and sympathy, her interest in money, and sometimes her manipulative ways. Yet he couldn't bring himself to end their relationship. He wasn't sure if it was love or addiction to sex. "You do know I care about you, don't you?"

"I just want to be sure." Her lower lip quivered as she looked up at him from studying her fingernails. "I don't want to lose you."

#

"C'mon in." Hector swung the door open and put his arms around Carol. He moved to give her a kiss, but Carol held him off. Hector frowned.

"How have you been doing, Hector?" Daniel gave his brother a quick hug, and stepped inside. "Man, it's cold out there. Hey, thanks for inviting us. Y'know, a final feast and a place to stay before we take off."

"Ah, you're family. It's the least I could do." Hector took their coats. "It'll only take a few minutes to get the food going. First, let's have a drink." He guided them into a living room where a fire burned in the fireplace. A large floral sofa and two armchairs formed a circle around the hearth. A bottle of white wine and three glasses sat on the coffee table. Magazines and books were stacked on the floor by one of the armchairs, which showed signs of wear from regular use.

"Sounds good." Daniel steered Carol to the sofa.

Hector poured three generous glasses of wine. "To your great adventure out west." He raised his glass.

"Let's hope it's a prosperous adventure." Daniel raised his glass and turned to Carol. "What d'you say?"

"Well, I hope your friend, Fats, has a job waiting for you." Carol sipped the wine and frowned as though she'd tasted something unpleasant. "D'you have something a little sweeter? This tastes sour."

Hector's eyebrows rose. "Hmm, you don't care for the wine?" His voice implied that something must be wrong with the taster. "It's a Mersault."

"I think it's fine." Daniel spoke quickly. "What're we having for supper?"

"An old family favorite," Hector said. "Paella."

"What's that?" The frown on Carol's face returned.

"Don't worry," Daniel said. "It's kind of like a fish stew. You'll like it."

Carol's frown deepened. "Fish stew?" Her voice was heavy with doubt.

Hector rose. "I'm going to get started." He headed to the kitchen.

Daniel took Carol's hand and explained the ingredients in paella and how it was made. He knew he had to get her comfortable and talking otherwise it would be him and Hector holding the conversation.

A half hour later, Hector brought them to the dining room. In the center of the table was a huge tureen filled with lobster, shrimp, crab and clams in a fragrant yellow sauce. Other dishes contained saffron rice, broccoli and carrots.

Daniel noted that Carol ate the lobster and shrimp, but ignored the other ingredients in the paella. She ate only a small amount of rice and vegetables. She also joined the conversation when directly addressed or asked a question. She spent a lot of time consulting her fingernails.

Hector insisted they try several more wine from burgundy, making several trips to the basement.

Daniel enjoyed the wines, finishing those left by Carol, who did not seem to enjoy them. By eleven, he realized he was 'medio borracho' or half hammered. He'd drunk enough to get double vision. He was glad they were staying with his brother that evening. Driving would have been an invitation to disaster.

\#

It was at first light on Sunday, March 2, 1970 when Daniel pulled his white Ford Econoline van out of Hector's driveway. He was hung over as he navigated the van through Kent, and a series of secondary roads until he reached US 224, heading toward Interstate 71. He glanced at Carol and saw her eyes were closed and her mouth was open. She was sound asleep.

By the end of the first day, Daniel was tired of the never-ending ribbon of concrete that was the newly built interstate highway. The hum of the tires never changed, the van's engine only grew louder when they hit the long uphill grades. The landscape, punctuated by a constant parade of billboards, was the dry tan of winter-seared farmlands. The bright sunshine of the morning had disappeared under a vanguard of slate gray clouds.

On the outskirts of St. Louis, he stopped at a neon-festooned Travelodge motel and got a room that cost thirty dollars. It was more than he wanted to spend, but night was falling and he didn't like the idea of searching for something cheaper. His eyes felt gritty and he needed exercise, but the onslaught of a cold, heavy rain kept him indoors.

Daniel watched Carol wander around the motel room. She examined every detail as though she were in a showroom and about to buy something. *It was*, he thought, *a standard motel, like many of those he'd stayed in while consulting.* Yet for Carol, it was as if he were showing her a whole new world.

"This is really nice, isn't it?" she said.

"Yeah, I guess so," Daniel said. Its furniture was nicer than his furnished apartment in Kent. "This is a queen-size bed." He patted the bed and winked. "Want to check it out?" He remembered his first time in a posh hotel had made him feel special, important and adventurous.

Carol smiled slowly. "Let's take a shower together." She began removing her clothes, her eyes locked on his eyes.

Daniel had a sudden urge of arousal. He wanted to grin, but he didn't. He knew when she said that, once in the shower together, she'd get him started with a quick blowjob and they'd go to bed where he'd go down on her. She seemed to like that a lot. "Sure."

#

In the morning, Daniel saw the rain had turned to

snow. The weatherman on the TV forecast a series of storms for the next week in the Rockies that would make the skiers happy and the mountain passes hazardous. Even though the van was weighed down with their possessions, it wasn't good on slippery roads. "Carol," he called. "A change in plans. We're going through Albuquerque instead of Denver." He pointed to the TV. "The weather isn't cooperating."

"Okay." She returned to painting her fingernails without a glance. "That's fine with me."

#

The longer southern route took them to Oklahoma City, where they took refuge in a Best Western motel. Again, Carol took pleasure in what she perceived to be luxury. They made love both on going to bed and before getting up in the morning.

Later in the morning, they headed through the high plains of Texas and up into New Mexico. At Tucumcari, Daniel pulled into a motel advertising rooms for fifteen dollars a night. It was the only motel in town. It was also time to seek more economical places to stay to stretch his money. An overweight Indian woman led them to a room in a long adobe building.

Inside, an overhead fluorescent lamp provided the only light. A small TV on top of a plastic-veneered dresser stared blankly at a standard double bed. A cobweb lurked in the corner of the ceiling. Daniel was relieved to see the cracked tile floor of the bathroom was clean. He pulled back the covers on the bed and saw the sheets were fresh.

"Okay, we'll take it." Daniel paid in cash, in advance.

The adobe walls softened the steady rumble of heavy trucks on Interstate forty. Daniel put a towel at the base of the door where a trace of dust crept under a warped wooden door that loosely cleared the sill. "Well, it's cheap."

"I liked the other ones better." Carol sniffed as though something didn't smell quite right. A trace of the astringent aroma of pine cleaner seeped from the bathroom.

"Yeah, I know what you mean, but we're not going

to live here." As he sat on the bed, it squeaked. "Want to take a shower with me?" A quick vision of their previous turns in showers filled him with hope.

"No." Carol pursed her lips. "You go ahead. I'll take mine later." She began to study her fingernails as though seeking an answer. He'd come to recognize that was a sign she wasn't happy.

#

Departing Tucumcari, the distance between shabby towns grew greater. Snow lightly dusted the almost treeless plateau. The van labored up and down the wide rolling countryside, empty except for the occasional building in the distance. The van's engine slowed on the long grade to reach the pass in the snow-covered Manzano Mountains of eastern New Mexico and the Sandia Mountains overlooking Albuquerque. After crossing the crest of the mountains, Daniel let the van coast down the long run into a dry, dusty Albuquerque, where they stopped for fuel and a snack.

The road out of Albuquerque was another long climb, this time into the Zuni Mountains. The highway went through widely spaced, stunted conifers lightly sprinkled with snow. Along the way, the desert turned into stretches of jagged, broken dark gray rock that made him think of pictures of the moon's surface he'd seen on TV. It was the lava fields of the Malpais, near the town of Grants. It was almost as though they'd become space travelers, now entering an alien world.

As the distance between signs of civilization grew wider, Carol grew quieter. In Flagstaff, they stayed at an inexpensive motel, whose tired rooms again disappointed Carol. Again, she refused to take a shower with him.

Shit, I can't win, thought Daniel. *I want to do the right thing, but can't she see the sense in not spending a lot of money on motels.* He'd suggested sleeping in the van, but she'd only given him a cold look of disapproval. This was the second night she'd given him a cold shoulder once they got into bed. It was as if there were a correlation between the amount he spent on the motel and the frequency of their lovemaking. While trying to get to sleep, he realized she hadn't offered once to share in the expenses, even though he knew she had a nest egg from the sale of her Corvair tucked away.

#

The next day, the road left the broad mesas, and they zigzagged down through the austere mountains of Arizona to cross the Colorado River. Out into the desert, the land flattened out and the saw-tooth horizon softened.

They'd left the ice and snow as the sun offered more heat. The desert of stark, barren flats, hemmed in by purple hills, was the emptiest and loneliest place he'd ever seen. Crossing the Mojave felt almost like a cleansing experience that made him feel as though the troubles left in Ohio had finally been lifted from him.

By late morning, they descended from the bald, brown hills of the Tehachapi Pass into the flat, tawny lands around Bakersfield, where vivid green patches of irrigated land popped up like oases. As the land grew greener and the road widened into a freeway, more gas stations and fast food restaurants appeared. It was as though civilization had reemerged. The weather grew warmer and the sunlight cast a golden haze over the countryside.

It's like a rebirth, Daniel thought. California, golden California was even better than Fats' description. The roads were wider and better paved, with more traffic than any place on their trip. The closer they got to San Francisco, a more prosperous California appeared. Houses became larger and more modern. Signs for restaurants and gas stations grew bigger at each highway interchange. Landscaping began to line the highways, reflecting the wealth of the communities. California truly began to look like the Promised Land.

Chapter 15

Ben Hodges paused and glanced at the glass-covered poster extolling the performance of STR tires. He used it as a mirror to adjust his tie to perfection and smooth his jacket. He stood straight, took a deep breath and pushed open the door to the boardroom. *This is it,* he thought. *They're going to promote me, make me an officer of the company.* He'd set his sights on being vice-president of production at STR and possibly even becoming a member of the board. Every time they invited him before the board, his hopes rose.

It was a scene he hoped would become even more familiar. Eight men and one woman sat in overstuffed red leather chairs around a huge mahogany table. Pale yellow folders lay in front of each person with papers strewn across the table. Recessed lighting illuminated the table, barely revealing the walls behind. The room had an aura of power. He loved it.

A sea of knitted brows and pursed lips silently greeted Hodges as he stepped to the end of the table. "Yes, Mr. Mansky?" He forced a smile and nodded to the other members of the board. One glance gave him a quick read of their mood. His hopes of being promoted faded fast. Not one face held even a glimmer of any forthcoming congratulatory comment.

"Yes, Hodges." Mansky tapped a yellow covered report before him. "The accountants' preliminary findings aren't good. Cost savings haven't met plan. Cash flow is below budget." His eyes narrowed. "Why haven't production costs been cut to the target levels you set?"

A trickle of sweat ran down Hodges' back. The collar of his shirt constricted. "Er, Mr. Mansky, I have cut production costs significantly and have instituted additional steps to reduce expenses even greater than targeted," he said. *If I haven't, I will.*

"STR needs an additional ten percent cost reduction across the board." Mansky waved a sheet of paper at

Hodges. "There will be no bonuses this year for any executives. None."

Hodges felt a tightening in his chest at these words. That meant that the STR's financial problems were really serious. Executive bonuses were almost sacrosanct to upper management. Long-time company tradition held the executives fed at the trough before anyone else. There are going to be a lot of pissed-off executives once the news of this gets out. "Yes, sir," he said. "I'll get right to it--"

"I want a report on my desk by Monday morning. It will spell out the details of your cost reduction steps and the expected benefit to STR." Mansky wagged his index finger toward Hodges. "Do I make myself clear?"

"Yes, sir. Absolutely sir." Hodges straightened his posture and fought the urge to salute. He pirouetted on his heel and marched out.

#

Hodges searched through his files. *What was it that young twerp, Robles, had done on cost reduction?* He felt an element of desperation and moved quickly. *Ah, here it is.* He leaned back in his chair to read the memo on burning tire scrap in the utility boilers. The words '...has the potential to cut coal usage by sixteen percent and save more than a million dollars per year...' jumped out from the page to his attention. His heart beat faster. He leaned forward to place the memo on the center of the blotter on the desk, smoothing it flat to read it again, in detail.

The memo referred to another memo about operating conditions, which Hodges made mental note to read. He realized he could exceed the cost savings demanded by Mansky in direct fuel costs immediately. *Maybe*, he thought, *this will finally make the board realize I'm truly top executive material.* He studied the memo carefully. *So, if we use our rubber scrap as fuel, we save fuel costs and even cut scrap disposal costs. It was a double-edged savings.*

He forgot about looking for the memo on operating conditions. His concern was cost savings, now.

"Grabowski," Hodges said into the phone. "Did you read the memo on burning scrap rubber in the utility boilers? Good. What will it take to get that underway?" He listened carefully for about three minutes. "Yes, yes, I know all about the operating parameters. What I want is that adapter for the stoking system built as soon as possible. We need to start using scrap rubber as fuel immediately, if not sooner. Do I make myself clear?"

Hodges nodded. "Of course I'll approve an A.F.E. to pay for the machine work and installation. Walk it up to me and I'll sign it immediately." He tapped his desk with a pencil and frowned. "Yes, of course I've read the background information. Remember, I'm an engineer, too." He pursed his lips. "Good. As soon as possible. STR needs this kind of innovation to remain competitive." He hung up the phone.

Now, he thought, *where's the rest of the memos that twerp, Robles, wrote? I've got to revise them and make the originals disappear. There's no need for his name to be involved in a project with this kind of impact. He's not around; he doesn't need his name on this. I'm the one implementing it.*

#

Getting the special conveyor-chutes made for the three utility boilers frustrated Hodges. It took two whole weeks to get the scrap rubber stoking system built even after he authorized it as top priority. The machine shop could only release two men to work on it due to budget problems.

There was another problem. It was Robles's report on the condition of the superheaters. It contained copies of an ultrasonic trace and calculations that said the superheaters were unsafe. *What utter nonsense,* he thought. *Those boilers were built back in the days when they knew how to build 'em right.* Yet, he didn't want that memo out where the union could get it and use it to shut STR down, which they might. He made a mental promise to track down all the memos and remove them from the files. *I've got to find the originals and*

78

destroy them.

"Okay, Grabowski, start it up." Hodges paced back and forth in the fueling room. The steady rumble of the furnace made conversation almost impossible and the heat made him sweat. The dark metal stoking equipment seemed almost malign against the silver painted insulation on the furnace.

A long rubber belt conveyor laden with chunks of tires and rubber scrap came through a rough opening in the dark red brick wall into the fueling room. The end of the conveyor, like a giant black, wart-covered tongue, stuck out over a hopper above the reciprocating metal coal-feeder that put fuel into the furnace.

"We're gonna start slowly," Grabowski yelled. "As we feed the rubber, we'll slow down the coal-feeder so we don't over-fuel the furnace." He wiped his brow with the back of his hand.

"Yes, yes, that's fine." Hodges began to feel almost faint from the heat. It was the first time in years he'd visited the boiler house and had forgotten how hot it could be. "Follow the procedure and report to me what happens. I want figures on coal and scrap rubber consumption every twenty-four hours. Is that clear?"

Grabowski nodded. "Yeah, right, Mr. Hodges, I understand."

#

When he returned to his office, Hodges called Robles. He'd looked all over and hadn't found the memos on the superheaters. He knew he had to find them, especially the originals. Robles should certainly know their location. Standing and staring out at STR's Research Center with the phone at his ear, he listened to it ring.

"I'm sorry, but the number you have dialed is not a working number..." said a tinny female voice.

Hodges checked the number in the personnel file again and re-dialed it. He got the same response. Damn. He leafed through the personnel file until he found information on next of kin. *Aha, he has a brother living in Kent. He should know where I can reach that damn Robles.*

"This is Ben Hodges, I'm plant manager of Schirmerling Tire and Rubber... Yes, that's right. I'm looking to contact, er." He looked down at the personnel file. "Daniel Robles, yes, that's right. Why? I have some questions for him about work he did here. Well, he still has a responsibility to us even if he has been discharged. You don't think so? Why not? Oh, I see. D'you know where he is? You don't? I see. Well, can you let me know when you do find out?"

Hodges felt a surge of anger as he gave his number. *This Hector Robles had a hostile attitude. Doesn't he realize STR is more important than his snot-nosed whelp of a brother?*

Chapter 16

Daniel and Carol stood on a street in Pacifica littered with paper and empty beverage containers. Near the corner, a car sat on concrete blocks instead of wheels. He checked the address. It was the right number. He knocked on the door.

The door opened a crack. "Hey, Fats," called a longhaired man. "Someone's looking for you." He turned away and disappeared inside the stucco cottage whose peeling pink paint and frayed window shades were several steps below shabby gentility. "Hey, Fats, out front."

"What the fuck?" Fats appeared in the doorway, face flushed, no shirt and a half empty beer bottle in hand. "Daniel? What the fuck are you doing here?"

"You invited us. We're here." Daniel was disappointed but not surprised at Fats' reaction. He'd seen it before.

"I thought you were shitting me. I never thought you'd come. Wow, man, I thought you were, like, stuck in Ohio."

"I called and left a message for you with someone that we were coming." Daniel heard music coming from inside the house. It was a tune he recognized from Van Morrison's Astral Weeks album. He smelled marijuana smoke and the cloying aroma of cheap incense. "You going to invite us in?"

"Er, yeah, well, I guess so." He turned and stepped inside.

Daniel and Carol followed. The room's dim light revealed a sagging couch and mismatched armchairs whose colors had been tempered with years of grime. A rectangular slab of scarred wood covered with overflowing ashtrays sat on two concrete blocks and pretended to be a coffee table.

A regular Salvation Army interior decór, Daniel thought. He also realized that something wasn't right – Fats' attitude was all wrong. "What's up, man? You look like

81

something isn't cool."

"Er, I've got a problem." Fats shrugged.

"Okay, what's the problem?"

"It's kinda complicated."

"So, tell me."

A girl appeared in the doorway of a darkened room. She was buttoning her only apparel--a long, blue flannel shirt open to her navel. She had no bra on and her small breasts barely dimpled the shirt's fabric.

"I have--" Fats hesitated, "a slight legal problem. I was, like, involved in an auto accident."

This is more than a fender-bender, Daniel thought.

A face appeared, peering around the edge of a doorway with an air of caution, as though poised to flee.

"How bad?" he asked.

The face disappeared and a door slammed shut.

"I totaled a couple of cars. I don't have any insurance."

"Anyone hurt?"

"Yeah, but no one seriously."

This isn't the whole story, Daniel thought. "So, what's the real problem? Cars can be replaced." He knew Fats' father earned good money at Kent State and had enough to bail out Fats – if he so chose. His father had strange attitudes about responsibility.

"Well, you see," Fats took a deep breath. "I was in North Beach. I'd been at the Camels Are A Coming--it's a nightclub. I got into an argument with Vianna." His voice dropped. "She's my ol' lady. Well, I was pissed off. I drove over the top of the hill at Union and Hyde an' lost it. I hit another car." He raised his eyebrows and shrugged almost apologetically. "It was stopped in the center of the road. It shouldn't have been there, but it was a cop car. They park any fuckin' place they want. The fuckin' pigs busted me n' tossed me in the slammer. I only got out when Legal Services intervened."

The shirt-clad girl came up behind Fats and slipped

an arm around his waist. She looked barely sixteen. Her right hand stopped moving when it reached the top button of his jeans. "This is Pat. I met her in the Park today. Say hello to Daniel and Carol. They're friends from Ohio."

"Hi." Her eyes were blank and her face was flushed.

"Hi. So, you've got to go to Court, right?"

"Well, yes, I was supposed to, but didn't. I forgot. Now the pigs are, like, looking for me. I ain't here if anyone asks." His eyes opened wide and he nodded. "You dig?"

High on dope, thought Daniel. "So, where're you living?"

"In the city. I'll tell you later." He rolled his eyes toward Pat and briefly touched his lips. "Er, there isn't room for anyone else. An' it isn't your kind of neighborhood. Most of the brothers don't like white folk."

"So where do we stay?"

"Maybe you can crash here for a while. Y'know, like, help with the groceries an' rent in exchange for some space." Fats shrugged as though it were unimportant. "I'll talk to Denny later. It's his pad now. He's kinda short on change. An' my Ohio connection dried up. No more crank to sell. I ain't been making any bread lately."

The girl's fingers slipped inside the top of Fats' jeans.

Great, thought Daniel, *I fell for the line about the golden state. I should've known better. What kind of place does he have in the City if this is so much better?* As his eyes became used to the dim light, he saw the threadbare carpeting had a collection of food scraps, some splattered with wax drippings.

The girl pulled on Fats' arm.

"Hey, something's just come up. Gotta take care of, like, now." He smiled and turned toward the darkened room as his hand slid under the shirt to grasp the girl's bare buttock.

#

That night, in a sleeping bag on a section of the floor

that Daniel had carefully swept, he curled up next to Carol. The house had finally become quiet. He could feel her warmth and reflexively, he reached for her.

"Not here," she whispered, pushing his hand off her breast. "We have no privacy. It smells in here." She was right. The place did have a strange musty odor.

"Sorry." *What a come down*, he thought, *the golden state.*

"I don't know what got into you today," Carol whispered, almost hissing, "buying all those groceries. You must have spent a hundred dollars. I could feed us for a month on what you spent. Then you gave Denny fifty dollars to help out when he said he needed money for rent. He seems to have enough money to buy dope."

Daniel had never seen Carol this angry before. "I thought I'd help out so we'd have a place to stay until we get our feet on the ground--"

"Daniel Robles," she said. "We could've stayed in a nice motel, with a bed, in privacy, for a week with that money. I hate it here. It's a dump."

"I'm sorry. I just thought we needed some place to stay until we get our own place." *Jeez, she's taking it badly.* Sure, it wasn't what he'd expected, but then, he'd done some primitive camping and this was good in comparison. Even though he'd visited San Francisco on business, he didn't know where to look for inexpensive apartments. "I thought it'd be nice if Fats could show us around and look for our own place."

"That's the first thing we do, starting tomorrow. Now shut up." Carol turned her back on him. "I want to sleep."

To Daniel's amazement, Carol fell sound asleep. He'd always known she could drop off into a doze whenever she wanted, but hadn't expected this, since she sounded so angry. It was several hours before he fell asleep. When he did, he was troubled by dreams of falling off a precipice.

#

"Are you sure you want to live here?" Carol wrinkled

her nose, and her mouth turned down at the corners.

"It's the cheapest place we've seen, and it's right on the bus line. In reality, it's the only place we can afford."

It'd taken Daniel a week to find this place, which was a furnished, single room studio apartment. It had been a week of steadily declining expectations. The cost of apartments in San Francisco was far higher than they'd imagined. They had been shocked at how expensive the rents were for even small apartments.

During their tour of San Francisco while looking for a place to live, they'd been accosted by pleas for 'spare change' at every corner in the Haight-Asbury. Gaunt-eyed bearded hippies offered a supermarket of drugs every time they slowed their pace while checking addresses. The Golden Gate Park had become a camping ground for legions of homeless, plus the news was full of deaths from drug over-doses. Daniel realized that the Summer of Love had turned into the winter of drugs and despair.

They found the apartment just off Mission Avenue in San Francisco that was a converted motel. It was furnished with an eclectic selection of motel leftover furniture: gaudy, plastic and much the worse for wear. The apartment cost two hundred and fifty dollars a month, twice what Daniel had paid in Kent. They also had to put up two months rent as a security deposit.

He'd also gone to the local State Bureau of Employment office and filed a claim for unemployment compensation, just on the chance California unemployment rules might be more liberal than Ohio. The clerk had said it would take a couple of weeks to verify his employment with the State of Ohio. She had also said she would help him file an appeal for benefits. The clerk hadn't held out much hope the appeal would work.

Daniel realized by taking this apartment, he'd be down to six hundred dollars. If they didn't take the apartment, they would continue to sleep on the floor. That meant he would continue to get the cold shoulder from

Carol. He couldn't take the frustration of no sex any longer while sleeping next to her. "Yeah, we'll take it."

"I'd expected something better than this," Carol said. "I thought California was supposed to be nice."

Daniel bit his lip. "Look, it's just for the time being until I get a job. Then we'll get one of those places you liked, y'know, one of those Victorian style places with a view of the Bay." He forced a smile. Those apartments cost six hundred dollars or more a month, half as much again as Carol had earned while working at Rick Box Honda. Even with a good job, that would be a stretch. She would have to work, also.

Carol inspected her fingers as though seeking guidance. "You promise?" She glanced up at him.

"Yeah," he said, "I promise." *Man*, he thought, *I hope this all comes true.*

Chapter 17

Grueden closed the file folder that contained the information on the drug lab investigation at Schirmerling Tire and Rubber. He glanced up. Diana, the departmental secretary, had just finished applying a generous layer of lipstick and was fluffing her hair, obviously admiring herself in the mirror. *Another hunting expedition*, Grueden thought. *Sooner or later, she's gonna catch some poor sucker.*

The office was warm, even stuffy. Two officers sat hunched over their desks, laboriously writing up investigation reports, which they'd later give to Diana for transcription. The glare from the overhead fluorescent lights reflected off four empty desks. It was quieter than usual, which Grueden appreciated. It gave him undisturbed time to think.

He'd just seen the detailed chemical analysis of the methamphetamine from the illegal lab at STR and had compared it to the drug traces found in Rogan's apartment. They were identical, right down to its trace constituents. *So,* he thought, *Rogan got his speed from the lab at STR, where he worked.* This begged the question whether or not he was making it. *If he made it there, he might have got his chemicals at STR, too. Better check it out.*

He checked the number before dialing the security department at STR. He didn't like the attitude of the STR guards who acted like they were equal to the regular Akron police. *Goddamn puffed up phonies,* he thought.

"Hello?" Grueden said into the phone. "Yeah, give me your head honcho, O'Brien. Yeah, I'll hold." He leaned back in his chair and stared at the off-yellow ceiling. *Needs painting*, he thought. He glanced back at Diana who was pounding out something on her IBM Selectric typewriter at a furious pace.

"O'Brien? Yeah, this is Grueden, Akron Police. I need to check on something connected with the Rogan disappearance. I need to see which chemicals he had access to." He frowned at the waffling response from O'Brien. "Look, I ain't asking you to pull your pants down in the middle of Market Street and bend over. I just want to see what chemicals he handled over the past twelve months."

Grueden frowned. "So, how long d'you reckon it'll take to get your legal department's okay?" He leaned forward and pulled a pad of paper closer and began to write. "Let me get this right, it's gonna take a week minimum? Is that right? Gee, Captain O'Brien, it just might be quicker if I got a search warrant. You follow me?

"I'll give you until the end of the week before I start talking to the judge, okay?" Grueden slammed the phone back into the receiver. *What the hell's going on?* he thought, *he's acting as if I'm trying to pull a fast one.* He put the file folder away and picked another from the in-basket. *Well,* he thought, *there's always something else to work on.*

#

"Yes, your honor," Grueden said. "I've asked nicely about seeing their records, but their security chief says their legal department believes we need a search warrant." He hunched over the phone and nodded. "That'd be great, it probably would work better that way. Thank you very much, Judge, I do appreciate your help." He gently placed the phone on the receiver and wiped a trace of sweat off his brow.

He looked up to see Officer Kincaid watching. "What did Judge Milano say? Did you get a search warrant?"

Grueden leaned back in his chair. "No search warrant." He wrinkled his nose. "The judge is going to call Mr. Mansky, the CEO of STR to 'suggest' he advise his legal and security department to cooperate, especially if he wants to keep this out of the newspapers. They know each other. Belong to the same club or something."

Kincaid frowned. "Is that a good thing?"

"Sure." Grueden tapped a pencil against his lower lip. "Cooperation is always better than coercion. Always."

#

"Yes, Mr. Mansky, I understand completely." Hodges frowned as he put the phone down. *Another aggravation*, he thought. *I did the right thing, firing that nosy-parker, Robles. Now the damn police want to search the chemical stockroom records.* He ran his hands through his bristly hair and glanced out the window of his office. There were traces of dingy snow lining the walkways outside. It was late March and winter was fading.

Hodges' office was warm, even cozy with its designer selected furnishings. It was his refuge against the noise and smell of the factory. He picked up the company phone directory and when he found the number, he made a call.

"Dieter? Hodges. Listen, I need you to do something for Mr. Mansky, right. The Akron police are sending a man over to check the chemical stockroom records at the Research Center. You're to escort him in and out of the building. Yes, that's a good idea. When he's done, give me a complete report on what he wanted and what he looked at. I need to make sure Mr. Mansky understands the thrust of the police investigation."

#

"Hello?" O'Brien put his walkie-talkie to his ear. "Cops just came in? They're going where? Ten-four." He frowned as he lengthened his stride. His shiny black shoes squeaked on the red and black-checkered linoleum, echoing off the pale green walls of the corridor that led from the accounting department to the stairwell. He knew if he hurried, he could reach the personnel department before the police arrived.

"Ah, Dieter." O'Brien forced a smile. "I understand the Akron Police are coming in. Perhaps I should escort them around, y'know, since I understand how they operate." He leaned against the doorway to the office, catching his breath. *These guys in personnel sure do have nice offices*, he thought.

William Dieter pursed his lips. "Well, okay. It's just

that Mr. Hodges also wants a report on what they're interested in. He'll want that in writing."

O'Brien nodded. "That's something we do all the time. No problem." He raised his eyebrows and nodded, seeking approval. That would give him a chance to make sure nothing reached management that cast him in bad light.

Dieter sighed. "I'm kind of busy with the colleges right now. Yeah, I'd appreciate it if you would take Detective Grueden to the Research Center chemical stockroom. He wants to check which chemicals Rogan took out over the past twelve months. I've already called Beckham and told him what to expect."

"Okay." O'Brien nodded. "Consider it done." *Now*, he thought, *all I have to do is handle Beckham so he doesn't reveal I've already checked those purchase records.*

Chapter 18

"Daniel." Carol pushed open the door into their apartment with a rush. "I got the job at Pacific Electric and Telephone." She smiled as though a victor in a hard-run race. She held her arms open.

"Great." Daniel pulled her close and kissed her first on the neck and then on the lips. "PE&T is a great company. What'll you be doing?" He leaned back to look at her and continued to hold her at arms length. It was the happiest he'd seen her in a long time.

"It's in the billing department." She wrinkled her nose. "I have to start as a clerk to learn the procedures. The manager, Frieda Carino, said if I do well, they'll train me to handle account auditing. She seems really nice. She even bought me lunch."

"That's terrific. When d'you start?" Daniel stepped back into the section of their one-room efficiency that functioned as a kitchen. He opened the door to the tiny refrigerator located beneath a counter of stained and scratched Formica. He retrieved a beer from within its cramped interior. Stroh's hadn't made it to the West Coast and with their present budget, he'd bought the cheapest variety of beer available. It was okay, but it wasn't as good as Strohs.

"She said I could start tomorrow, if I wanted." Carol looked down at her fingers for a moment. "I said I would."

"That's fine," Daniel said. "Now, let me tell you what I've been up to." He smiled. "I stopped in at Fluor—they're one of the biggest engineering firms in the country. I've got an appointment for an interview tomorrow. They're looking for a power system engineer."

"D'you think you could get a job with them?"

"Better than an even chance, but wait, there's more." He smiled. "I called a friend at Bechtel, here in the city. He set up an appointment for me on Wednesday. He said they need engineers, too. I've got two interviews with first-class engineering companies. Both are looking for engineers with exactly my experience." He put his arms around Carol and squeezed her tightly. "Things are going to work out, you'll see."

#

Daniel walked hand in hand with Carol in the garden next to the DeYoung Museum. His feet were sore after a marathon sightseeing session in the Steinhart Aquarium and the museum. The late afternoon sky was clear with a brilliant blue that is unique to California. Sunlight provided enough warmth to linger for a while. "So, how d'you feel about the job at PE&T after a week?" he asked. "D'you think it's okay?"

"Yes." Carol nodded. "Frieda has been very helpful in showing me how things are done. It's so much more professional than the Honda dealership in Kent. People are nicer, too. The department is all women, so there are no creepy men to bother me." She shrugged.

"Good." Daniel hoped that things would work out. The tension between them had caused their love life to suffer. "I figure I'll hear from Fluor and Bechtel this coming week. Both sound like they want me. I know I can do what they need." He paused and pointed at a bench beneath a parade of severely pruned sycamore trees that stood guard in front of the museum. "Want to sit for a while?"

"Sure," she said.

They sat on a low granite wall that held flowerbeds. Nearby was a thin, young man with stringy blond hair and a vacant look. He was aimlessly swinging his legs. "Nice day," he said, smiling.

"Yeah." Daniel nodded and smiled. "Really nice."

The blond man slid along the wall to join them. "Here." He pulled out a slender, tightly rolled joint and lit it. "Try this. It'll make it an even nicer day." He held it out.

What the hell, thought Daniel, *it's a part of the California experience.* "Cool." He accepted the joint. He'd

92

tried marijuana a couple of times back east but found it screwed up his head for work. He regarded it as an equivalent of drinking hard liquor--something you didn't do when you had to go to work the next day. But he had nothing on his agenda for tomorrow. He took a hit and offered it to Carol.

Carol shook her head and frowned, "Don't you have enough problems without becoming a dope fiend?"

Daniel shrugged. *It doesn't matter what I do*, he thought. *She always seems to find fault with anything that's outside her narrowly prescribed mode of behavior. It's like she's training me to what feels like an impossible standard.*

After a few tokes, Daniel found that life had a softer edge. Serious problems faded to consideration of the pleasantness of the day. He traded a series of obvious observations with the blond guy on the state of the sky, the warmth of the sun and how nice it was. Lacking anything else to say, he found himself talking about pollution control, just like he was back at work. It had been on his mind for the last week, ever since his interviews with the two engineering companies. However, Carol had no interest in that subject.

"Hi," said a stocky man in jeans who had a down vest over a red wool shirt. He'd been sitting on the wall of a nearby flowerbed, close enough to hear them and smell the smoke from the joint. "It's sure a nice day, isn't it?"

"Yeah, like really." It struck Daniel that there was a level of civility and hospitality in this encounter he'd not previously noticed in San Francisco. Coming to California hadn't been as he'd expected--it wasn't friendly; maybe it was even a little hostile. Now he wasn't even sure what he wanted. He only knew he had a feeling of being apart, alienated.

The man in the down vest asked Daniel several questions about pollution control, nodding at his answers as though finding them sources of inspiration.

Is it me? Daniel wondered, or is it this maraweenie? All at once, people seem nicer.

"Y'know," the man in the down vest said. "Your ideas about controlling pollution sound great. I know that my wife would love to hear them, especially about protecting the environment. That's one of her interests. Would you be willing to talk to her?"

"Sure," Daniel said. "I'll talk to her." *It was, after all, currently a trendy topic. The way he felt right now, he'd even talk to Tricky Dick Nixon.* "Where is she?"

"She's not with me today." The man in the down vest frowned as though seeking an answer in his memory. "You know, we're having some friends over for dinner next Sunday. This might be a little forward, but why don't you join us?" He nodded encouragingly. "By the way, my name is Joe Winston."

"Hi, I'm Daniel Robles and this is my girlfriend Carol Meadows." Daniel looked at Carol. She gave him the go-ahead nod. "Sure. Can we bring anything?"

"No, it'll be catered. We're having a small group over. Perhaps you and my wife, Marilyn, could chat after the piano recital."

Catered? Piano recital? Mentally, Daniel raised his eyebrows. "How formal is it?" He wasn't sure how to dress for this, even though he did have several nice suits.

"Oh, casual. Jeans and a sweater, nothing special." A wry smile flickered over Joe's face. "Here's my address." He fished out a business card and scribbled on it before handing it over.

Daniel glanced at the card. "Woodacre." That was somewhere in Marin County. He turned the card over. "Joseph Winston, Owner. Winston Plumbing and Heating. Six locations serving the Bay Area." *Hmm, looks like he does more than just twist a wrench to fix leaky pipes.* "Cool."

#

Carol looked up from reconciling a billing problem and saw Frieda watching her. She was a tall woman with wide shoulders and solid build who kept her hair cut very short. All the time Carol had seen her, Frieda wore severely

94

styled wool suits whose fit concealed her generous hips and large breasts. The way she was watching made Carol feel as though she was undressing her with her eyes. Yet it was different than the slimy looks that Schmidt at the Honda dealership gave her. It was almost she was being admired and that was flattering.

Frieda strode over to her. "Do you have any questions about this billing procedure?" she asked with a smile. Her hand strayed to Carol's shoulder for an instant.

"I think I've got it." Carol looked up and found she was smiling too. "You've been very helpful."

"Which way do you come to work?" A hint of a frown touched Frieda's forehead. She sat on the edge of Carol's desk and glanced over the billing section floor, with its dozens of clerks toiling with comptometers and punch card machines.

"Oh, I walk up Mission," Carol said. "It isn't far and the walk does me good."

"I had to drive over to a satellite office in the Mission last night on the way home, which is near where you live," Frieda said. "That isn't the best of neighborhoods, you know."

"Well, I haven't had any problems coming and going," Carol said, "and I don't go out at night. I'm trying to save money so I can get a nicer place."

Frieda smiled and leaned closer. "I understand, but please be careful," she said softly, as though trying to keep anyone else from hearing what she was saying. "When I first got a job here in San Francisco, I had to do without, too. It's not easy getting started."

Carol nodded without saying anything else.

"Look," Frieda said, "you could stay with me for a while, to save money. I think I'm a good judge of character. I think you and I could be quite compatible living together. I like to think we're becoming friends, and could become even better friends." She nodded as though to encourage her. "I live near the City College. It's a nice area, safe, and there're some good restaurants nearby."

Carol nodded slowly. "That's very generous of you. Let me think about it for a little while. You see, I've got a security deposit with the apartment, which means I have to give notice, otherwise I lose it." She pursed her lips, wondering whether she should tell Frieda about Daniel. *No, I won't,* she thought, *she wants to help me because she thinks I'm all alone.*

Chapter 19

"Next Sunday?" Nancy Chanson Benét scribbled rapidly on a piece of paper. "Sure, I'll be happy to play something. I'll give Marilyn a call once I've picked out a piece." She juggled the phone against her ear. "Anyone new coming?"

"Who did you say it was?" Nancy listened as Joe Winston rambled on. "An environmental engineer, really? I might be interested in talking with him, too. Does he have any particular expertise?"

Phillipe Chanson paused at the entrance to Nancy's office, a frown creasing his forehead. Her father mouthed the question, "Got a minute?"

Nancy nodded and held up a finger gesturing for her father to wait a moment. She spoke into the phone. "Right. I've got the details. Consider it settled." She put the phone down and beckoned to the chair alongside the gray metal desk. "What's on your mind, Papa?"

Phillipe passed a sheet of paper across the desk as he sat heavily in a timeworn wooden armchair. "I've run the numbers on the impact of this stupid EPA no-burn order. We have to find a way of dealing with it."

Nancy ran her eyes over the sheet. "I didn't realize the cost of transportation was so high." She knew that trucking the vineyard waste from their main operation in the Caneros region of Napa Valley to their new vineyard in Lake County was expensive, but hadn't realized its full cost.

Chanson Vineyards had eighty acres of vines, mainly the Chardonnay varietal, which was their signature wine. Phillipe had planted the vines shortly after the Second World War when he emigrated from France. He was originally from Beaune in Burgundy and had brought the knowledge and skills to make superlative wines. In the last ten years, demand for their wine had soared, and he had taken on significant debt to expand operations and put in new plantings.

Nancy knew the new plantings would require five years before any grapes could be harvested, with their full potential requiring at least ten years. She had grown up with conversations around the dining table on the art of making wine and understood the risk her father was taking. She had worked at every job in the winery alongside their regular employees and was unafraid of getting her hands dirty.

"We need to do something about it and soon." Phillipe sighed and his full sixty years showed briefly as he sagged in the chair. As owner and manager of Chanson Vineyards and Winery, he had shared his worry about the debt with Nancy.

"This soiree at the Winstons, next Sunday." Nancy paused.

Phillipe smiled briefly. "The one where you're the free entertainment?"

"Oh, you know that I enjoy playing a little classical piano from time to time. Besides, I get all the latest gossip about what's happening in the valley." She leaned forward. "I understand that Joe Winston invited some environmental engineer he just met. Maybe this guy will have an idea or two about how to solve our burn problem."

"Really?"

"Yes, Joe said the young man sounded like he knew what he was talking about. He said that his area of expertise was combustion." Nancy paused. "Of course, it was on a Sunday, and we all know how Joe likes to get relaxed on his day off." She raised her eyebrows.

"Talk to him and see what you can find out." Phillipe rose and headed to the door where he paused. "I'm counting on you to move all of our recent bottlings to market. I don't plan to cellar any wine until the new vines start producing."

"That may not be so easy."

"Oh?" Phillipe leaned against the doorjamb. "Why not?"

"Supposedly the economy is slipping into a

recession. At least, that's the reason the distributors give when they ask for lower prices on our wines." Nancy pulled a sheet of paper out of the in-basket. "I intended to get together with you to review this later, but since you brought it up." She pointed to the chair. "Want to hear the details?"

Phillipe shook his head. "Just a quick summary."

Nancy took a sharp breath. "It seems that all of our distributors are peddling the same story. They all want a price break. In a word, our cash flow is going to take a hit."

"Damn." Phillipe tightened his lips. "This comes at the wrong time. We've committed to our expansion plan. We need to keep our cash flow up. We'll have to figure out something."

Chapter 20

Ben Hodges stood before the window and stared out. All the snow had melted, leaving a line of litter around the edge of the parking lot in front of the Research Center. Shrubs and bushes still had not recovered from the weight of snow and cowered close to the ground. It was a gray, overcast day, which was the tint that colored the landscaping.

First quarter would be over in two days, Hodges realized. Cost cutting efforts hadn't produced the savings Mr. Mansky demanded. It was too soon to say if using scrap rubber would work out the way projected in Robles' memo. He knew there would be some serious ass chewing in his future if he didn't produce results. If that weren't bad enough, he'd just had a call from personnel who wanted to know what kind of reference they should provide for Robles. Two major companies were interested in hiring him.

He still felt angry at Robles. *No references for you, you insubordinate whelp*, he thought. He picked up the phone. "Dieter? Hodges here. About the reference for Robles. Right, tell them we do not wish to discuss his tenure at STR. That's right, exactly like that. I know how they'll take it. That's exactly how I want them to take it." He put the phone down and resumed his gaze out the window.

Hodges leaned back in his over-stuffed leather executive's chair and closed his eyes to think. The ringing of the phone interrupted his reverie. "Yes? What is it, Grabowski?" He leaned forward and listened intently. "Leaks? What's the matter, can't you fix a simple steam leak anymore?" It was irritating to get calls about something so stupid, especially when he had been thinking what it would be like to be the Vice-president in charge of manufacturing.

"Oh, so you know how to fix a leak, then?" Hodges snapped. "More than usual? You're blaming the use of scrap rubber as fuel for that? Well, adjust the feed rate and fix the leaks. Don't be late with your fuel consumption report." He slammed down the phone, shaking his head.

That reminded Hodges that Robles' brother still hadn't revealed the twerp's whereabouts. It was time to do something about it. He picked up the phone. "O'Brien? He's not there? This is Hodges, tell him to stop by my office. Right." He put down the phone and leaned back in his chair to think.

#

"Mr. Hodges, you want to see me?"

Hodges looked up to see O'Brien's muscular shape filling the doorway to his office. *He really should cut his hair shorter,* Hodges thought, *then he just might look military.* "Yes, come in." He pointed to the sofa and headed to the armchair that sat opposite, back against the window that looked out on the Research Center. He liked to sit in that location since he would be backlit, which made it harder for those sitting on the couch to read his expressions. He believed it gave an advantage in dealing with people.

Hodges took a deep breath and forced himself to speak slowly and calmly. "I need to find someone, yet I don't want to make a fuss about it." He paused to see what O'Brien would say.

O'Brien pursed his lips and nodded.

Hodges felt warm, as though perspiring. "I need to find a former employee, Daniel Robles."

"Isn't he the spic who called the cops about the alleged meth lab in the boiler house?" O'Brien's eyes narrowed as he leaned forward.

"Yes, that's the one." Hodges felt momentary surprise, for he hadn't realized Robles was a wetback. *Maybe that explained his un-American attitudes.*

"He do something wrong?" O'Brien eyebrows narrowed as though angered.

"Ah, no. Well, not illegal, at least I don't think so." Hodges decided to tell O'Brien. He knew the man had a reputation for being close-mouthed. "I need to find out what happened to some of the files he worked on. I can't locate some of them. I need this kept, er, quiet." He nodded, as though seeking agreement.

O'Brien slowly nodded. "Okay, I can do that. First I'll search his office and check the warehouse to see if he sent anything over there." He smiled with the warmth of a snake anticipating a good meal. "Always do that to avoid having the perp, I mean the individual point out the missing items were in our possession."

"Good idea."

"Only then will I start to make inquiries."

Hodges cleared his throat. "I believe he's in San Francisco. Two companies, Fluor and Bechtel, called checking his references. However, they wouldn't give his address to our personnel people."

"D'you have the phone numbers of these companies? Mebbe they have his address. I may have a way of getting it out of them."

"Good." Hodges handed O'Brien a folder. "This is a copy of his personnel file. It's in there along with the phone numbers of Fluor and Bechtel. However, he may not have taken the files with him. He may have left them with his brother."

"Where does Robles's brother live?" O'Brien asked.

"In Kent."

O'Brien read slowly and silently. "Okay, this is enough for a start." He rose to his feet. "I'll get the goods on him."

#

"Mr. Hodges."

Hodges looked up. O'Brien stood in the doorway to his office. *That man has the habit of just showing up unannounced,* he thought. The hardness of his features and the scars above his eyebrows hinted that he'd seen much violence. Hodges felt a shiver of apprehension. "Yes, O'Brien, what d'you have for me?"

O'Brien stepped into the office and silently closed the door. "I didn't get anywhere with those California companies. They didn't have a phone number or address for

Robles. Something about him being new in the area, so he arranged to contact them. I told them Robles had good reason to hide where he was living, that I was a cop and was trying to locate him. They seemed surprised. So, I hinted there was a warrant out for his arrest in Cleveland." He smiled thinly, as though tasting something sour.

Hodges felt a warm glow of satisfaction, knowing the reaction of large companies to any hint of criminality would disqualify a job candidate. "Excellent. What else?"

"I asked around where he lived in Kent. I found out he was shacked up with a chick who worked at the local Honda dealership. A couple of phone calls got me the chick's mother's phone number. So, I called her, telling her that her daughter had money coming from a refund, but I could only send it to her directly. After a little prodding, she gave me a phone number in San Francisco where she works."

"Did you get Robles' phone number and address?"

O'Brien wrinkled his nose. "I don't think he has a phone, leastwise, not yet. I called the chick in San Francisco—she works for Pacific Electric and Telephone—who said I could send the stuff to her at her work address."

"So no phone number or address?"

"Not yet." O'Brien raised his eyebrows. "It's going to take some footwork in San Francisco to find out. Is this important enough to pay the freight?"

"Freight?"

"Either you send me, or you hire a private dick out there. Either way, it'll be a couple of grand." A trace of a smile cracked O'Brien's face. "I'd enjoy smoking him out."

Hodges thought for a moment. "I'll get you the money." That would use up most of the production department's travel budget. It had already been slashed from the previous year's amount. No one would go to any technical meetings or training programs this year, not even Hodges.

Chapter 21

Nancy Chanson Benét jogged up the driveway, finishing her regular three-mile run through the side streets of Napa. The morning breeze on her damp tee shirt felt cool. The eucalyptus trees lining the city street scented the air with a hint of astringency similar to that of cough drops. She felt limber, free and alert. She loved starting her day this way.

Dark green vines laced the tall white walls of the Chanson Winery and reached for its crown of red clay tiles. A man in yellow rubber boots hosing down stainless steel equipment on the concrete pad in front of the cooperage building glanced up, waved and smiled at Nancy before returning to work.

She passed the large building, tall, square and white. It was aromatic with scents of oak and fermenting fruit. Ahead was a sprawling Spanish style house with its familiar pink walls. She felt secure in the knowledge no matter what happened, she would always belong here. This was home, with her family. It gave her a sense of peace and belonging.

#

Nancy dropped the towel and examined herself in the full-length mirror on the door. The bathroom was tiled with tiny pale blue and white tiles in an ornate Rococo pattern. A crack ran across the width of floor that was a souvenir of an earthquake that occurred when she was a child. The walls had blue wainscoting and the white porcelain pedestal sink matched the toilet and bidet. A freestanding Mahogany armoire held a generous supply of fluffy, white towels.

Not bad, she thought, *one hundred and twenty-five pounds and everything still looks good.* She examined her make up in the mirror and pursed her lips. *Perfect,* she thought, *perfect for kissing. It has been a while since someone I love has kissed me. Ever since that swine, Claude.* The thought of him brought a touch of sourness to her stomach. *Lord, I was such a fool.*

#

It was five years ago, in Paris, on the second day of classes at the Universite de Paris Sorbonne when everything was new, different and exciting. Nancy thought it was a new world without any rules when she met the most charming, debonair man in the universe. Claude Benét, an instructor who took the time to help her with her rusty French. He was ten years older than her, with just a hint of gray on his temples. Tall, slender and with a smile she found engaging.

He offered, no insisted that they visit the places she'd only read about, like the Louvre and famous restaurants. In a matter of days they became lovers. After their quick civil marriage ceremony, Claude changed.

He started to come home late. He said he had to go to 'conferies' or meetings on the weekends. Nancy stayed home and waited patiently for his return.

Their relationship began to unravel the day she went to his class to surprise him and go to lunch on a spontaneous impulse. She saw a pretty young woman, blonde and petite hanging onto him, gazing at him the way she did, devoted and obvious with her desire. In an instant Nancy saw herself, sick with passion, wanting him. All at once, she was looking in on a relationship that was supposed to be hers and hers alone.

Nancy tried to push thoughts of Claude away, but thoughts came, unbidden, to the surface. *I should have confronted him. But no, naive little fool that I was, I ran back to their apartment and cried. When he came home, I even believed his story that the woman was just a student who needed a little encouragement to succeed. Succeed? Merde alors! Succeed at what? An advanced degree in seduction? Then I was desperate to believe him, and so I did.*

She still could not believe that the money she gave him for a deposit on the larger apartment in the seventh arrondissement was gone. She recalled seeing Claude shrug in that Gallic manner and give her his famous smile, the one she saw given increasingly to other women. He said it was due to his expenses of living. She might have continued to forgive him, until that day he came home bearing the scent of another woman. She was so humiliated that night when he turned his back on her in their bed. He had raised her senses to new levels, and now, rejection.

It was their first and only big argument. It was their last. He told her that, as his wife, she had to understand that men like him needed other women from time to time, and her duty was to him and him alone. What a selfish bastard.

That was the night she left and ended up in a small tourist hotel smelling of leaking toilets and garlic. It was filled with the incomprehensible babble of people from the Middle East. She cried most of the night, feeling betrayed and degraded.

She remembered when she came home and had to tell Phillipe, her father, what had happened to her marriage. It was necessary to bare her soul to him, for she knew he accepted her unconditionally. He held her close and whispered she wasn't stupid, only young and infatuated. He promised her she would always have a home at Chanson. That was when Nancy made the vow to herself she would never again have anything to do with a man who was dishonest or unfaithful. She had met many since who failed her standard.

#

Nancy stared at herself in the mirror. *So, why are we getting ourselves all tarted-up, hmm? Is it because we haven't been with a man for a while, eh, cherié?*

She was conscious that she'd just turned thirty. She wanted children. The question was, with whom? And when? *So, will my Prince Charming be at the Winstons after the piano recital?* She sighed. *Fat chance. It'll be the same crowd. Men who drink too much, make suggestions of assignment and whose wives or girlfriends fume silently at me.* It would be nice to find a smart, competent hardworking man who is honest and faithful--a good man who wants to settle down and have a family.

Chapter 22

It was the first Sunday in April. Carol had misgivings about going to a dinner based upon an invitation from a stranger in the park while smoking dope. "I really don't want to go all this distance, go to the front door and have the people ask me who the hell I am," she said.

Daniel listened as he drove over the Golden Gate Bridge. "Look, the guy wrote down his name, address and phone number, along with time and date." Daniel focused on driving the van and trying to find a hole in the traffic. No one was changing lanes, even though the pace was relatively sedate. "What did you want? An engraved invitation?"

"That's not the point." Carol consulted her fingers. "We don't know these people."

"Well, let's just go to the door and introduce ourselves. Joe did say it would be catered." Daniel braked hard to avoid a car that changed lanes without signaling. "It's a chance to get a good feed."

"I'm not sure we should be going if it's going to be rubber chicken and soggy potato salad. I like food too much to put up with that." Carol did like to eat. He'd noticed she'd gained some weight lately. "I don't want to go any place where there're drugs, either."

"Okay, okay," Daniel said. "If it's a bust, we'll split. We can always find something to eat somewhere."

"That wouldn't be polite."

Crap, a no-winner, Daniel thought. He concentrated on driving. Once off the bridge, he picked up the pace.

It took them another twenty minutes to reach Woodacre and twenty more to find the address. It was a huge, rambling contemporary style house set well back from the road among tall redwoods.

"Hi, we're Daniel and Carol. We were invited--"

"Yes, yes, of course, you're the people Joe met last Sunday. Do come in," said the woman who answered the door with a big smile. "I'm Marilyn. Joe's told me all about you. I do so want to talk with you about controlling pollution. It's such a problem in the Bay Area. Let me take your coats. I'll introduce you to some people." Marilyn ushered them inside, talking non-stop.

Marilyn was a tall, round-faced woman with dark hair and a friendly smile. There were at least twenty people in the room representing all age levels. The crowd had an undeniable air that whispered money. The room was huge, with bay windows at one end and a fireplace at the other end that was topped with an ornately carved mantle piece. A huge, red oriental rug covered much of the polished wood floor. Original oil paintings covered the walls.

"You're just in time for the recital," Marilyn said. "Nancy is playing selections from Chopin." As she spoke, a young woman started to play a grand piano set against the wall near the window. She was perhaps thirty, with a long patrician nose set in a narrow face with flashing green eyes and reddish-brown hair. She wore a sleeveless black cocktail dress that revealed a slim physique.

Marilyn showed them to seats and then returned with two Scotches, light on the wash.

Daniel drank both because Carol didn't like Scotch.

Daniel felt moved, listening to a piano recital in a living room, even though there didn't seem to be enough room to do justice to the majesty of the work. The Scotch landed hard on his empty stomach, for both drinks had been poured with a generous hand. He forced his attention on the performer.

Daniel couldn't help noticing that the muscles in the pianist's slender arms rippled like ropes as her hands ran up and down the keyboard. He found that he was paying more attention to her than the music. She seemed competent and gave a faultless performance. Well, it seemed that way to him.

After the recital, Daniel sought refuge in Club soda, for more Scotch would be a disaster. *When*, he wondered, *are they going to serve the food?* The event became more like a normal cocktail party with waiters circulating drinks and appetizers.

Marilyn brought over the pianist and introduced her to them. "This is Nancy Benét."

"Robles?" Nancy said. She inflected his name in the Spanish manner. "¿Es usted de España?" She asked if he was from Spain.

Daniel swallowed. "No, Señora, soy norteamericano. Mi familia eran de la Ciudad de Mexico." He felt a blush heat his face, as he told her his family came from Mexico City.

"You have a Spanish name." She shrugged and nodded. "Mi mamá fue de España. Murió cuando fui joven." She explained that her mother was from Spain and had died when she was young.

"Lo siento." I'm sorry to hear that. "This is my friend, Carol," Daniel said quickly.

Carol stepped forward. "Hello."

"Pleased to meet you." Nancy nodded, face neutral.

Marilyn piped up, "He's the one that Joe talked to about pollution control and waste minimization."

"Really?" Nancy's eyebrows rose. "Is it a hobby or your profession?"

"I'm an engineer. I've worked in the field--"

"Where did you go to school?" Nancy asked almost brusquely as she picked up a glass of white wine from the tray of a passing waiter. She sniffed the wine carefully and wrinkled her nose. Her eyes returned to Daniel.

"I have an undergraduate degree in chemistry from Kent State and I went to Case for engineering." Daniel shook his head at the waiter who offered him a glass of wine from a tray. "They're in Ohio. Do you have an engineering background?"

"No." Nancy shrugged. "I have undergraduate degrees in oenology and the French language from Davis, with post-graduate studies at the Sorbonne. Spanish came from my mother. Tell me, what kind of pollution control work did you do? Who've you worked for?" Nancy took a sip of wine and aspirated it before swallowing, her eyes narrowing in concentration.

Gee, thought Daniel, *this sounds almost like a job interview*. "Matlock Consulting and Schirmerling Rubber, where I worked on waste to energy and combustion projects." He briefly described using scrap tires as fuel to generate steam. He mentioned that he had handled a variety of pollution control projects.

"Did you have project responsibility?"

"Yes--"

"And you know combustion? Hmm." Nancy briefly pursed her lips. "The California Air Resources Board ordered my father to stop burning grape vine prunings. The Napa Valley is under a no-burn order due to its air pollution problems. However, it's not economic to have the waste disposal service pick them up. Is there anything we can do instead of open burning? Is there some way to dispose of them that complies with regulations and is economical?"

Wow, thought Daniel. *She doesn't waste any time.* "I'm not sure. I've never dealt with prunings. If it's like yard waste, perhaps composting might work. What kind of volume?"

A trace of a frown flashed over Nancy's forehead for a moment. "I don't know. It's from eighty acres of grapes. My father's been trucking them to our Lake County vineyard and burning them there. There're a lot of vines, and it's expensive." She smiled briefly, as if to encourage him.

"I see," Daniel said. Nancy was almost his height and kept looking directly into his eyes. Her trace of a smile grew, which he found appealing. "It's not something I can solve in ten minutes over cocktails." He felt a growing sense of excitement. "Perhaps if I saw the operation, I could offer a suggestion."

"When would you be available to come out?" Nancy looked over the glass of wine that she had just sipped, eyes twinkling. "My father is there all the time. He's the one who'd provide the details."

Daniel found himself smiling. He wanted to go and see this operation, and maybe Nancy, too. "Well, I'm, as they say, currently between positions. I could stop by next week." He felt Carol squeeze his arm. It was a warning.

"Good. Let me have your business card," Nancy said.

"I just arrived in California. I don't have any cards."

"Okay. How about I call you early on Monday?" Nancy put down her drink and opened her purse. "What's your number?" She took out a black leather address book and looked up. "I'm certain that my father would want to talk with you."

Daniel took a deep breath. "We don't have a phone yet. We just moved into an apartment." He looked toward Carol. "It's short term until we find something more suitable." He felt a twinge of discomfort saying this.

"Here, let me give you my phone number." Nancy pulled a business card out and scribbled something on the back. "Give me a call at the office and let me know when it's convenient."

Daniel glanced at the card. Chanson Winery, Family owned and operated, Dealy Lane, Napa. Nancy Benét, Sales & Marketing. On the back, she'd written: 'Please do call. Nancy.' She'd underlined 'do' and signed her name with a flourish.

"What's your father's position at Chanson?"

Nancy's smile widened. "He owns it."

"Oh," said Daniel. "The name difference threw me."

"I was married for a while." Nancy's mouth pursed as though tasting something unpleasant and a frown briefly rippled her brow. "It didn't work out. So, I came back to the family business."

"I didn't mean to pry--"

"Oh, it's no secret. I was too young and I married a guy who wasn't meant for me. He kept ending up with others."

"I'm sorry to hear that," Daniel said and meant it. There was something happening between them that felt electric.

"Call me. Perhaps we could do lunch, too." Her smile grew as she ran the tip of her index finger around the edge of the wineglass making it vibrate and almost sing. "Maybe try a good Chardonnay, like one of ours?"

Daniel felt Carol squeeze again, much harder than the first time. It was a distinct warning. He'd not included Carol in their conversation, and he felt a twinge of guilt. He tried to think of a polite way to end the conversation. "Er, yes, we'd like to do that, sometime." He suddenly felt desperate for something to say. *Yes, she is very attractive, but I'm with Carol, right?*

Nancy's easy smile widened. "I'm looking forward to it."

"I think Marilyn wants us." Daniel intercepted a gesture Marilyn had made vaguely in their direction. "I'll be sure to call," he said, holding up the card. This time Carol squeezed his arm much harder. "I, er, enjoyed your performance."

"Thank you," Nancy said with a smile. She grasped his hand and shook it. Her hand was warm and strong, and it lingered for an instant longer than necessary. "Nice meeting you, too." Her nod to Carol was abbreviated.

"Likewise." Carol didn't smile either.

"Daniel, I want you to meet Charlie Evans. I told him all about you." Marilyn beamed. "He's the editor of our local newspaper. He's very interested in all things about the environment." Her eyes had a sparkle. She obviously enjoyed her role as hostess.

Charlie Evans was the editor for a Marin County weekly newspaper. He provided insight as to what was happening on the local scene. Daniel glanced at his watch. It was already three o'clock. The volume of talking had become much louder. The food had not been served and the drinks continued to flow. As usual, alcohol had lubricated the vocal cords. If he didn't get something to eat soon, he'd have to leave.

Magically, a buffet appeared, with white uniformed (including gloves) young men who were "so pleased to serve you." The roast beef was rare and tender, the sourdough bread crunchy and fresh, the horseradish hotly pungent. For Daniel, the rest of the dinner party was a blur of quickly forgotten names. Except for that of Nancy Benét.

#

"You ate like a pig," Carol said as the van headed south toward the Golden Gate Bridge. "You had three helpings of food, two more than anyone else. I was so embarrassed. We'll never get invited back." She stared out a side window, consulting her fingers.

Daniel suppressed a belch. "That was my first meal today. If I'd known they were planning to serve the meal so late, I'd have had breakfast. I thought it was going to be a brunch."

"Well, you should have restrained yourself," Carol said, "And you kept staring at that woman who played the piano."

"I wasn't staring at her."

Carol held out her hand. "Let me see that card you got from that woman."

Daniel struggled to get the card. He glanced at it to make sure he'd got the right one. "Here it is," he said in a neutral tone. *Now, what does she want with it?*

Carol cracked the window and pushed the card out. "You don't need to work for free. You need a real job."

"Aw, Carol, did you have to do that?" Daniel glanced in the rear view mirror but saw no trace of the card. "How d'you know it wouldn't lead to something hot?"

"The something she'd lead you to is hot all right. It isn't old grape vines that're on fire. Bitch." Carol's words came out in a tone that meant trouble. "You encouraged her." She was silent for the rest of the way home.

Daniel knew that it would be a cold evening once

they got home. Still, he could not put Nancy Benét's face out of his mind.

Chapter 23

"I see." Daniel nodded as he leaned against the phone booth door to seal it against the traffic noise. Market Street was still busy even though the rush hour was officially over. "So, there's no position open at Fluor? Oh, to me? Why?" He took a deep breath and gritted his teeth. "I'm sure I can do the work. Well, thank you very much." He resisted the urge to slam the phone into its receiver. *They don't want me? A bad reference? It's got to be that Fascist prick at Schirmerling.*

It was his third rejection of the day. It had started out with rejection. He'd tried to kiss Carol before she left for work, and she'd given him an elbow in the ribs for his efforts. When he called Bechtel, they said the position had already been filled. Now Fluor, telling him he had a bad reference. *Now my best job prospects are gone,* he thought as he looked up and down Market Street. *I better call information. I need to find out how to contact Chanson Winery.*

#

"Mr. Chanson," Daniel said, "I think I found a way to make this work. There are six golf courses in the area that send their grass clippings to a landfill at an average cost of five-fifty per ton. Now, if you offer to do it for two-fifty or three dollars per ton, that'll cover your transportation costs and it'll give you a source of nitrogen to compost the shredded vines."

As he spoke, he stood in the doorway of Phillipe Chanson's office in the winery. It was a small room with an old wood desk and a row of battered filing cabinets along one wall. Other walls held family photographs and ribbons for award-winning wines. Three cardboard boxes with wine bottles sat next to the desk. There was no place for him to sit.

"I'm a wine maker." Phillipe shrugged. "I know nothing about making compost." He was six feet tall, had a long face with bushy white eyebrows and a full head of silver hair. His jeans were faded and his brown wool sweater had leather patches on its elbows.

"Think of it this way," Daniel said. "Your disposal cost disappears and you get an income stream. I've got vendors sending written quotes on the equipment needed for the job. Based upon information I got over the phone, the economics look like this." He placed a sheet of paper before Phillipe.

The room grew quiet as Phillipe studied the economic model. Outside, a tractor chugged past and then faded into silence. "This is a whole new business," Phillipe said. "One which might have significant profit potential, if it works the way you say it will."

Daniel nodded. "The golf courses would like to lower their disposal costs, plus the five local landscapers I contacted buy enough compost to consume your output. Currently they're buying bagged compost that comes from Milwaukee. You can beat their price easily." He put several sheets of paper in front of Phillipe. "This is the equipment information and the names of the people at the golf courses and landscapers, and this is the equipment layout."

Phillipe leaned back in his chair and nodded. "You did a lot in the few days you've been here. I'm glad Nancy talked you into coming. Let me think about this for a while and do some checking on my own." He glanced at his wristwatch. "Meanwhile, I believe Nancy said something about the two of you having lunch. She's in the front office." His smile was warm as he winked. "Bon appétit."

#

Daniel felt a rising sense of excitement as he stared over the top of the wineglass. This was their third lunch together this week, during which they shared their life histories. He knew they enjoyed each other's company, which troubled him because of his relationship with Carol. He hadn't told Carol that he'd been coming to Chanson Winery every day this week.

"I hope that we can continue to see each other." Nancy put her wineglass down and patted her lips with a cloth napkin.

A gentle breeze fluttered the edge of the white cotton tablecloth. Sunlight filtered through the overhead trelliswork covering the patio. Purple tinted hills rose in the distance, backstopping the neat, geometric rows of bright green grapevines. "I'd like to think that we've become friends." She smiled.

Though he'd only drunk one glass of wine, Daniel found his tongue thick, making it difficult to speak. "Nancy." He found that he savored the sound of her name. "This isn't easy for me to say. I like you, enjoy your company, but I think I should stay away from you, because I might be tempted to do, or say something I'd regret. I have a relationship with Carol. I hope you understand."

Nancy looked down and sighed. "Then you do know how I feel about you? Have I been that obvious?"

"It's not that you're being obvious, it's mutual. If I were not in a relationship, I would try to spend every spare moment with you." He looked away, feeling as though he were about to do something stupid and lose something very precious. "I shouldn't have said that. I apologize."

Nancy grasped his hand. "Daniel, I understand. I don't like it, but I respect you for being the way you are." She released his hand and looked down.

For several moments, they said nothing. In the silence, sparrows hopped close to their feet, seeking out crumbs. Their eyes met and they stared at each other for long seconds. "I should be going," Daniel said, feeling awkward.

"Promise you'll stay in touch with me?" Nancy said. "I know that my father wants you to come back if he decides to do this composting thing. If he doesn't, I still want to know where you are and what you're doing."

It felt like a compromise to Daniel, one with which he could live. Carol didn't know he'd been coming over to Chanson Winery every day this week. His burden of guilt had grown enormous. *I am with Carol,* he reminded himself. *I am not screwing around with anyone on the side. I don't do that.* Yet he still felt a bond, an attraction to Nancy. She came from a culture he understood and had a familiar feel. "Well, okay." It felt as though he was betraying Carol's trust.

Nancy picked up her purse and rummaged inside. She pulled out a card and wrote on it. "This is our inward WATS number," she said. "Use it when you call me. You can call me from anywhere in the U.S. It's a toll-free, direct line into my office."

Daniel took it and hid it deep inside his wallet.

Nancy stood up and smoothed her dress. A brief flurry of worry lines appeared between her eyebrows. "I hope that we can do lunch again, and soon." She smiled. "Oh, before you leave, see my father. He has a check for you." Her smile grew more relaxed. "He said you were very thorough and worked hard this week. He believes in paying people who work for him. I think he likes you, too."

#

"What gives with the references?" Daniel nestled the pay phone's handset against his ear with his shoulder. He'd found a phone booth on a quiet tree-lined street. He'd called Dieter in STR's Human Resources department using the WATs number he'd been given. He listened to Dieter tell him how Hodges had ordered a bad performance review in his personnel records. "He told you not to give out any references? Yeah, well, that screwed up my chances for a good job with Fluor and Bechtel. Thanks for the info. Talk to you later. 'Bye."

The walk back to the apartment seemed to take forever. He didn't look forward to telling Carol what he'd learned.

Chapter 24

April 30, 1970.

Carol climbed the concrete steps to their apartment.
As she opened the door, she thought, *only one more day of
work left this week, then two days of freedom*. Their one
room apartment held the kitchen, dining and sitting areas,
plus a fold out couch. Even the apartment's bright pastel
colors now seemed garish and cheap. It seemed to get
smaller each day. One glance told her Daniel had bad news.
"Hi, how'd it go?"

The lines in Daniel's brow deepened. "Nothing," he
said. "Or worse than nothing."

"What d'you mean?"

"I talked to Dieter at STR. He told me Hodges
refuses to give out a reference." He shook his head.
"Someone has been spreading the word at the engineering
companies that I'm a suspect in some kind of crime."

"How d'you know that?" Carol felt her stomach
lurch.

"When I called the personnel department at Fluor
Engineering, they asked me what crime I'd committed.
When I told them I didn't know what they were talking
about, they said the police had called, that they were looking
for me." Daniel shook his head. "I asked them what police;
they said it was from back east. I don't understand it. I
haven't done anything wrong."

"What're you going to do?" Carol felt a twinge of
fear. She wanted, no, needed him to have a secure, high-
paying job if they were to have a good life together.

"I don't know. I may have to find another line of
work. Anything to get by on."

Carol felt a brief surge of hope. *Well*, she thought, *he
is bright and does work hard. Maybe he can find something*

else. An outside thought struck her. "D'you have enough money for next month's rent? It's due on the first."

"Yes, but not much more." He sat down and put his head in his hands. "I may have to ask you to help out in the future." He stared at the floor.

Carol had never seen him so depressed. She put her arms around him and pulled his head to her midriff. She sensed this might be the time to ask him something she had been thinking about. "If we had a permanent relationship," she said. "If we were married, then you wouldn't have to ask about things like that."

Daniel looked up sharply, a frown creasing his face. "Married? How can you think about something like that now? I can't support you."

Carol released her hands and turned away. *I have to get the words right,* she thought. "You do love me, don't you?"

"Yes, of course I love you," he said. "But getting married won't solve these problems. I need a job so we can afford a nice place to live." He stood up. "Look, we've only known each other for six months. This is the first time we've faced tough times together. I think we'll know how well we can get along once this is behind us."

"You're making excuses." Carol looked at her fingers while struggling to come up with a compelling reason. She knew once they were married, she wouldn't have to try as hard to please him, to pretend she enjoyed everything they did together. She could make him change into the kind of person she really wanted. "I left home for you. I broke with my mother for you. I think I gave up more for this relationship than you did." *There*, she thought. *Try to top that*.

"Carol, I'm sorry about what happened between you and your mother, but please try to understand. I need to find work, and soon. I'm confused about this screwed-up reference thing. Yeah, I guess if STR doesn't want to give me a reference, that's their right. This thing about the cops has me worried. In my present frame of mind, how can I even think about getting married?"

Carol stared at him, feeling her anger grow. She stared at her fingers for a moment. "You don't really love me," she said. "You're like all the other guys. You just want me for sex."

"Aw, that's a bunch of crap." Daniel's voice rose. "Carol, please," his voice softened and he put his arms around her. "You're the only woman I've felt this way about."

Carol used her elbows to free herself. "I was right," she said. "You want to use sex to avoid discussing our future."

She wished they had a bedroom, for she wanted to go somewhere where she could slam the door in his face and be alone for a while to think. She let tears come to her eyes, hoping they'd work their usual magic, but Daniel didn't seem to notice.

Maybe I ought to take up Frieda's offer and move in with her for a while. Then he could find out how much he needs me. That might make him realize my idea about getting married isn't such a bad idea after all. In fact, she thought. *If I cut him off from sex for a while, maybe he'll get the message.*

"Well," she said with a sniffle as she headed toward the counter that served as their kitchen. "We're having franks and beans for supper. That's all we can afford since you aren't working." She bumped and banged the battered pots more loudly than usual to let him know she was still annoyed. Soon the sounds of food preparation dominated.

Daniel had settled down on the couch and turned on the TV for the evening news. He liked to watch what was going on with that stupid war in Viet Nam and other boring business stuff.

"Carol," Daniel said. "The economic news isn't good. There's a rise in unemployment. I think the economy is slipping into a recession." He didn't sound happy.

#

About nine-thirty, Daniel unfolded the couch and made up the bed. After a quick shower, he got into bed. "Carol, are you coming to bed?"

Carol took a deep breath. *Well*, she thought, *I guess I must.* She went into the bathroom and took her time in the shower. *It would be nice to have a tub to take a nice long soak, like Frieda had mentioned. A bubble bath.* That sounded appealing.

After she dried off, she put up her hair. It was time. She eased into the bed, wondering whether there would be another argument. She knew Daniel would try to make love with her as a means of getting over their spat. Well, tonight that wasn't going to happen.

"Carol." Daniel slipped his hand over her, "I'm sorry. I do love you--"

"Don't," Carol said, perhaps more loudly than she'd intended as she removed his hand from her breast. "I'm not in the mood." She rolled over and presented her back to him.

Chapter 25

May 1, 1970.

After Carol left for work, Daniel stopped in at the apartment manager's office and paid the rent, counting out the bills carefully. He then headed to the phone booth on the quiet side street just off Mission. It was warmer than yesterday and the sky was blue, cloudless except for a trace of fog drifting above the distant Twin Peaks.

Daniel emptied his pockets of his last handful of change and dropped them into the phone. "Hello, Hector?" Daniel needed to talk things over with his brother. The job situation and Carol's coldness had left him twisted and hurting inside. "What's happening?"

"What's up?" Hector said. "How's it going in the land of milk and honey?"

"Well, I hate to complain, but STR and someone else has royally screwed me in the job market," Daniel began, and told Hector what he'd experienced.

"Y'know, I got a call from that Nazi at STR, Hodges. He's looking for some of your memos and other stuff. I think it was about the boiler or superheater," Hector said. "He was very demanding, so I hung up on him. He sounds like a real cabrón."

"Yeah, he's a real son of a bitch. He's got no interest in safety either. One of these days, he'll go too far."

Hector cleared his throat. "So, what're you going to do?"

"I guess I'll keep looking for a job. Maybe outside my area of expertise, anything to keep going."

The operator's tinny voice cut in, demanding more money.

"Gotta go, I don't have any more change."

"Well, if things get too tough out there, you can always come home. Okay, take care, kiddo. Call me anytime."

Daniel knew Hector would give him money, but he hated to ask. That would be the last resort. He wasn't a freeloader and wasn't about to start.

#

O'Brien caught a shuttle from the San Francisco airport into the city. He dozed on the bus. He'd had two very busy days in Las Vegas where he got lucky both at the gaming tables and with a blonde call girl. He had enough money and then some to do the task he set for himself.

He got off the bus at Union Square and glanced at the Fairmont Hotel, wishing he could afford to stay there, but gambling and the ladies came first. He headed west, into the Tenderloin area, and found a cheap hotel. He knew he'd only be there a couple of nights, which, if things went well, would leave enough time to spend each evening with a different hooker. He liked variety.

After changing into a suit, he studied the photograph of Carol Meadows he'd torn out of the Ravenna High School yearbook. He'd found it in the library while researching her background. He had to recognize her to make his plan work. He glanced up at the building that contained the PE&T offices. *Now*, he thought, *find a way to visit the billing section and spot this bimbo.*

#

"So where do I go to get this bill straightened out?" O'Brien asked. He waved a piece of paper. "I need to talk to a person, face-to-face." He smiled and shrugged as though it were just another task. "I have trouble communicating over a phone."

The corpulent guard sitting in the polished granite desk looked over the top of his half-frame glasses as though studying O'Brien. He pointed to the sign-in sheet.

O'Brien signed Daniel's name.

The guard covered a yawn and ran his finger down a plastic-covered sheet on the desk. "Accounts receivable, floor twenty-one, room twenty-one oh-five. Elevator on the left." He waved vaguely behind him.

"Thanks." O'Brien headed to the bank of elevators. Before taking the elevator, he studied the directory until he found what he wanted.

Once in the accounting department, O'Brien stopped at the front desk and smiled. "Say," he said, "they sent me here, but this doesn't look like the computer section." He winked at the receptionist. "That dress looks really nice on you."

The middle-aged receptionist smiled. "Why, thank you." She retrieved a directory from a drawer and studied for a few moments.

O'Brien methodically studied the women working. There were long rows, each engrossed in her work. He spotted one wearing a gray sweater. She seemed to look like a Carol Meadows. She was the only one that looked to be in her early twenties. Most of the other workers were either middle-aged or overweight.

"The computer section is in room twenty-five oh-one," the receptionist said, looking up.

"Uh, I see," O'Brien said. "I got the numbers twisted up."

"Is there anything else?" She smiled.

"Ah, no, thank you. You've been a sweetie." He winked again and left.

#

Following Carol after she got off work proved to be simple. She walked the whole way and in the rush-hour crowds, it was easy to get close and not lose her. When she climbed the stairs of an old motel just off Market Street and went inside, O'Brien felt a little rush of excitement. *Outside doors*, he thought, *no secured entrances to worry about. This is gonna be easy.*

He headed back to his hotel. *First, a quick meal and then a hooker to haul my ashes. Then off to bed, so I can be up early in the morning.*

#

O'Brien watched Carol leave the apartment a little before eight o'clock in the morning. He had to wait another hour before Daniel appeared. Five minutes after Daniel left, O'Brien slipped on a pair of gloves and opened the door to their apartment. It took him less than thirty seconds to release the latch.

His search was quick. He tossed every drawer, seeking the memos. Nothing. He looked around and eyed the furniture. He opened his Buck knife and slit open every piece of upholstery and bedding. Still nothing. He began to realize that either they weren't here, or Daniel carried them with himself.

Well, phase two, O'Brien thought. He put a small bag of marijuana under a cushion on the damaged couch. He also put a hypodermic syringe and vial of speed with a smoke-stained spoon beneath the sink.

When he left, he checked the time. It had taken only thirty minutes. *Now,* he thought, *that's payback for calling the cops about my lab. You Spic bastard, now you're gonna have to talk to the cops about this and you ain't gonna enjoy it.*

#

Daniel headed back to the apartment to get lunch. He opened the door and saw the mess in the room. *Ah, shit,* he thought, *we've been robbed. Better call the cops.*

He went downstairs and got the manager, a skinny, middle-aged man with a potbelly and a perpetual scowl. "Hey, man, call the cops. Someone busted into our apartment this morning. Aren't you supposed to keep an eye on things to prevent robberies?"

The manager's scowl deepened. "Lemme see," he said. He followed Daniel out to the apartment. He glanced inside and without a word, headed back to the office to call the police.

The police arrived an hour later. Their first comment was that that there was no sign of forced entry. Inside, they examined the apartment for clues. An officer paused, sniffing deeply, which led him to the cupboard beneath the sink. He opened the door and said, "We gotta call vice. There's drug activity going on in here."

"What're you talking about?" Daniel said.

"Step outside," the officer said. "We need to investigate this further. We need to check for fingerprints."

The apartment manager stared hard at Daniel. "According to your lease, drugs are cause for eviction. Buddy-boy, you're outa here, like now--"

"Hey, we don't do drugs. D'you think I'd call the cops, then leave drugs in plain view?" Daniel said. "I just paid the rent yesterday."

"Tough shit," the apartment manager said. "I'm gonna hafta get new furniture, an' clean the place. Your security deposit an' rent will barely cover it." His scowl deepened. "Druggie."

"C'mon, man," Daniel said. "That's old furniture, can't cost that much." He had a sinking feeling his situation had gone from bad to worse.

"I'm putting your stuff on the street," the manager said. "If you want it, fine. If not, someone else might."

"You can't do that--"

"Buddy-boy, if you give me anymore shit, I'm gonna press charges of malicious destruction of property. You'll do time in the slammer." The apartment manager wagged his finger at Daniel. "I don't hafta take your shit."

#

"Carol, you know we don't do drugs," Daniel said. As they sat in the van, he stared at the door of the office. Carol had just begged the manager to let them keep the apartment. It was to no avail. The manager had been adamant about their eviction.

"Well, you did do drugs that Sunday, at the DeYoung Museum." Carol examined her fingers carefully.

"Aw, that's different. I haven't bought drugs. I don't do dope, you know that."

Carol looked up, tears forming in her eyes. "I came

127

out here with you and you said that you'd take care of me."
She sniffled. "Where're we staying tonight?"

Daniel realized with a sinking feeling that he had two
hundred dollars and change in his pocket. He thanked God
they hadn't left money in the apartment, or that would have
been gone, too. "Maybe we can find a cheap motel," he said.
"I don't have much money left. I'm going to need your
help."

Carol's eyes narrowed. "I've got enough money for a
plane ticket home. I can't spend that. It's for emergency use
only."

Daniel knew that Carol had sold her Corvair for six
hundred dollars and while she lived with him in Kent, he had
paid all of the bills. In addition, she had several paychecks
from PE&T. She hadn't spent a penny of it since then;
everything had come out of his pocket. He knew that she was
holding out on him. It was time to call her bluff. "Okay, if
you don't have any money to spare, then we'll just have to
stay in the van."

Chapter 26

May 4, 1970.

Carol thought the weekend would never end. She hardly spoke to Daniel the entire time, even as they ate their meals together. At night, the sounds of the city penetrated the metal walls of the van. The rush of vehicles past their parking spot on Sunset Avenue made for uneasy sleep. Even though she had almost nine hundred dollars, she was determined she wouldn't start paying for <u>him</u>. She remembered what her mother had told her about her father. He hadn't worked and kept taking her money until it was all gone. Then she kicked him out. It was a matter of principle, she decided.

Daniel found out they could take showers at a Salvation Army station under the severe frowning gaze of uniformed men and women of indeterminate middle age. Carol felt it was another level of dignity stripped away.

Carol woke before first light. "I have to go to work," she said. "My job is now more important than ever."

"Okay," Daniel said, "I'll drive you in and drop you off."

Carol nodded and ate a bowl of dry cereal. Later, after brushing her teeth, she said, "I'm going to ask around at work to see if I can find a place to stay. I'm not staying another night in this van. That's final."

Space was tight in the van and it got cold at night. Not having access to a toilet or bathroom was a real drag. Everything was such a hassle. Right now, the thought of her mother's home and even Daniel's old apartment in Kent, seemed pretty nice.

"I'll call you later this afternoon about three-thirty or so, okay?" he said. "If you've got something, fine. If not, we'll make do."

"I'm not spending another night here, don't you understand?" She raised her voice and glared at Daniel. "I won't put up with this any longer."

"I understand," he said.

His appearance came into sharp focus: His face was long and he needed a shave. He was beginning to look like some of the bums she saw on the way to work, those that hung out on lower Market Street.

#

The office at PE&T seemed almost palatial. Its bright, clean and shining bathroom was almost like a refuge. Carol washed her face and fixing her make-up when Frieda entered the bathroom.

"Hi, Carol, how was your weekend?" Frieda asked

Carol started to answer and found herself crying.

"Come into my office and tell me what's wrong." Frieda steered Carol, hand on her back, into her office and closed the door. She guided her to the couch across from her desk. "Let me get you a cup of tea."

While Frieda got the tea, Carol managed to wipe her eyes dry and blow her nose.

"Well, d'you want to tell me about it?" Frieda looked over the top of her half frame glasses. She placed two mugs on the coffee table and sat next to Carol.

"We got evicted from our apartment."

"We?" Frieda's eyebrows rose.

Carol blew her nose again and began explaining the circumstances that led up to her present predicament. "Now I don't have a place to stay. Daniel doesn't seem to mind staying in that van. It's horrible."

"Well, this Daniel guy is a bit of a surprise, but I think we can work things out." Frieda patted Carol on the knee. "Why don't you and Daniel come and stay with me for a while until you find something?"

"Could we?" Carol said.

Frieda stood and nodded. "Yes, for a little bit."

Carol rose to her feet and found Frieda's arms around her, holding her tightly. Frieda's lips whispered in Carol's ear, "Things will work out, trust me." Carol felt like clinging to her, for she was the only security she knew any more.

Frieda released Carol. "Now, not a word to any of the other women. There's more than enough gossip going around as it is."

For just an instant, Carol wondered what kind of gossip was going around the office. Most of the women in the office left her alone and didn't share their confidences with her. She had wondered why, but assumed that it was because she was younger than most of them and was new to the company.

#

Daniel seemed uncomfortable, standing in the sitting room of Frieda's apartment. The apartment, near Balboa Park, was modern and had new, stylish furniture. It reminded Carol of the better motels in which they had stayed, only nicer. *This was more like it,* she thought. *This is what I want. It's something like places I've seen in magazines.*

"So," said Frieda. "Carol and I will share my bed, while you have the couch." She glanced at Daniel and smiled.

Daniel frowned. "I'm not sure I like that arrangement."

"What, you want to share my bed? A nice little threesome?" Frieda chuckled. "I don't think I know you well enough for that."

"Wouldn't it be better if Carol and I shared the couch together? That way, it would be less of an imposition on you."

"Oh, I don't mind. What d'you think, Carol?" Frieda's smile widened.

One glance at the couch was enough. *It would be more than cozy on that couch*, Carol decided. "Are you sure there's enough room in your bed?"

Frieda beckoned and led Carol into a dimly lit room.

A huge double bed was set against a wall and covered with fluffy pillows. Its four posts supported heavy velvet curtains that were tied back. It looked like something out of an exotic movie set. Compared to the van, it was like a

131

dream. Carol took a quick breath at the idea of such luxury. "Oh, it's only for a short time, I think I'll sleep with Frieda."

Frieda smiled even more widely.

Daniel frowned. "I don't think you know what you're getting into." He turned toward Frieda. "With all due respect, I prefer to keep Carol close to me."

"Daniel, be reasonable," Carol said. "Frieda has been very generous in her offer to share her apartment. I don't think you should ask her to give up her bed and sleep on the couch so we can be together, do you?" She looked quickly at Frieda, seeking support.

Frieda nodded.

His eyes went back and forth between them. "No," he said. "I can't accept that. I thought we were together."

Frieda's smile faded.

Carol frowned at Daniel. *Why is he being so obstinate? This isn't forever. I don't want to sleep all scrunched up on that couch. That bed looks so nice and I do like Frieda. So it wouldn't be a problem.* "Well, make up your mind. Are you going to take Frieda's offer or not? I'm staying, whether you do or don't."

A smile crept back onto Frieda's face.

Daniel's mouth tightened. "Okay, if that's how things are, I'll see you around." His shoulders sagged. He turned and headed for the door.

"Daniel, wait," Carol called.

He stopped and looked back. "Well?"

"Please be reasonable. I'm not sleeping in that van, ever again. You know that. Frieda has offered to let us stay here, and you're being selfish. Please, stay. You've got a couch to sleep on and I can stay with Frieda in her big bed."

Daniel shook his head. "You really don't understand, do you? She wants you, in her bed, away from me."

Frieda stepped forward. "Out," she said. "I've been patient, but you've gone too far. Now, get out."

Carol felt a wave of astonishment at seeing this tough side of Frieda. Up until now, she had always seemed gentle.

"Okay, Carol," he said. "You've made your bed, now sleep in it."

#

Daniel slept poorly that night, waking often to think about Carol and what was happening to their relationship. *Comfort has clouded her reasoning, or does she really like that dike? What am I going to do? Maybe it's time to go back to Ohio. There, at least, I've got family who'll give me a place to stay while I get things back together. I'm calling Hector in the morning.*

Chapter 27

May 5, 1970.

The rumble of traffic grew louder. Daniel pulled the sleeping bag over his head, but sleep didn't come. He sat up and looked out the van's windshield through a layer of heavy dew. It was morning, dim, gray and cold. It was time to face the day. He felt lost, almost naked, with everything stripped away. He no longer had a job, a girlfriend or friends. He shivered. It wasn't just from the cold.

The beach across the Great Highway faded into a misty distance. Just days ago, laughing, playing people filled its bright golden sands; now the beach was sterile, cold and damp. He tried to shake the fog of depression that gripped him like a form of paralysis, but there was nothing he could grasp to lift his spirits.

I'd better call Hector, he thought. *Maybe I should go home. I'm not making it out here.* Once dressed, he reached into his pocket to find he had only one hundred and fifty-seven dollars left. *Man, I came out here with over two thousand dollars and it's almost all gone.*

It took three tries before the phone rang. "Hey, Hector, it's Daniel--"

"They slaughtered our students! It was a massacre. Those fuckers, they killed them without warning." Hector's voice, loud and high pitched, sounded almost out of breath.

"Whoa, man. What're you talking about?" Daniel raised his voice over Hector's torrent of words.

"They sent the army on campus, and they shot a bunch of students, just for protesting against the Viet Nam war--"

"Who sent them?" Daniel demanded. "Who was killed?"

"Those fuckers, Nixon and Rhodes, those bastards sent in the National Guard. They shot unarmed students, killing them in cold blood." Hector's voice cracked. "Four dead, cut down without warning, and more wounded, in critical condition." He took a deep breath. "Haven't you seen the news? It's a national crisis."

"No, I haven't seen the news. I'm staying in my van. We got thrown out of our apartment, and Carol's not with me--"

"Oh, my God. Everything's happening all at once, the whole fucking world's gone crazy." Hector's voice cracked into falsetto.

It sounded like Hector had started to cry. *This is some serious shit*, he thought, *that isn't like him*. "Hey, listen, I was thinking about coming back to Kent-"

"No, you don't want to do that. It's too dangerous. They might kill you, too. It's insane, totally insane."

"Who's going to kill who?"

"The fucking pigs, man. The military-industrial complex is taking over. This it the first step of a fascist putsch--"

"Hey, Hector. Listen to me. I'm going to check the news and find out what's going on. Then I'll call you back." *Geez, he's in bad shape*, Daniel thought. "Say, in about two hours, okay?"

He listened for a while. "Yeah, I understand, nothing like this has ever happened before. I can't talk for long. I'm almost out of change... Right, I'll call about ten o'clock, or one your time. Okay?" He hung up the phone and stared down the street.

Hector may be a liberal, he thought, *but he usually gets his facts right*. He knew there were a lot of protests over the Viet Nam war and there had even been violence in Chicago at the Democratic Convention. *But the Army's killing students?* He found it hard to believe. It was scary just to think about what Hector had said.

The boxy pastel colored houses in the quiet neighborhood of the Sunset District looked quiet, peaceful. Cars drove slowly down the street, obeying the speed limit. It looked normal to Daniel, but if what Hector had said was true, he knew the world would never be the same after this.

#

At a small diner near the City College, he lingered over a second cup of coffee and watched almost an hour of news. Hector had the basic facts correct. There were four students dead in Ohio, killed while protesting the Viet Nam war. National Guard troops called onto Kent State's campus by Ohio's Governor Rhodes had shot them. By the time Daniel left, he made up his mind to go back east.

He glanced at his van and decided there wasn't anything that he could do to get ready except check the fluids. *I can't afford anything else. If it breaks, well, I guess I'll have to hitchhike. I'll just drive easy. It should be okay, I've always taken care of it. I'm just going to have to trust it.*

I'll get gas when I get into Oakland, he thought. *It'll be cheaper than here in San Francisco. California has been a bust for me. The only thing that went well was that one-shot consulting job at the winery.* Images of Nancy filled his mind and a wave of conflicting emotions rippled through him. Unbidden, the thought came: *Why isn't Carol more like Nancy? Why couldn't I have met her when things were going well? I'd better get going.* He pulled into heavy traffic and headed downtown.

Once he was over the Oakland-Bay Bridge, he stopped at a Chevron gas station and got fuel. Moments later, he found himself at a pay phone dialing the inward WATS number Nancy had given him from memory. As the phone rang, he wondered at the wisdom of making the call.

"Chanson Wines."

Nancy's voice took him back to the time they'd been together. He could see her, smell her perfume and felt an overwhelming need to see her. "This is Daniel-"

"Hi, Daniel. It's nice to hear your voice. How're you?"

Daniel hesitated a moment. "I'm leaving. I'm going back east. Have you seen the news about Kent State?"

"Oh, my God, it's terrible," she said. "Doesn't your

136

brother teach there?"

"I talked to him this morning. He's more than upset. He's losing it. I'm worried about him. Plus there are other things that have happened." Daniel told Nancy about losing the apartment and his separation from Carol.

"Look, we've got a small apartment above the cooperage barn that's not being used. You could stay there until you get on your feet."

"Thanks, Nancy, that's a very kind offer. But I've got to go and see my brother. I talked to him twice and he sounds, well, like he's having a nervous breakdown. I owe him for all he's done for me. He's my only family."

Nancy's voice softened. "I understand. Family and loyalty, plus you care." She paused. "I respect that. I appreciate you calling me. Daniel, please, don't forget to call again. I'd hate to think I'd never hear from you again. In the short time we had together, I know that you are special."

Daniel took a deep breath. *I know I must go home*, he thought. *If things were different in Kent, I might be tempted to stay. Carol's still here*, he thought and his emotions surged into a conflicted mass. "Nancy, I feel the same way. I will call and we will see each other again. I just don't know when or under what circumstances."

"Remember this number and do call."

Daniel hung up the phone and turned to leave, but hesitated. *I'd better touch base with Carol.* He still felt they had something special, even if it was rocky at the moment.

"Carol?" Daniel held the phone tight and stuffed a finger into the other ear as a large truck rumbled past. "Listen, I've decided to go back east. No, I'm not running out on you. I don't have a job. Hector doesn't sound good, so I'm going back to Kent. Did you hear the news about what happened at Kent State? No?" Daniel gave her a short summary of the events, but it was obvious it meant nothing to her.

"I want you to come with me. Quit another good job? I didn't think you cared so much. No, I don't have money to stay in nice motels or any motels. Money? No, that wasn't the reason. I wanted you to come with me. Well, 'bye for now."

Daniel smarted from Carol's comment he wanted her to quit another job so she could come with him to pay his way home. Yeah, the money would have useful since he had only one hundred and seventeen bucks and change in his pocket.

I've paid her entire way ever since she moved in with me in January and now she doesn't give a shit about me? Well, maybe that's a little strong, but she didn't seem depressed, not at all. In fact, she sounded almost happy. Frieda wants her to stay with her? Maybe she likes that idea. I wonder... no, I can't let myself believe that. Maybe some time apart will be good for us, to sort things out.

Daniel hung up and climbed into the van. As he drove north on Interstate 80, he realized the route would pass close to Napa. It would take less than an hour to be at the Chanson Winery and Nancy. The thought was delicious with its implications, especially after Carol's comments. *No*, he thought, *I've said goodbye and Hector needs me. I'm going home.*

#

Nancy put the phone back on the hook carefully and leaned back in her chair. She looked out the window at the dry vines, but saw little of it. *What about Daniel?* She thought. *He's so different from the men I've dated since I got back from France.* She realized that he was almost formal in the way he behaved, and his Spanish was the polished speech of an upper class Mexican. *Plus he's smart and worked hard, and my father likes him. But there's something else about him.* She shook her head, rose from the chair, and went to the glass door that overlooked the vineyard.

It's not a physical attraction, or is it? She tried to be analytical. *He isn't big or handsome. It's the way he is. He worked hard on that assignment for my father, he's loyal to his family. And he didn't make even a hint of a pass at me, even when I encouraged him.* She leaned against the door, the glass cooling her cheek, making her realize that her cheeks had grown warm while talking with Daniel.

She shook her head. *How could he affect me this way? We've never even kissed, and I get aroused thinking about him. Maybe it's because I know he's attracted to me, and he stayed away because of his girlfriend.* The image of Carol came into her mind, remembering her barely concealed scowl she had worn at the Winston's party. *Now she's out of the picture.*

Now he's free of her, what should I do about it? Could I do anything about it? He has gone east, and does that mean I'll never see him again? God, I hope he comes back.

Chapter 28

Thursday, May 11, 1970.

Barry Mansky, CEO of STR, rubbed his eyes and looked up from the notes at the pale and drawn faces of his staff in the boardroom. It was already ten p.m. and the recessed lighting in the ceiling barely revealed the boardroom's walls. Papers, coffee mugs and paper plates with half eaten food littered the huge table. "Okay, we'll resume tomorrow morning at seven-thirty a.m."

He'd got a call at four a.m. about an explosion at Utility Boiler Number Three. It was worse than he feared, much worse. Two operators, a maintenance man and a cleaner died when the superheater burst. From what he'd patched together, they were in the section behind the superheater, working on a leak when the superheater had ruptured.

STR's Number Three boiler house was missing one side from where the superheater section had blown out. The explosion had released a blast of high-temperature steam, which caught the four workers while they were outside the manifold room. The sound of the explosion and the subsequent sound of steam screaming from the boiler had attracted immediate attention. He'd learned the emergency workers rushed the injured employees to Akron Superior Hospital in record time, but the combination of asphyxiation and third degree burns was too much. They died on the way. All of them had families.

The news media had set up shop at the entrance to STR's Plant ready to pounce on any bit of information. Mid-morning, Mansky held a press conference and gave out the names of the workers who died. He'd already talked to their families, which depressed him even more. It had been one of the most difficult tasks he'd ever faced. The news media asked pointed questions, suggesting they wanted someone to take the blame for the accident. When he refused to answer further questions, the press conference almost degenerated into a brawl of pushing reporters yelling their questions at him. He escaped with the assistance of the plant security guards.

Mansky picked up the phone and dialed Hodge's number. "Yeah, keep the two other boilers running, but I want your people watching the steam pressure like hawks. Right. No more screw-ups, understand?" He was sure that someone had done something wrong to cause the explosion. They were old, low performance boilers that should run forever as long as they weren't stressed. STR's consulting engineers told him they suspected the superheater had been overheated, producing steam pressures beyond its capability. That meant something had changed in the operating parameters, and by God, he was going to find out.

"Hodges, get me the operators' reports for number three." Mansky paused. "And all memos detailing the history and maintenance on Number Three. I want them on my desk tomorrow morning, by eight a.m. Got it?"

#

Mansky reread the memo on using scrap rubber as fuel and compared it again with the operators' reports. If the primary combustion zone expanded and rose into the superheater section, that could cause higher pressures. A trickle of sweat ran down his back when he realized it was highly likely the fuel change might have caused that problem. He grabbed the phone. "Hodges. Are you still burning scrap rubber? You stopped? When?" His stomach soured when Hodges told him it was only after the explosion had taken place.

"Were the operators following the recommendations in this memo? This memo by--" Mansky flipped back to the first page, "er, Robles." He listened carefully. "What about controlling the fuel feed rate to prevent post-boiler combustion? What d'you mean, you're not sure?" He felt another surge of acid wash through his stomach. "Well, you better God-damn well re-read the memo. Someone has

141

fucked-up big time. You'd better find out who let the operating conditions get out of control. I shouldn't have to remind you, but this is going to have a very negative impact upon STR. And that means it will affect you the same way. Have I made myself clear? Good." He slammed down the phone.

"How the hell did he ever become production manager?" Mansky looked at Cooperthwaite. If only his favorite financial analyst knew as much about the manufacturing process as he did about the numbers, he'd make him production manager.

"Er, I'm not sure. I think he has a track record of cutting operating costs, but high personnel turnover. That has been a concern for sometime." Cooperthwaite wiped his brow and pushed his long, thin blond hair back over his balding head. "He recently claimed he could save one million dollars in fuel costs by including scrap rubber in the fuel mix." He busily sorted through a stack of papers before him. "Ah, here it is."

Mansky glanced at memo. He'd seen it earlier, except this one had Hodges name on it as the author. "That's nothing compared with what this is going to cost us. Someone is going to pay--big time."

Chapter 29

May 6, 1970.

Daniel woke to the sound of a truck's rumbling exhaust. It was a delivery vehicle backing up at the rear of the shopping center where he'd parked overnight. *This is Sacramento, right? Well, I'd better stock up on provisions for the trip here, before I head east. It'll be cheaper here.*

He waited until the Safeway supermarket opened and bought a loaf of bread, a jar of peanut butter and a bag of apples. *Ah, the perfect well-balanced diet. Should be enough to get me home*, he thought. *And keep me regular.* At nine-thirty, he departed. As he drove, he calculated how much he needed for gas to get back East. He hoped he had enough. He drove within the speed limit and coasted on the downgrades with the engine turned off.

As he approached the Donner Summit, he slowed his pace, for the van's engine temperature had begun to rise. At a rest area, he stopped and walked around through the tall conifers. This was a part of California he hadn't seen before. He wished he had time to sightsee and even visit the nearby ski areas. With a sense of regret, he climbed back into his van and departed. At Truckee, the grade began to go downhill, and he slipped the van out of gear whenever possible to coast and increase his gas mileage.

At the end of the first day, he stopped in Elko, Nevada. It was a small, dusty town with two thriving businesses; a casino and a bordello—he could afford neither, even if he had had any interest, but he didn't. Gaudy, clinking slot machines made their presence felt everywhere-- even in the bathrooms. Gas was cheap, and the casino, over-endowed with neon lights, had people coming and going at all hours. Daniel figured that its parking lot would be a safe place to stay overnight.

After a breakfast of an apple and a peanut butter sandwich, all washed down with water from the gas station's bathroom. He reminded himself to vary the order in which he ate them--variety is the spice of life. The food odors coming from the casinos tempted him until he counted his cash. It was now eighty-nine dollars. It would be close.

By late afternoon, the soaring, distant mountains of Nevada parted to reveal the blinding white vista of salt flats of Utah. The road twisted and turned as it descended down into the huge basin. The road straightened and flattened into an almost hypnotic drive. He found it difficult to keep his speed down and began chanting, "Fast eats fuel, fast eats fuel." He shook himself at regular intervals to stay alert.

In the distance, Salt Lake City appeared, framed by the white tipped peaks of the Wasatch Mountains beyond. He knew there was yet another set of mountains to cross, and that would burn a lot of gas. Soon, the sparkling waters of the Great Salt Lake appeared. 'Sea Air,' the resort on the south shore with its quaint, gingerbread style, was not far from the city limits. It vaguely reminded Daniel of Cedar Point in Ohio, more by location than appearance. *I must be getting homesick.*

He stopped in Salt Lake City and walked around and visited the Mormon temple in downtown. He gathered an impression that Salt Lake City's people were polite and courteous, especially when he recalled how people had treated him in San Francisco. *Well,* he thought, *with certain exceptions.* Peoples' faces here rarely carried frowns, and they'd flash a trace of a smile if he looked them in the eye and nodded. They seemed less uptight, not at all like the hurrying crowds on Market Street in San Francisco.

Now, let me find a place to park for the night. Better here in the valley than up in the mountains. The Wasatch peaks still gleamed whitely with snow. Even in May, skiers plied the slopes. It would be cold up there. He found a shopping center a short distance from Interstate 80 in South Salt Lake and parked well away from the stores and settled

144

in for the night.

Before first light, the increasing rumble of early morning traffic woke him. After a quick breakfast, he made a trip to the bathroom of a nearby gas station, where he washed himself and brushed his teeth. Refreshed, he resumed his trek east.

#

The remainder of the trip became a blur. Each long day of freeway driving was followed by a brief glimpse of a new place. Laramie and Cheyenne with their ubiquitous Stetson hats and battered pickup trucks signaled the end of the mountains. Once he put the last of the Rocky Mountains behind him, the road flattened, and along with the steady wind from the west on his tail, distance between fuel stops became longer. The pace of traffic picked up, but he maintained a steady sixty miles per hour.

Across the relentless rolling lands of Nebraska through Omaha to Iowa, now freshening with the brilliant green of spring, his van chugged on, a faithful steed. He crossed the mighty, muddy Missouri River, the hillocky terrain of Iowa rolled by, and into the hurly-burly traffic around Chicago.

At the border of Indiana, signs advised him that Interstate 80 would become a toll highway. That forced him onto secondary roads, for he had almost no money left. His pace slowed. At the end of the sixth day, he pulled into a roadside park somewhere in central Ohio. He felt exhausted and depressed. Yet he had no sense of homecoming.

While driving, Daniel had thought, no, obsessed, about his relationship with the two women in his life. *I tried hard to make things work with Carol, but things just seem to keep going against me.* Her attitude on the phone had surprised him. He'd thought she would have missed him, but it didn't seem that way. As he cast his mind back, he realized there were times she had manipulated him to get her own way.

Maybe, he thought, *it was because we were lovers*

and I was blinded by sex. As for sex, there had been less and less as time has gone by. He realized they made love when he did something that pleased Carol, which seemed to revolve around him spending money on her.

The drug stuff in their apartment still puzzled him. He knew it wasn't his, and for damn sure it wasn't something Carol had brought in. *So, how did it get there?* He suspected it might have been the apartment manager, seeing a sucker who would forfeit a large security deposit that would be enough to buy new furniture. Daniel wasn't sure, but it was too late to do anything about it. Besides, he'd left before the cops had gotten serious about their investigation and they didn't even have the license number of his van.

Then there's Nancy, he thought. *She's different than Carol. A lot more mature, sophisticated in ways Carol wasn't—she has a good education, knowledge of wine and is well traveled. She's everything I ever wanted in a woman, plus her mother was Spanish. She speaks the language and understands my culture. She has also got me thinking about using engineering in the wine industry. I wish I had met her earlier.* He found her attractive, stimulating, and yet he felt comfortable with her. *What am I going to do about her? I know I want to see her, but I've got a commitment to Carol. Or do I? What do I have with Carol?*

As he drove, his mind went over his relationships with Carol and Nancy again and again. He barely saw the road.

Chapter 30

May 12, 1970.

In the back of O'Brien's mind was the fear the Akron police might discover he'd got the chemicals from the stock room for his 'meth' laboratory. After he'd racked his brains, he came up with a solution that gave him a great deal of satisfaction. He'd hang the responsibility for the drugs on Robles.

I'll get even and more with that smart-ass Robles, he thought. *I gotta admit, it was a stroke of genius putting drugs in his apartment after tossing it. That dumb spic was so predictable; I just knew he'd call the cops.* He'd heard on TV the San Francisco cops were hell on wheels about dope ever since a plague of drug overdoses and deaths had swept the City. They'll be sure to indict him and maybe even give him time in the slammer.

The idea of Robles being put into a cell with hard-core criminals and raped pleased O'Brien to no end. *That's fitting punishment for him fucking with my laboratory. Fuck with me, and I'll get you fucked. In the meantime, I've got to finish the job.*

He put copies of the requisition forms he'd used to get phenyl acetone, the precursor for making speed, in Robles's files. Then, when the SF cops start to make a case against him, he figured it would be time for an anonymous tipster to let them know about the speed lab at STR.

O'Brien felt proud of himself. That should be the final straw for asshole Robles. Let the cops fight over him. Maybe they'd convict him in two states. Then he'd get time in two different slammers and get porked by two whole different sets of butt-bangers.

As midnight approached, O'Brien slipped into a set of blue coveralls that the maintenance workers used. He knew nobody would be around when the shift changed, for

147

the workers usually took showers when going off work, and the incoming shift would change into work uniforms. That gave him fifteen minutes to get into the files in the office that had belonged to Robles without being seen.

The bluish lights of the mercury vapor lamps lit up the area in front of the boiler building. It was as he expected--deserted. The factory still hummed, but was quieter than during the normal full production period. Steam drifted from the top of the undamaged section of the boiler house.

He shivered. Spring had been cool this year.

The door to Robles' office was unlocked. The office was dusty, for no one had taken Robles' place and it was no longer used.

O'Brien carefully closed the door behind him and headed for the filing cabinets at the back of the room. He knew he would have to put the files in the section where copies of the requisitions for supplies and equipment for working on the boilers were kept. Except these memos would go at the very back of the files, as though being hidden. He pulled on the handle of the file cabinet, but it wouldn't open.

The file drawer hung up.

"Damn," O'Brien said. He put the requisition forms on top of the filing cabinet so he could use both hands to pull open the drawer. It opened with a squeak and a rattle. He paused, to listen for the sound of footsteps.

Nothing.

It took a moment to put the requisitions into the files. He carefully closed the drawer, looked around and left. At the entrance to the boiler house, he paused and scoped out the open area. As he went down the steps, he caught a glimpse of someone coming around the corner of the building. It was a short man, pudgy with a crew cut.

Shit, he thought. *That looks like Hodges*. He lengthened his stride, lowered his head, hunched his back and walked in the opposite direction, into the factory as though he were a production worker facing another midnight

148

shift. *I can't let him see me,* he thought. *Had he?*

#

"Damn." Hodges tore the sheet of paper out of the typewriter. He was using Miss Krieger's IBM Selectric typewriter because she typed all the departmental memos and its type would match. However, it wasn't going well, for he had never learned to type. This was his third hunt-and-peck effort to make a replacement first page for the memo on the use of scrap rubber as boiler fuel. He'd already changed it once, to remove Daniel Robles's name. Now it had to be revised to show Robles was the one who had recommended using higher amounts of scrap rubber in the Number Three utility boiler.

Hodges also planned to include a recommendation on the amounts the operators had been instructed to use. He took a deep breath and inserted another sheet of paper into the typewriter. Hunched over, he began again, one character at a time and started to peck away.

It was almost eleven p.m., and the normally open curtains were drawn to cover the windows of his office. He had told his wife he needed to be at work due to the crisis caused by the boiler explosion. However, he'd come to his office to make sure the paper trail led responsibility to someone else—to Robles.

He knew he had to get this done tonight, completely changing all the memos. After all, he was a valuable member of the STR team, a critical component. Robles was a nobody, a Hispanic reaching above his station in life. He reasoned that Robles hadn't warned him specifically as to what might happen, so Robles was really responsible for the disaster. Now he just had to make the paperwork reflect that fact.

He held up the memo and examined it carefully. *I think I've got it.* He finished the last replacement memo. Earlier, he went through every file Robles had sent him on the boilers, to verify he had all the memos that made any mention of fueling them. He had a list of where they had to go.

The last thing I have to do, he thought, *is make copies and replace every memo mentioned on the distribution list. That shouldn't take long, since they're all in the production department central records, as well as Robles's office. It was fortunate Robles had no one else on his carbon copy list.*

Hodges spent fifteen minutes substituting memos in the production department files. It was almost midnight.

Satisfied, he headed toward Robles's old office in the boiler operations office. The office was just off the front entrance inside the utility boiler house. As he turned the corner, approaching the boiler house, he saw a tall, burly man in blue coveralls hurrying away from its front entrance. There was something familiar about the man's profile. *Probably one of the operators,* he thought.

He promptly forgot about it.

Hodges focused on a pair of battered green filing cabinets that sat next to two tall bookshelves full of three-ring binders and out of date catalogs. The office was dusty, for no one had taken Robles's place and it was no longer used. The dust on top of the filing cabinets seemed disturbed, as though someone had put something on top. For a just moment, he wondered who needed to access these files. He returned to the task at hand.

It took Hodges only five minutes to replace the memos in the files, for he found they were neat and in order. Carefully closing the last file drawer, he glanced around the office to see if there was anything else he needed to do. *Maybe I should have this office emptied out,* he thought. *All those three-ring binders and catalogs are long out of date. They're nothing but useless junk. No, not until this matter is settled. Then I'll get someone else to do it.*

He glanced at his watch. It was twelve-fifteen. Time to go home. Tomorrow would come soon enough.

Chapter 31

May 12, 1970.

The windshield wipers slogged back and forth in a futile cadence. Daniel leaned forward, as though seeking to penetrate the mist and spray as he wended his way into Kent. The road disappeared into a haze of rain, twisting through the countryside. *No wonder it's so green, with all this damn rain.*

The fields and trees had the luminous emerald tint that came from freshly emerged leaves. Spring had arrived in Ohio later than usual. Though the road was familiar, it had the strangeness that comes from absence and seeing it through refreshed eyes. He'd chosen to cross Ohio on Route 30, and once through Canton, he swung north on State Route 44 and followed it until he reached Rootstown. That's when the rain changed from a drizzle into a downpour.

He left the main highway and took secondary roads past Sandy Lake and Brady Lake, seeking the back way into Twin Lakes, which was on the north side of Kent, where Hector lived. It was like he wanted to sneak back, unseen, like the failure he was.

Turning into the driveway of Hector's home, a white center-hall colonial, he felt a sense of relief, as though it was a place of refuge. He put his head on the steering wheel and rested a moment, gathering his thoughts to tell Hector what had happened.

The front door swung open. Hector was red-eyed, his reddish beard longer than usual and his ears covered by hair. "Come in, quick," he said. "Don't let them see you."

"What's going on?" Daniel asked, all thoughts of carefully prepared remarks evaporating. He didn't like the wild look in his brother's eyes.

"The fucking pigs, man, they're in cahoots with the guardsmen. Nobody's safe anymore. The word is they're going to off everyone connected with the university."

Hector's words came out in a torrent. His hands shook and he had a twitch on the left side of his face. The house smelled of stale food. Newspapers littered the floor.

"Hey, man, slow down," Daniel said. "Why don't you tell me the whole story? Preferably after you've given me a Strohs." He had a sudden thirst, a need for something alcoholic. Something was very wrong with Hector. He'd never seen him like this before.

"Oh, sure." Hector headed for the kitchen. It was as though the request had given him focus.

Daniel followed into the dim kitchen. The sink was full of dishes, the counter covered with pots and pans, and all the blinds were drawn.

The refrigerator spilled a gash of light on the floor as Hector retrieved a beer from within. "Let's go to the basement rec room," he said. "They can't see us there."

Oh, crap, thought Daniel. *Either he's losing it or the world has really gone to hell.* And the beer was Pabst, not Strohs; that confirmed the world really had gone to hell.

"Okay, why don't you start at the beginning and tell me what happened? I've been on the road for six days and out of touch." The news he'd heard on the AM radio jumped from one news flash to another without any details. He knew there'd been a massacre, but hadn't heard anything about martial law.

Hector started, first speaking rapidly, bouncing from topic to topic about the Kent State massacre. After an hour, he slowed down and became more precise in telling what had happened. It was as though he found relief from talking about it. He kept coming back to his statement that martial law had been declared in Kent, even though the news media referred to the restrictions as a curfew. In addition, the University had closed and sent all of its students home.

Now that Hector had slowed the pace of his account and become more methodical, Daniel realized his brother had returned to what he'd always known him to be. However, he learned there had been a great deal of panic after the shooting. After the University closed, the State police had shut down the city of Kent. Daniel realized it was the lack of information that distressed his brother.

"Oh, yes," Hector said, after he'd brought Daniel up to date on the massacre. "There was something in the news yesterday about the company you used to work for."

"STR?"

"Yeah, something about a boiler explosion." Hector got up from the overstuffed armchair and retrieved a newspaper out of a bin. He flipped through several pages. "Ah, here it is."

"Let me see." Daniel read quickly. When he saw that four workers had died after the number three utility boiler exploded, his throat tightened. *I know those men. I worked with them. They were good men. They put in an honest day's work. They knew the strengths and weaknesses of that boiler. How could it have happened?* He reread the article, but like most journalism, it was full of fluff and few real technical details. It sounded to him as though it were an explosion in the manifold section, or, possibly the superheater. He couldn't tell. It had an all too familiar ring.

"Also," Hector said. "I've had a couple of phone calls from someone at STR who's looking for you. Got nasty with me last time, so I hung up on him."

"What was his name?"

"Um, something Irish, I think." Hector frowned.

The word Irish prompted Daniel to say, "O'Brien?"

"Yes, that's it. The way he talked, he sounded to me like he was a pig." Hector used his favorite word for the police. "I told him I didn't have to answer his questions and he said I'd better, if I knew what good for me. That's when I slammed down the phone. I hope I busted his eardrum."

#

The next morning after Daniel had washed all the dishes in the sink, tidied up the house and done the laundry, he went with Hector to a tavern in Twin Lakes for lunch. He noticed Hector's attitude had improved since he first came home.

Sitting at a window that gave them a view of the East Twin Lake, they made small talk as they waited for their food to arrive. The waitress, an over-weight lady of near retirement age and a head full of silver hair, finally brought them two generous burgers dripping grease and a basket of French fries.

After a couple of bites of burger and a half-glass of beer,

Hector said, "I need to get away for a while, away from phones, TV and people. I'm going to take a trip to Warren Forest in Pennsylvania and camp out for a couple of weeks or so. Nobody will be there, since all the rest of the schools are still in session. I think a change of scenery is what the doctor ordered. Why don't you come with me? It'll be like old times." He referred to the camping trips they'd made to the national forest when Daniel was in high school.

Daniel chewed his burger slowly, enjoying its flavor. It was the first time in a long time he'd had a burger, and this was a good one. With memories of sleeping in his van fresh in his mind, he picked his words carefully. "Normally, I'd jump at the chance." He put the burger down. "However, I've got to start looking for a job right away. I'm broke, really broke this time around. The trip out west was a disaster."

"Here's a few bucks." Hector handed Daniel the contents of his wallet, some fifty-five dollars. "I'll get more after I cash a check."

"Thanks. This is really good of you." Daniel went on to tell what had happened, finishing with the strange discovery of drugs in the apartment. "I don't do drugs. Neither does Carol, so I really have no idea where they came from." He took a deep drink from his Stroh's beer.

Hector frowned. "So, what did the pigs say about it?"

"I dunno. We didn't stick around to find out. And I didn't leave a forwarding address."

"There might be a warrant out for you."

"Yeah, I know," Daniel said. "Carol is now staying with a girlfriend. The apartment manager didn't know where she worked, so she should be all right. There wasn't any parking available at the apartment, so the manager doesn't know my van's license plate number. And I'm long gone." In the back of his mind, the thought nagged at him he'd have to find out sooner or later and clear himself. He drained the last drop of beer from his glass and glanced around the tavern. "Why don't we head back to your place? We can drink cheaper there."

"Bueno, I've got some packing to do." Hector paused. "Y'know, if that O'Brien guy calls again and finds you here, he might cause trouble."

Trouble? Daniel knew O'Brien was pissed off about his calling the police to inform them of the illegal laboratory. And O'Brien might have a private agenda. He also knew he'd be no match against O'Brien if it came to a fight. The guy was big, and he had an aura that said don't mess with me. "Maybe I can stay with the Terzillos," he said. "They'll want to know what Fats has been up to."

Hector smiled. "They just might like that."

Chapter 32

May 13, 1970.

Later that afternoon, Daniel met with Professor Terzillo, relating the problems that his son, Fats, had encountered in San Francisco. "So, I'm not sure what he's doing at the moment. I kind of lost track of him."

"Look, he left home. He's got to learn to take responsibility for his actions. People don't learn if they're always getting bailed out. I know he's my son, but he'll be a better man when tempered by real life. That's how it was for me." Professor Terzillo glanced at Daniel and shrugged. "I'm boring you. Look, why don't you join us for dinner?"

His physique reminded Daniel of a bowling ball: His face was round, his stomach was round and even his shoulders were round. He obviously enjoyed food and often said he had no desire to do the hard physical labor of his parents. They had been immigrants from Italy who had swung pick axes in the coalmines of West Virginia. His once brawny structure and poorly set nose evidenced a tough upbringing. "That way we can catch up on your West Coast adventures." He seemed to take lightly the problems his son had experienced with the police. It was almost as though he regarded it as minor transgression, like the sowing of wild oats.

"That sounds great, prof." Daniel knew that Mrs. T was a wonderful cook and would take the opportunity of having a visitor as an excuse to whip up a feast. Over the past week, he had lost weight on his apple and peanut butter diet. He could just imagine the meal that Mrs. T would make. His mouth watered and his stomach rumbled at the thought. Proof of her culinary skills showed in Professor Terzillo's waistline. "What time?"

"About six. We can have a few drinks before dinner." He chuckled. "You still drinking that Stroh's crap?" He'd often tried to get Daniel interested in drinking Italian wines. However, red wine never sat well on Daniel's stomach and even less on his wallet, especially the Barolos, which he'd tried often at the Terzillos. Stroh's was more within his budget.

"Yep, I am. Stohs sounds great."

#

Daniel pulled up to the late-fifties ranch-style house that had white doors and trim offsetting its pink siding. Neatly trimmed evergreen bushes guarded the base of the building and the garage door had a diamond shaped window. As the front door opened, Daniel caught the smell of garlic and meat cooking. His stomach lurched in anticipation. He hadn't eaten really good food in a long time. Even though Hector was a good cook, in his present state of mind, food preparation was low on his list of priorities. Carol was a reasonably good cook, however, her tastes ran to simple fare and never used garlic or other spices. It was almost like he had been on emergency rations in comparison to what he knew was coming this evening.

"C'mon in." Professor Terzillo led the way to the kitchen.

Mrs. T. straightened up from the oven and wiped her hands on a towel, a smile creasing her face.

"Daniel." She wrapped her arms around him and gave him a generous hug. "How've you been? Was San Francisco fun? We always had a good time there, what with its restaurants and nightlife. I bet it was just up your street." She laughed as though the whole world existed for good times. She was short, buxom and jiggled when she moved. She reminded Daniel of a white version of the Aunt Jemima seen on pancake syrup bottles. Daniel often wondered how they met, for Mrs. Terzillo had no interest in politics, which her husband enjoyed. It didn't matter, for they were happy together.

"Well, it wasn't quite like that for me," Daniel said. "Let me tell you what I know about Fielding." He always used Fats given name with his family, but nowhere else.

"My, Daniel, but you look as though you've lost weight." Mrs. Terzillo frowned. "We'll just have to fatten you up and get you well."

Daniel laughed. He knew that it was her objective to feed the men in her life and make sure they were well nourished.

"Before you get settled," the Professor said. "How about a bottle of your favorite swill?" He was amused that Daniel preferred beer to a good Italian Barolo. "I got a case of Stroh's, so you don't run short." He chuckled as though it were a private joke.

Daniel felt a strong thirst for his favorite beer; it had been almost three months of doing without. "Sure, I'd love one." He popped the cap and got down to recounting what he'd seen of their son's life style on the West Coast. He urged them to encourage his return. Daniel could only see bad things happening to Fats should he remain in San Francisco.

After he'd polished off two generous helpings of Sicilian style lasagna and six Stroh's, he called Hector. His brother told him that he was leaving for his camping trip early the next day and wondered if he'd made arrangements to spend the night with the Terzillos. They both thought it a good idea, especially if someone from STR should come looking for him. Hector ended the conversation with the suggestion that Daniel and the professor tie one on together.

Daniel asked the professor if he could stay. The professor quickly agreed. He'd always felt at home with the Terzillos. They openly accepted him as if he were a close relative. He'd often stayed with them when Fielding lived at home and he'd always done chores whenever he was there. After dinner, they settled down for some serious conversation and drinking. He learned more about the Kent State massacre and its impact upon the City of Kent.

His discussion with Professor Terzillo reinforced what his brother, Hector, had said. He realized the shootings and the martial law would go into the history books. Now he understood why Hector was so upset. The professor suggested this awful event would change the course of the nation. Daniel found he'd missed this type of conversation. For the first time in a long time, he felt like he was really home.

Chapter 33

May 17, 1970.

"Yes?" Hodges snapped into the phone. Ever since the boiler house explosion, he'd felt as if he were on the edge of a cliff. Even his office, normally a comfortable refuge filled with mementoes of his successes, was now more like a prison. He'd come to fear the ring of the phone for it never brought good news these days.

"This is Bill Dieter in personnel," the voice said. "I just saw something in the Akron Beacon-Journal concerning STR. It's about the boiler explosion. It's on page two. It doesn't sound good."

"I'll take a look at it." Hodges put the phone down without another word. He retrieved the newspaper from Miss Krieger's desk. She frowned as she looked up at him. She usually had a smile for him in the mornings. At times, she would lean forward, which offered a glimpse of her ample cleavage. But not today. Something was wrong, he sensed. It wasn't going to be a good day.

He felt his blood pressure rise as he read the article. "God damn yellow journalism," he said to no one in particular. "They're trying to crucify us."

The newspaper article suggested the boiler explosion could have been prevented if STR had done necessary basic maintenance. The newspaper cited unnamed sources within STR who were familiar with its boiler operations. The article implied it was a case of criminal negligence.

The more Hodges thought about it, the more nauseated he felt. His only consoling thought was he'd made sure the paper trail led away from himself and toward Robles. The ringing of the phone dragged him away from the third reading of the article.

"Hodges, what the fuck is this shit in the newspaper?"

Mansky's voice produced a surge of bile in Hodges'

gut. "It's a crock," he said. "We ran those boilers under the direction of a professional engineer--"

"He'd better explain what happened, right now. Get him up here on the double."

Sweat trickled down the center of his back. "Er, the engineer's no longer with the company--"

"Why not?" Mansky's voice boomed from the telephone.

"I, er, discharged him for insubordination--"

"Get your ass up to my office," Mansky said. "Bring everything you've got about changes in boiler operation. I need to get to the bottom of this, right away."

Oh, shit, Hodges thought. *Another ass-reaming.*

#

Mansky leaned forward over his desk. "I've already had a call from the attorney-general's office in Columbus. They're hinting the explosion might have been the result of criminal negligence. I need to find who's responsible for getting STR's name dragged through the mud."

It's gotten worse, Hodges thought. *Mansky is looking for a scapegoat.* He knew that Mansky wouldn't hesitate to throw him into the legal grinder to save himself. He had absolutely no doubts about that. Mentally, he patted himself on the back for establishing a paper trail that pointed the finger in a different direction.

"I'll need an hour to go through the files to make sure that I've got them all."

"No." Mansky took a deep breath. "I'm sending someone from the legal department to help you. Don't start until they arrive." Mansky pointed to the door.

Hodges' stomach twisted into an even tighter knot as he left. That meant Mansky suspected he might try to destroy files. He was looking to establish legal defense to protect himself.

As he returned to his office, he could hear Miss Krieger saying 'yes, sir,' repeatedly into the phone. It was silent for a moment. She appeared at his door.

"Mr. Hodges?" she said. "Mr. Mansky's secretary just called and asked me to watch the files until Mr. Wolf from the legal department arrives." Her frown deepened. "Is something wrong?"

"It's the boiler thing." He hesitated. He realized he really didn't know where Miss Krieger's loyalties lay. In fact, he didn't know if he could trust anyone at this point, which forced him to say, "Something about chain of custody of the records. Y'know, one of those funny legal requirements."

"Oh," she said, "is that all it really is?" The tightening of her lips and deepening of her frown showed a cloud of doubt. "Well, since it was Mr. Mansky's request, I'd better do it." She pursed her lips primly. She turned and disappeared into the outer office.

The sick feeling in his stomach threatened to erupt. *I can't let this happen. I've got to appear in control.* Hodges took a deep breath. *I hope those memos work. In the meantime, I'd better not go near the original memos Robles had sent me.* He was sure they would be safe in his desk. He'd hidden them within the little-used file folder that covered legal correspondence. *I'll dig them out later and destroy them.*

#

"So, this is where y'all keep copies of the departmental memos?" Herbert Wolf was a tall thin man with a gray pallor, bushy eyebrows, a beak of a nose and a poker face. He spoke with an Arkansas accent that caused some to assume his mind was as slow as his speech. They only made that mistake once, usually to their detriment. He'd directed his question to Miss Krieger.

"Yes. I have an index to everything in there." Miss Krieger pointed to a row of filing cabinets in the room off her office. "All the departmental records. We have a central filing system. They go back for seven years. Those older get sent to long term storage."

"That's real handy." Wolf nodded his approval.

"Why, that sounds like you do things just right in here."

She smiled as though she'd just won a spelling bee, for Hodges had never shown interest in her efficient operations.

"Y'all don't mind if I have a copy of this, Miss Krieger?" Wolf fingered the list while peering down his nose at the sheets of paper.

Miss Krieger glanced quickly at Hodges before she said, "I'll make you a copy right away."

"Why, thank you, that's mighty nice of you."

She hurried out of the office.

Hodges watched Wolf wander around the office, casually inspecting its contents.

Miss Krieger returned and silently handed the list to Wolf.

Wolf sat down behind Miss Krieger's desk and resumed study of the list. He glanced up at Hodges. "I think I'm going to rely upon you to pull out those memos that Mr. Mansky wants. Why don't you and Miss Krieger work together and round up those files." He pivoted his chair so he could observe the file room.

"Now?" Hodges felt cornered. So far, Wolf had shown no interest in Miss Krieger's files.

"I believe there's about forty minutes left of the hour Mr. Mansky gave you." Wolf's smile was like that of an executioner getting a commission. "I don't think I'd be late, if I were you. Now, y'all don't mind me. I'll just sit here and keep an eye on things." He waved his hand as though flicking off a fly. "Just a formality, y'understand."

#

"Mr. Mansky, I swear we followed the directions of the engineer," Hodges said. "I'm sure they're in those files, somewhere." He pointed to the stack of files he'd brought from the departmental filing room that was outside Miss Krieger's office.

Mansky's office was warm, even cozy with its pale-maple-paneled walls and plush beige carpeting. Mansky sat behind an eight-foot wide blond wood desk. Its matching credenza had two phones and a large rotary file of phone numbers. The files were the only item on the desk.

"I think we ought to get these copied. I can have my people take care of it," Wolf said. "I haven't had a chance to go through them yet, but I think they could be critical to our legal position, especially if they document actions that lead to a reasonable belief for the cause of the boiler explosion." His face had become longer and grayer.

"Which means?" Mansky said.

"Criminal negligence is a most serious charge, especially when human life is lost." Wolf's eyebrows went up. "It could have serious adverse consequences for STR."

"God dammit," Mansky said. "As if we don't have enough problems. Look, Wolfie, we've got to have some kind of defense, maybe sabotage. Yes, that's it. Tie this to that engineer. Show he was acting independently of STR. Figure out some way to show it was deliberate on his part."

Wolf's eyebrows rose further. "Well, I need to have credible documentation or some kind of evidence for that type of defense. Lemme see what I can find in these here files." He turned to leave and paused. "Oh, yes, as an officer of the court, I need to make sure I can testify our files are safe. I'll get special locks put on those files to ensure they're safe." He smiled at Hodges. "I'm sure y'all understand."

Hodges' stomach tightened. *Damn,* he thought, *now all I need is a chance to destroy Robles's original memos. I hope those replacement files are the proof Mansky and Wolf want.* He forced a smile. "Nice to know that you're thinking of everything."

Chapter 34

May 19, 1970.

Herbert Wolf parked his reading glasses on top of his head and leaned back in his chair. Most of what he'd found in the files didn't point the finger clearly at the engineer. There were comments about operating the boiler within specified limits. From the production record, it showed the amount of scrap rubber used as fuel on Number Three boiler was within specifications. The engineer had given STR no warning about any problems with the superheater. So what made it blow up?

He also discovered that Robles, the engineer, had his own set of files, which were in the boiler house. Those had proved to contain much of the same memos as those in the departmental records, with certain exceptions. Those files puzzled him, for they contained stockroom receipts for chemicals. Even though he'd been around the rubber industry for many years and knew much of its chemistry, he didn't recognize the names of these chemicals.

It was only after he'd spent some time looking them up in the CRC Handbook of Chemistry, he decided he needed some help. He picked up the phone and dialed. "This is Wolf," he said. "Who's a young hot-shot chemist who can tell me what certain chemicals are used for?" He addressed his question to Dieter in personnel, who was responsible for college recruiting. He'd found Dieter often had a better idea of what the new employees could do than their managers. That bothered him, but he knew many managers focused their attention on those above them rather than developing their people.

"What're the chemicals?" Dieter said.

"Er, phenyl acetone, methyl amine."

"Hmm, doesn't ring a bell right away." Dieter took a deep breath. "Can I get back to you on that?"

"Well, as long as it's before you go home tonight,"

Wolf said. "I need the information, and soon."

\#

Dieter put the phone down and looked around his office. The oak desk, matching credenza and guest chairs still had the gleam of newness. Yet the decor seemed cheap and confining to him. He'd just realized Wolf had been turned loose to find a scapegoat for the boiler explosion. Dieter had obtained a lot of information about the chemicals from talking to a chemist who worked in the Research Center.

He reached for the phone. "Mr. Wolf? Phenyl acetone and methyl amine were tried in the lab to make blocked curing agents for urethanes. That work was done by Zack Rogan. He was the chemist who disappeared. No, they weren't successful. What else? Well, they can be used as drug precursors, to make a drug called methyl amphetamine." He paused as Wolf commented he'd heard about it. "Right, yes, those are the same chemicals that were found in the drug lab in the boiler house. Do you remember that was what Robles reported to the police?" Dieter paused.

"Kinda odd Robles should have blown the whistle about something like that," Wolf said softly.

"Why do you say that?" Dieter hoped that Wolf would say more. The phone clicked in his ear, followed by silence.

Dieter put his hands behind his head and leaned back in his chair. *Is there a connection between those chemicals and Daniel? If Daniel were somehow involved, then Daniel could be in a world of trouble.* He knew Wolf was ruthless in protecting STR. He also knew the company needed some way to deflect blame for the superheater explosion. They just might decide Daniel was convenient for that purpose. He found it hard to believe Daniel had anything to do with drugs, for he'd always worked hard and stayed focused on his projects. And he had been very good to Carol, better than any of her previous boyfriends. He just seemed like a good guy.

I may regret this. He reached for the phone. "Yes, this is William Dieter. Can I leave a message for Daniel Robles? Oh, he's not there? Can you give him my number so he can call me?" He nodded as Hector Robles made a vague commitment to pass on the message.

Ten minutes later, the phone rang. "Dieter, personnel." When he recognized Daniel's voice, he leaned forward over his desk and cupped his hand around the phone. "Yeah, it's me. Look, I just learned that Wolf in the legal department, found stockroom receipts for drug precursor chemicals in your files." He listened for a moment. "I believe you. Wolf is dangerous, that's all I can say. I've got to go." He felt a wave of heat flow through himself. He wasn't sure if it were guilt or fear. He just knew he had opened himself up to the possibility of being fired. Yet he couldn't bring himself to believe Daniel had been running an illegal drug lab at STR.

#

"Lemme speak to Detective Grueden," Wolf said into the phone. He bounced the eraser end of a long, yellow pencil on the top of a stack of files. The desk, mahogany with a worn, burnished patina of many years, was covered with stacks of manila file folders as was the credenza and the floor alongside the desk. The carpeting, worn and stained, had at one time been beige. It was now a collage of coffee brown and off yellow colors.

"Detective Grueden? This is Wolf at STR. Y'all remember that case where an alleged drug lab was found in our boiler house? Well, let's not quibble over something that's not been adjudicated." He picked up a coffee mug and sipped. Even though it was cold, he still had to have it. Fuel, he called it, and he needed a lot of fuel.

"Well, in checking the files of one Mr. Daniel Robles, we discovered he had a collection of chemical stockroom receipts for some of the same chemicals found in that alleg-ed drug laboratory. Yes, I thought y'all would find that interesting." He put the mug down and leaned back in his chair. It squeaked. "Where is the said Mr. Robles? Why, I do believe he took off to hippie heaven, y'know, San Francisco."

Wolf had learned from O'Brien that Robles had been traced to San Francisco after companies there had sought references from STR. He also knew Robles hadn't been employed by any of those companies. "No, Mr. Grueden, I do not have his current address. Perhaps you could use your contacts with the po-lice in that city to help find him?"

#

Grueden put the phone down. The rest of the office was quiet, for most of the officers were out on calls. It had been a busy week; there had been several shootings over drug deals gone bad. The Mayor had renewed his campaign to stamp out the flood of drugs. He'd made appearances on the six o'clock news several times with his demands for action and how he was putting more pressure on the police to perform.

He'd just learned the San Francisco police wanted to talk to Daniel Robles. Grueden felt almost angry, for he'd thought all along that Robles had been an upright, law-abiding guy. Now he'd learned that methamphetamines had been found along with other drugs in his apartment in San Francisco. *Son of a bitch,* he thought, it was all misdirection. *Maybe he even had something to do with Rogan's disappearance. The guys were about the same age. Maybe they had hung out together. Maybe they even did drugs together.*

The San Francisco police sent him a complete trace analysis of the methamphetamine found in Robles' apartment over the department's new facsimile machine. When he had it compared with the drug analysis from the illegal lab in STR's boiler house, he was astonished to see they matched perfectly, down to smallest traces of impurities. They were from the same batch.

Well, Mr. Robles, he thought, *it's time to face the music. You got some serious questions to answer.* He rose to

168

his feet, feeling almost weary. *Sometimes my instincts screw me up.* He knew he had to send a copy of his analysis to the San Francisco police. He had no doubt they'd issue a warrant for Daniel Robles' arrest. He, too, wanted to have a chat with him and learn if he had any dealings with Zack Rogan.

Chapter 35

May 20, 1970.

Daniel put the phone down. Hector had relayed a message from Dieter, and he had returned the call. Dieter told him of his conversation with Wolf of STR's legal department, who was suspicious that he was involved with drug manufacture. The news struck him as ludicrous but frightening. He suspected the police would want to question him. He needed time to think, to get away for a while. For a moment, the idea of going with his brother to the wilds of Pennsylvania appealed to him. They'd never find him there in the back woods he knew quite well. But those were the actions of a guilty person. He wanted to get a job and a normal life.

He'd already made up his mind he had to get out of Kent and away from the Akron area. The aftermath of the Kent State massacre had left the town under a curfew; it was almost like martial law. Cops everywhere. It wasn't like the town where he'd done his undergraduate work any more. He figured it was time to call some old classmates and take them up on their long-standing invitations to visit and start networking, looking for a job. He had to let the Terzillos know he was leaving today.

"Professor Terzillo," Daniel said. "I've to go out of town. There's something I've got to take care of. I hope you understand."

"Well, Daniel, you've got to do what you've got to do." Professor Terzillo's enthusiasm for Daniel's presence had faded after the first day, even though Daniel had done a number of maintenance chores that had been neglected for some time. The Professor liked to talk above all else, and most obvious topics had been thoroughly exhausted at this point. It was obvious the coin of conversation had become devalued.

"Yeah, well, it can't be helped." Daniel shrugged. "Thanks again, and tell Mrs. T. I haven't eaten this well since I last stayed here. She makes the best Italian food in the whole world. I really enjoyed it."

At the door of their home, Daniel paused for a moment. He really did like the Terzillos and felt like he was running out on them. "If I hear anything about Fielding," he said. "I'll give you a call and fill you in."

"Thanks, it would be nice to hear from him. You take care of yourself, Daniel." Professor Terzillo nodded seriously. "You're always welcome in our home."

As Daniel started the van, he glanced back at their tidy house with its green shutters and neat landscaping. *I wonder when I'll next see them,* he thought. He'd already decided that he'd visit Stevie Huff, a former classmate from Case-Western Reserve who was working on his doctoral thesis about some aspect of metallurgical engineering. Even though he hadn't talked to Stevie since leaving Kent, he knew he had a couch in his living room he could use. Since Stevie was busy doing research and writing, there would be time to think and figure out what to do. Besides, Cleveland had a far larger job market than Akron and Kent combined. And at Stevie's apartment, all Cleveland phone calls would be local, which would save money.

#

Traffic in University Circle moved slowly and the Euclid Epworth Methodist Church with its famous verdigris colored oil can spout spire was a familiar sight. He turned left down East Boulevard, passing the Greco-Roman style edifice that was Severance Hall, the home of the Cleveland Orchestra.

Several turns later, he reached the quiet side street where Stevie rented the third floor in a turn-of-the-century home that wasn't aging well. Graying wood showed through the flaking white paint of the rambling Victorian style house. Three cars occupied the driveway. One car had a flat tire and weeds growing around it. He cruised down the block until he found a parking place into which he squeezed his van. As he walked to Stevie's home, he received several hostile glances.

171

The race riots of 1966 had left Cleveland a polarized city and many in the black community expressed open hostility at white interlopers.

Daniel went up the back stairs on a path beaten through litter and a thick layer of dust. He moved cautiously across the dim floor of the second landing. The overhead bulb, bare and dangling, had the dark tine of burnout.

"Hey, Stevie, it's me, Daniel." Daniel had called earlier and agreed to show up at lunchtime. Since he'd eaten with Stevie many times while they were in school together, he knew that it would be a cheap, fast lunch. Stevie was efficient; he didn't seem to care what he ate as long as it had calories and was quick. His familiar face framed the doorway and gestured for him to come in.

"Daniel, what's happening, man?" Stevie was slight of build with frizzy Afro that formed a halo around his dark brown face. He wore heavy black-rimmed glasses with thick lenses that perched on the end of a wide nose. "I thought you were seeking your fame and fortune in California with that fox, Carol." He beckoned, opening the refrigerator. "Wanna beer?" The almost-bare refrigerator had just two Stroh's among miscellaneous packages of food.

"No, thanks. Well, things didn't work out the way I thought they would--"

"That's obvious, man," Stevie said. "You wouldn't be on my doorstep unless you were in some kind of shit." Stevie had always had keen insight on Daniel's activities. "You eat yet?"

"No, not yet."

"Okay. I got some hot dogs in the 'fridge. Won't take a minute to get 'em ready." Stevie pointed to the couch. "So what's really happening, man?"

As Stevie moved around the cramped kitchen, efficiently removing items from battered cupboards and a refrigerator that had seen service since the Depression, Daniel recounted what had taken place.

"Someone got the idea that you're into drugs?" A

frown washed across Stevie's face. "Are you, man?"

Daniel sighed. "No, I don't do drugs."

Stevie nodded. "Yeah, you ain't changed. What about Carol? I thought you were serious about her. She really had your nose opened."

"I was--or am. I don't know. I'm confused about her. I still feel for her, yet, I don't know why she stayed in California." He didn't want to get into how they broke up.

"You talk to her lately?"

"No, I'm short on bread, so I haven't called her."

Stevie pointed to a battered rotary phone sitting on a scarred end table next to a sway back couch of uncertain color. "Why don't you call her and find out? You got enough uncertainty in your life. Eliminate some. I gotta do some serious library time this afternoon. I'll be back at six. Make yourself at home. 'Bye." He picked up his book bag and went out.

#

"Carol?" Daniel held his breath for a moment. "It's me, Daniel. How're you?"

"Where're you?" Carol said. "Are you back in town?" The clatter of the office sounded faintly in the background.

"I'm in Cleveland. I've run into some problems. I'm staying with Stevie. Y'know, the guy I used to room with in college. I told you about him." Daniel explained what had happened. Carol listened in silence until he finished. He couldn't bring himself to tell her that he loved her, even though his heart still ached for her. He took a deep breath. "I'm broke. I might have some legal problems. I'd hoped you could help me."

"Me? Help you? Why did you leave me? You said you would get me a nice apartment here," Carol said. "But no, you had to run off to Ohio, to your rich brother and his fancy friends."

"I thought you wanted to stay with Frieda, since she offered to let you stay there for free. Isn't that working out?"

In the back of his mind, Daniel had a strong suspicion that Frieda's interest wasn't entirely altruistic. He felt a surge of hope his fears had been unfounded.

"You knew she was a lesbian and had the hots for me," Carol said. "I didn't realize it until she was in bed with me."

"What happened?" Daniel held his breath.

"What d'you think happened?" Carol's voice pitched lower, "I had to do it, so she wouldn't throw me out. If I didn't, I'd have lost my job and had to live on the street. It's all your fault." Her voice rose. "Can you send me five hundred dollars? I need it for a deposit on an apartment. I found a nice place in the Avenues, just off the Muni line."

The image of Carol, naked, with Frieda, surged thought his mind, overwhelming him. He felt anger, jealousy and hurt. It was a feeling of betrayal, for he still had a hope that they belonged together. He chose his words carefully and spoke in a controlled fashion. "Right now, I've got less than fifty dollars to my name, and I'm probably going to have to give that to Stevie for this phone call and--"

"You don't have any money? I thought you'd gone to see your rich brother. Can't you get it from him?" Carol's voice had become louder, harder.

Daniel winced at hearing her words. "Carol, please, understand. I don't freeload off anyone, not even my brother."

"So that means you won't ask him for the money, but you're willing to freeload off me?"

"No. I can't and won't."

"Thanks a lot, yet you're hitting me up for money? Don't call me until you can help me." The phone went silent.

Daniel put the phone down and stared out the window, seeing nothing.

Chapter 36

May 20, 1970.

"Hodges." Mansky's voice rang like a hammer on an empty oil drum.

Ben Hodges jerked the phone away from his ear. "Yes, sir?"

"You remember what I said about cutting costs?"

"Yes, sir."

"That did not mean cutting production. You understand?"

Hodges frowned. "But, Mr. Mansky, we lost number three boiler. That cut our superheated steam output by one third--"

"Look, the banks don't give a shit about number three boiler, nor anything else. All they want is their money. If they don't get it, they get nasty." His voice was loud and breathy, as though he'd been running hard. "Nasty, like calling their loan, which means bankruptcy. Now do you understand? Just get production up--right away."

Hodges stared out the window of his office at the research center, thinking how easy the researchers had it, just concentrating on hare-brained ideas with no responsibilities. For an instant he wished that he'd taken up chemistry instead of industrial engineering. Sweat trickled down his back. He was sure the State was desperately seeking to divert attention from the Kent State massacre. STR's problems were a convenient smoke screen for them. "I'm not sure we can make up the shortfall from number three--"

"What part of what I said did you not understand? Production up? Or right away?"

Hodges rose to his feet. "Yes, sir, Mr. Mansky, right away." He almost saluted. He caught himself and sat down when he realized Mansky was no longer on the phone.

"Grabowski, we need more steam from number one

and two," Hodges said into the phone. "Cut the back pressure on the condensers and increase the amount of rubber scrap in the fuel mix." He knew that would increase the flow of superheated steam into the tire curing section at a lower temperature. It would make the system less efficient since greater volumes of steam would be needed to cure the tires, but production came first. He hoped the change would make enough steam. If it wasn't, he knew he'd have to figure something else to increase in output. If he didn't, he knew next thing to explode would be Mansky.

He called production operations to advise them of increased steam availability and ordered a revision in the production schedules, upping the output. *There*, he thought, *that ought to make a difference.*

He knew he had to make sure the State investigators had the right party in their sights when they aimed the charge of criminal negligence. He was sure the documents retrieved by Wolfe from the files in Miss Krieger's office were the right ones. And, he'd come in early yesterday and managed to destroy the original memos from Robles.

#

"Hello, PE&T billing. How may I help you?" Carol answered almost automatically from within her glass walled cubicle. The background chatter of punch card machines running outside was barely audible. Frieda had promoted her to customer relations in the billing department, which meant more money. It was also more interesting work since she got to investigate why there were problems with bills. She met a lot of the other workers in the department. The fact they knew she lived with Frieda meant they treated her with more respect, or was it fear? Carol didn't really care, since it was better than being on the bottom.   "Carol Meadows?" The male voice was deep, authoritative. It almost sounded like her father's voice, with a roughness that came from drinking whiskey. It wasn't him.

"Yes?" Carol glanced down at the phone and then realized the call had come in on an outside line. She should have denied being that person since the company policy required no one give out their name. "Who's this?"

"You can earn a significant reward for information leading to the whereabouts of Daniel Robles."

Carol waited to hear more, but she could only hear the sound of his breathing. Money always interested her. "Er, how much?"

"Five hundred dollars, cash. Tell me now, and you'll get the money today." Again silence.

"Let me think about it," Carol said. "What's your phone number?"

"I'll call you this afternoon. If you can't help me, the money goes to someone else. I have other leads." The phone went dead.

Carol thought about the money. *That would cover the deposit for that cute apartment out in the Avenues with a little left over.* For a moment she had the idea of giving the address of Daniel's brother in Kent to the man. She knew it would be the first place anyone would look knowing Daniel had gone back east. She went to Frieda's office and knocked.

Frieda smiled and beckoned through the window to come in.

"Can I ask you a question?" Carol said.

Frieda glanced around as though to check whether anyone was with hearing range. "You can ask me anything, sweetheart."

"Well, someone asked me where Daniel is. I don't know whether I should tell them or not." Carol looked down at her fingers.

A trace of a frown crossed Frieda's forehead. "He is out of your life, isn't he?"

"Yes." Carol continued to stare at her fingers.

"Why should you care who's looking for him?"

"I guess you're right." Carol turned to go.

"Would you like to go down to Ghiradelli Square this evening and eat at Fisherman's wharf?" Frieda leaned back in her chair, eyes twinkling and a smile playing on her lips.

"Oh, yes, that'd be super." Carol enjoyed going out to eat, and Frieda liked to take her to fancy places. Carol had found Frieda was as easy to control as most of the guys she'd dated. She also knew that after a good meal and a bottle of wine, they'd go to bed after they got back to Frieda's apartment. She was enjoying sex more and more with Frieda. She'd learned there were a lot of women with women in San Francisco who believed this type of relationship was perfectly normal.

Maybe I don't need to get my own place, Carol thought. *I can't afford to eat out at those places Frieda takes me to. But five hundred dollars for an address?* It was too easy.

She had mixed feelings about being with Frieda, for there was always the strict guidance of her mother, straight-laced and firmly Baptist in the back of her mind. But, she had to admit she liked Frieda's attentions, even the first night with her.

On the first night Carol stayed with Frieda, she encouraged her to try a bubble bath after she made mention of it while looking in at the bathroom. She'd agreed and Frieda helped her get started. Once in the tub, soaking, Frieda had come in and insisted she scrub her back. That back scrub had eventually moved to her breasts. Frieda also had helped her to dry off using those wonderful big fluffy white towels. Then she had produced a frilly little nightgown.

Once in bed, they'd talked and while Frieda had rubbed her back. It was only when Frieda had started to kiss her and touch her, she realized where this was going. She had protested, but Frieda had put her finger on her lips and said, "You can leave if you want."

It was at that instant Carol realized she had no choice but to go along with whatever Frieda had in mind. She remembered her nervousness had changed to pleasure, for Frieda knew how to touch her in all the right places. She actually ended up enjoying what happened. However, guilt did nag at her for a while. As time had gone by, the guilty feelings had become less and less.

Do I really want to move out...? I don't think so.

#

O'Brien hung up the phone. *She'll come through*, he thought. He'd learned from the landlord at the apartment that Robles and Carol had shared, the landlord had heard her complaining about money several times to Robles. *Money, that's what every bitch wants. They'll do anything for money.*

It had taken less than a day to track Carol down. He'd told Carol's mother her daughter had a settlement coming from a class-action lawsuit. He'd used a news item about the Corvair, the car she'd previously owned as the cover story. Carol's mother had given him Carol's work phone number since she didn't have one for a home address. He guessed her mother wouldn't call Carol, but would wait for her daughter to call first. He knew Carol's mother had very little money. He guessed she came from a culture where long distance phone calls were something one made only in emergencies.

He waited until three o'clock before calling Carol again. "Hello, Carol?"

"Yes? Who is it?"

O'Brien felt an involuntary smile coming. She sounded eager. "Where can I find Robles?" he said.

"When do I get my money?" she said.

"Today. I've got it with me, right now."

"Well, er, maybe after work." Carol paused.

"Where's Robles? Five hundred dollars for the information, today." He knew he had to keep the pressure on.

"If I tell you, how do I get my money?"

"I'll be outside the front door on California Street. Look for a guy carrying a bunch of yellow roses, that's me. I'll have an envelope with five hundred dollars, in cash, for you."

Carol hesitated for a moment. "Okay, I'll tell you then."

"What time do you get off? Gimme something to

recognize you." O'Brien softened his voice.

"Four-thirty. I'm wearing a maroon sweater and black slacks," she said. "I've got long, blonde hair."

"Okay, got it. Remember the roses." He hung up the phone.

#

"Hey, lady." O'Brien flashed a smile. "Are you Carol?" He waved a bunch of yellow roses at her. He had picked up a dozen roses, which he was sure would be enough for his purposes.

Carol hesitated for a moment. "Yes."

O'Brien handed her the roses. "These are for you."

Carol took the bunch of long-stem rose and sniffed them. "They're pretty."

"This is for you, also." O'Brien held out a thick envelope. He opened the flap and revealed a thick wad. It looked like a lot of twenty-dollar bills. "When you tell me where Robles is."

Carol moved the flowers into her left hand and reached for the envelope. The bunch of flowers almost slipped from her grip. She struggled to keep them from falling.

O'Brien did not release the envelope into her grip.

"He, he's staying with a friend in Cleveland, a student at Case-Western Reserve University. I don't know the exact address. It's on Belleflower Street, just off Euclid Avenue——"

"Yeah, I know where that is," O'Brien said. "Who's the guy he's staying with?"

"Er, his name is Stevie Huff, he's black, a negro"

"What kind of student is he?"

"I'm not sure. I know he's in a doctoral program of some kind." Carol frowned.

"Okay, that should be enough. Here's your money." He released the envelope into her hand.

Carol peeked inside the flap of the envelope with one hand, and as she did, the flowers impeded her view. It looked like a wad of crisp twenty-dollar bills. She quickly stuffed the envelope into her purse.

Dumb bitch, she fell for it, O'Brien thought, *the flower trick works every time. Women can't resist roses, and that made it difficult for her to take out the money to count it.* He'd put a couple of twenties on each side of sheets of paper cut to the same exact size as the money into the envelope. "Thanks," he said. "Have a nice day." He smiled, nodded and headed for Union Square. He stepped into the street and dodged traffic as he crossed the street. He was sure that Carol wouldn't follow him.

One more phone call, O'Brien thought. *Then I'm off to the airport.* He dialed a series of numbers and fed a fistful of change into the pay phone. "Lemme speak with Detective Grueden. Yeah, tell him I've got info on the whereabouts of Daniel Robles, the suspect in the drug case."

Chapter 37

May 21, 1970.

The pounding on the apartment door surprised Daniel. He knew that Stevie had few friends and none that would come to visit without first calling to make sure he was in. He opened the door just a crack. "Yes?" It was his second day here.

"Daniel Robles?"

Daniel peered past the partly opened door into the grubby stairway hall outside.

A slim man wearing a grubby tan raincoat stood in front of the door. He was middle-aged with a long and thin face that was framed by sideburns. He held up a gold badge. Behind him was a large, uniformed policeman who had a red face and a trace of closely cropped ginger hair showing from beneath his peaked hat.

"Yes?"

"Police. Open up," the man said.

Daniel felt his stomach lurch. He was sure that no one would find him here in Stevie's place. "What the--"

"I'm Detective Grueden. You're under arrest..."

Daniel barely heard the rest of the words about his rights, and suspicion of illegal activities under the Ohio Revised Code. For just an instant, the hallway seemed to brighten and took on an almost luminous appearance, stretching off into the distance forever. It was like a dream, a bad, bad dream. When the policeman tightened the handcuffs behind his back, everything came into sharp, clear focus. "Ow, you're pinching my wrists."

"Shaddup," the large uniformed policeman said. "Get moving." He steered Daniel down the stairs, with one hand firmly grasping the back of his collar.

The way down was more difficult than Daniel had ever imagined. The loss of his hands to aid his balance made him stumble, and the beefy hand of the big police officer pulled him upright with a jerk that almost strangled him.

The ride in the police car seemed to last forever.

Daniel realized the car was heading south, toward Akron. Eventually they pulled up at a grimy, three-story building with a limestone façade into which went a steady stream of police officers. The busy activity of the uniformed men made him think of blue bottle flies.

Once inside the building, the big policeman guided him through long corridors and down a flight of stairs into the basement to put him into a bare, dingy yellow room with a table and two chairs. The officer made him sit in the chair that faced the door and then left, slamming the door shut. He was alone. He realized his world, as he knew it, was over. He'd never imagined anything like this could happen to him. Words Dieter said about drug manufacturing came back. *That must be why I'm here*, he thought. *But how could that be tied to me?*

#

"Will you accept a collect call from a Daniel Robles?" Carol heard on the phone. Since she had phone privileges and it would cost her nothing, she accepted it.

"Carol, I need help. I've been arrested." Daniel's voice sounded faint, almost tinny. "I can't get hold of my brother, he's on vacation. I don't know how to reach him."

"Where are you?" she asked, fearing what his call meant.

"I'm in the Akron City jail. I need bail. You have no idea how horrible this place is. I've already been in one fight with a prisoner who tried to force me to . . . Never mind. Can you help bail me out?" His voice sound strained, as though he were in pain. "Please, Carol."

"What does that mean, bail?"

"I need a bail bond, to get out of jail. Bail is five thousand dollars, which means I need five hundred for the bail bondsman . . ." He paused and the silence grew.

"Five hundred dollars? Where d'you think I'm going

183

to get five hundred dollars from?" Carol already had more than twice that amount in the bank from the money she had brought from Kent, plus saving every penny she earned at PE&T, because Frieda paid all her expenses. "If, if I could scrape it together, when do I get it back?" she asked.

Daniel cleared his throat. "That's the fee for the bond," he said. "Look, I'm in jail. They're not going to let me out unless someone posts bond. As soon as Hector comes home, then I could ask him to reimburse you for the bond."

"Oh, so it's like a loan." Carol pursed her lips and thought about the nasty man who had cheated her out of five hundred dollars he'd promised her. Many of Frieda's friends had told her of the bad experiences they'd had with men, to which Carol could now relate. All they ever wanted to do was get in her pants. Now he wanted to take her money when he got himself in trouble. Just because they'd been intimate together gave him no right over her. "Daniel, I'm sorry, but I can't help you." She put the phone down and for just an instant felt powerful for what she'd done.

#

Daniel felt a wave of depression sweep over him. His world had shrunk into a small cell defined by a row of steel bars and walls of concrete, the ever-present stench of stale urine mixed with vomit and cigarette smoke. He was sure his nose had been broken fighting off Slam, a tattooed hulk who'd said, "I'm gonna make you my bitch." Even though not as large as Slam, Daniel was in better physical condition from running regularly and working out. They had an uneasy truce, based upon a mutual physical thrashing, which the guards had found amusing.

Daniel hurt all over, his clothes were filthy and torn and his pants kept sagging after the loss of his belt. Not only was his freedom gone, he also felt degraded. He returned to the cell, knowing there was little chance Hector would return soon and bail him out. He knew Carol had money. Mentally, he tallied up the money she should have had while living with him. It came to more than nine hundred dollars. *And she can't help me? Even after everything we had together?*

Maybe I can call someone at STR, and they can bail me out. "Hey, guard, I need to make another telephone call!" Daniel called down the grimy corridor between the colonnades of steel bars. Water puddled on the cracked concrete flooring.

"One call per day," the guard called. "You've already had yours for the day, pretty boy."

Chapter 38

"Personnel," Dieter said. Spring recruiting season was in full swing. Even though STR had no plans to hire new college graduates, there were a lot of contacts he wanted to maintain. He knew the business cycle went up and down and he was determined to preserve his entree into the universities. His oak desk was covered with resumes and transcripts sent in by job hopefuls. It was the only untidy spot in his office.

"Dieter, this is Daniel Robles."

Dieter took a quick breath. "Where are you?"

"In the Akron City jail. Look, I need help. My brother is away camping and I have no way of contacting him. I need to post a bond so I can get bailed out." Daniel's voice sounded strained, almost hoarse.

"I dunno, Daniel. How much is the bond?"

"It's five thousand and the bondsman needs five hundred."

"I don't have that kind of money," Dieter said. "You know I have a family, kids. That takes every penny. I'm sorry, but I can't help you with your problem." After he spoke, he realized he'd emphasized the word "your." He waited for Daniel to speak.

"If, if you know anybody that can help, please ask them. I've got to get out of this hell-hole." Daniel's voice cracked. "Please." His voice sounded even more strained. "You have no idea what it's like."

"Let me think about it, okay?"

"Look," Daniel said, "they're accusing me of making drugs. You know I had nothing to do with chemicals or lab equipment. I know my files would show that."

"There was quite a fuss made about your files, something about the boiler..."

"Number three was dangerous." Daniel's voice rose, strong. "I sent a memo with proof its superheater's wall was corroded below a safe thickness. I even prepared an AFE to get it rebuilt."

"I heard that Wolfe said the files are highly incriminating against you and you never said anything about an unsafe boiler in the reports you wrote. They have the records of the chemicals you requested, the ones used for making drugs."

"What chemicals? I never used any chemicals the whole time I was at STR."

"Supposedly, they found stockroom receipts for chemicals that were used for making drugs. Those receipts were in your files." Dieter felt uncomfortable in giving this information to him.

"Were these chemicals phenyl acetone and methyl amine?"

"Er, yes. So, you do know these chemicals?" Dieter suspected his knowledge came from using them. It pointed toward his guilt.

"I reported a drug lab in the boiler house. That's where I saw those chemicals. I called Akron Police and reported the drug lab to them. They should have a record of that. But make drugs? Never."

"Oh, I see." Dieter paused. "Are you sure?"

"Call them, you'll find out."

Dieter remembered the comment Daniel made about the boiler. "What did you mean that number three was dangerous?"

"Well, I prepared report on number three, which pointed out the unsafe condition of the boiler. I recommended its superheater be replaced. I provided Hodges with an analysis and trace that showed its walls were below minimum safe thickness. I bet they're still there."

"What's in these files?" Dieter knew Hodges was interested in everything that Daniel had done.

"It was a complete report on the condition of the boilers. It had measurements, calculations and analyses. It was a complete report and I sent it to Hodges in late January."

Dieter took a deep breath. "I haven't heard anything about that report or the files that came with it."

"Someone must have done something to the files. There's another set of the original copies of the reports on the condition of the boilers I gave Hodges. I specifically warned him about the unsafe condition of the superheater of number three boiler, along with the original trace of the ultrasonic scan. That was the real reason he fired me."

"Where're these reports?" Dieter felt his heart begin to pound. This was something central to the current crisis over the boilers. "Tell me."

"No. I put them in a secure place. You bail me out and I'll get them, but not before. Uh-oh, gotta go. Someone else's turn on the phone."

Dieter put the phone down. He'd suspected something like this would happen. He didn't believe Daniel was involved with drugs. *But, he'd gone to San Francisco, there might be a connection. After all, everyone knew Haight-Ashbury was the center of the drug trade, right?*

This thing about the superheater of number three boiler was important. He knew the legal department had been through every file connected with work done on number three. He wrestled with his loyalties for a moment before realizing if it ever came out he knew about the files and hadn't passed the information along, he would lose his job. He reached for the phone. *What do I owe Daniel anyway?*

"Mr. Hodges? This is Dieter in personnel. I just got a call from Daniel Robles, who is being held in the Akron City Jail. Yes, I believe the charges brought against him have something to do with drugs. Yes, he's trying to get bailed out. He also said there were another set of files hidden within STR. Something about safety and the superheater of number three boiler. No, he didn't tell me where they were. Yes, he said he put them in a secure place. Thank you, sir." He gently placed the phone in its receiver. *Now no one can accuse me of not being loyal to the company.*

188

Grueden scratched his head. Forensics had been through Robles's van, yet they hadn't found any trace of methamphetamine, not even any marijuana. So they'd gone over it a second time, even more thoroughly. This time they found traces of horsehair, grasses from both the Mid-west and the West coast, even perfumed talcum powder. But no drugs, not even tobacco. The presence of these other components negated the possibility the van had been swept by a professional. It had begun to look to him like Robles didn't use drugs, at least not in his van. They had done a similar check on his clothing and had come up negative there, also.

Grueden picked up the report from the San Francisco police. It gave the analysis of the medicine vial of speed found in Robles's apartment. It was identical to the speed found in the illegal meth laboratory at STR. *And there wasn't a trace*, he thought, *found in the suspect's clothing, either. This doesn't make sense. It's the same batch of speed. He worked there, but there's nothing on him.* He picked up the file and started going over his notes--once again. This didn't make sense.

Daniel awoke, somewhat rested. Slam had disappeared into the justice system. His current cellmate, Paul, had been busted for smoking a joint and wasn't hostile. It was the first time in three days he slept without fear.

Hours crept by until it was his turn to use the phone. There was only one person left he might call. He knew it would be a long shot. He'd thought about calling professor Terzillo, but he remembered what he'd said about his own son learning from hard knocks. He had almost given up hope. He dialed the number and waited as phone rang and rang.

"Chanson Winery," a familiar voice said.

Chapter 39

May 26, 1970.

Nancy entered a tall, blocky structure covered with dark green vines. It was Chanson's main winery building. Her hair was still damp from showering after her regular morning run and she had the warm glow exercise always brought on. As she climbed the stairs to her office above the winemaking operation, she heard the phone ringing. She hurried to her desk, leaned across and picked it up. It was the WATs line. "Chanson Winery." She maneuvered herself around the desk toward her chair.

"Nancy, it's Daniel--"

"Daniel, so nice of you to call. I was thinking of you. How're things going?"

"Not well, in fact, I'm in a real jam. I'm in jail, in Akron, Ohio." His voice sounded strained.

"What?" Nancy sat down heavily and leaned into her arms, cradling the phone closely as if it would get her closer to Daniel. "Tell me what happened."

"I've only got five minutes on the phone," he said. "I've got drug charges against me. I need to post bond to get bailed out of jail. My brother is away, and there's no one else who can help me."

Nancy heard him take a deep breath.

"Can you help me? Please."

"How can I help?"

"Could, could you post bond for me? Please."

"Of course, how much is it?" Nancy didn't hesitate. She knew, just knew Daniel wasn't into drugs. More importantly, she was sure he was a good man. As Daniel told her the details, she scribbled them down. She realized she would have to use Chanson Winery's law firm to make things happen quickly. "Sit tight," she said. "I'll make some phone calls. Daniel, don't worry, I'll get you out one way or another."

She heard him sigh.

When Daniel spoke, his voice cracked and it sounded like he was swallowing hard. "Thank you, Nancy. You have no idea how much this means to me." She heard a loud voice in the background. "I've gotta go, 'bye and thank you."

It took her only a few seconds to look up the number and dial of the winery's legal counsel in San Francisco. "Yes, get me Sidney Jefferson, please. This is Nancy Benet, Chanson Winery..."

"How can I help you?" came the smooth, melodious voice of Sidney, who had originally been hired as a 'token' of racial integration. He proved to be hardworking and productive. As result he had risen to become one of the firm's most effective litigators.

Nancy found him to be efficient and quite cost effective. "Sidney, Nancy Benet of Chanson Winery. There's a friend of mine, Daniel Robles, who is in jail in Akron, Ohio. He needs to post a bond to get bailed out. How do we do make this happen today?"

"With one of our correspondent law firms," Sidney said.

"Then let's do it, right away, please. I'll hold."

"Can you hold for a moment, please?"

"Of course."

The phone went silent.

Nancy tapped a pencil against the desk. Outside, birds sang. It would be another sunny, cloud-free day, yet her heart felt as though a dark, cold cloud hung over it. The phone remained silent. There was a long list of calls she had to make, she reminded herself, to generate sales for the winery, made more important now, since her father had bought additional grapes to meet growing demand. *Father drives himself too hard*, she thought, *and he's beginning to show signs of his age. We need someone to relieve his workload.*

"Miss Benet?" Sidney's voice, now crisp and

businesslike, broke her reverie. "I have Hamilton Pogue on the line. He's with the firm, Jones Knight that handles our business in Cleveland and northern Ohio. Please tell him what you need."

Nancy quickly recounted what she'd learned from Daniel and the need to bail him out of jail quickly.

"Mr. Jefferson has told me that you're a very good client of his firm and that's good enough for me. I'll call the bail bondsman we use in Akron and send him over to the jail. Should have this man out within an hour or so."

Nancy felt the dark cloud hanging over her begin to dissipate. "Very good," she said. "Please instruct the bail bondsman to ask Daniel Robles call me as soon as he can."

"Consider it done."

"Thank you." Nancy briefly wondered what this would cost, then she realized that she didn't care.

#

As the plane lifted off from San Francisco into the night sky, Nancy wondered if she was embarking on a fool's errand. She remembered her father hadn't objected. *I think it's because he knows how I feel about Daniel.* He'd even wished her good luck and sent his regards.

How do I really feel about Daniel? She knew he was the first man in many years, who while attracted to her, had remained faithful to his girlfriend, even when she let her feelings be known. When he'd called after getting out of jail, she'd learned some of the details about the charges against him. She'd learned his girlfriend hadn't gone back east with him and had also refused to help him. That secretly pleased her. *Am I in love with him? I just might be. This is crazy...*

"Ma'am, would you like a pillow and a blanket?" a stewardess asked, a bright smile on a face framed by bleach blonde hair stiff with hair spray.

"Yes, please." Nancy accepted them, for she knew she should try to sleep on the 'red-eye' to Cleveland. She couldn't believe Daniel made drugs. Sure, he was technically competent, but everything she knew about him told her he wasn't involved with that kind of activity. It just didn't seem possible.

#

Nancy woke to the smell of coffee. She could see the pink color of the sky peeking through the small window next to her seat. The pilot announced they were only one hour out of Cleveland. She yawned and warmed to the thought of Daniel meeting her at the airport. Frowning stewardesses rushed the snack service in preparation for landing.

As the plane jerked to a halt at the gate, she peered out the window, eager to catch a glimpse of Daniel. A row of faces that were dimly visible in the windows of the terminal were unrecognizable in the reflected light of the newly risen sun. It seemed to take forever before the passengers began to move. She got off the plane and entered the bare concrete corridor leading into the terminal. Her heart began to race, wanting him to be there as she walked into the concourse. A wall of strange faces stared at her.

"Nancy," a familiar voice called.

She saw him amidst the crowd. His face was bruised and his nose swollen, which made him look almost like a prizefighter. He also seemed thinner, almost gaunt with a sallow pallor. For a moment, she worried that this might be the result of drugs, then she remembered he'd been in jail.

He clasped his arms around her, his face in her hair. "Nancy, it's so wonderful to see you. I can't ever thank you enough for everything, for getting me out. I'm so glad you're here." He leaned back to gaze at her, a smile on his face.

She leaned forward and without thinking, kissed him. She felt a shiver run through him and his arms tightened around her. His lips sent an electric charge through her. It wasn't a light buss of friendship, but a kiss of passion.

He broke their embrace, cocked his head slightly and looked at her. "I've wanted to kiss you ever since I first saw you."

Nancy felt a surge of emotion and even arousal. She forced herself to focus on the reason for her trip. "Me, too."

193

She laughed. "First, we've got some problems that need attention. What did Ham Pogue have to say?"

"He thinks their drug case against me is weak. However, he cautioned me there's another serious charge pending, one of criminal negligence or even manslaughter, connected with a boiler explosion that killed four men. It seems STR is claiming that I made recommendations that caused the explosion."

Nancy felt a frown begin. Another problem? "Did you?"

Daniel shook his head. "That's just not true."

"You're sure?"

Daniel halted and took each of Nancy's hands in his. He looked her straight in the eye. "I warned the production manager of the condition of the boiler's superheater. I let him know it needed repair, but he didn't want to hear about it. He told me to destroy the memos, and I suspect that he did. However, there are copies, hidden away."

"D'you know how to get them?"

Daniel smiled. "Sure. I talked with Mr. Pogue about it for an hour. I think you should get his opinion on it. He said he'd recommend an attorney in Akron if it goes to trial."

Nancy felt reassured by his words. "Yes, I need to talk to him about the bond and other items too." She glanced around. "How do we get out of here?"

Daniel pointed. She looked up at him and smiled, oblivious to the heavy flow of travelers who were hurrying to catch morning flights. As they walked along the concourse, she slipped her hand into his. It seemed a perfectly normal thing to do.

Chapter 40

May 26, 1970.

"O'Brien, I have another job for you. It's Robles again." Hodges leaned over his desk, cupped his hand over the phone, and spoke softly. "I think he's absconded with some STR files, which we'd like to recover for, er, confidentiality reasons."

Hodges' head pounded and sweat ran down his back. Dieter's account of what Robles said disturbed him. If Robles had squirreled away files that proved he'd warned STR management about the condition of the boilers, it would be a problem. No, it would be more than a problem—it would be a disaster.

Hodges realized if those files did exist, they might make it look as though he'd done something wrong, even when his intentions were only for the benefit of the company. *That damn snot-nosed spic hadn't warned me properly about the dangers of using rubber scrap in boiler number three.* Then he remembered the report about an ultrasonic test on number three; that was an even bigger problem. Fortunately, he'd destroyed that report a long time ago. *But where is the original scan? That report can't emerge,* he thought, *absolutely not.* The pounding headache and trickle of sweat increased.

"Yeah, what d'you need?" O'Brien picked at his lower lip as he leaned against the closed door of Hodges office. "Right now, he's in the slammer facing drug charges. The San Francisco police sent evidence to the Akron Police. Now they believe he's the one who set up the illegal drug lab over in the boiler house. That oughta hold him for a while."

"Yes, yes, I know that," Hodges said. "The State investigators also believe he might be criminally negligent in the work he did on the boilers."

"Really?" O'Brien's tone of voice brightened. "He

sure was up to all kinds of mischief, wasn't he?"

"I just learned that Robles might have a set of files that could be damaging to the firm," Hodges said. "However, we're not sure where he hid them. I need you to track them down."

"They're not in his office?"

"No. We've been through it. Twice. They're not there."

"How about his set-up in the boiler house?"

"Not there either."

O'Brien took a deep breath. "The police went through his van pretty thoroughly. I'll check with them to see if they found any STR files. If they're not there, then he probably left them with his brother, y'know, the one who lives in Kent."

Hodges nodded. "Look, O'Brien, those files are important. Do whatever you have to do to get them, understand?"

"Anything goes?"

"Yes, anything."

"I'm going to have expenses on this job." O'Brien's voice became quieter. "I'll need an advance. In cash"

"How much?"

"Let's start with five hundred, okay?"

Hodges felt a lump in his throat. He knew he couldn't justify a miscellaneous cash advance of that amount from STR. He'd already cleaned out the production department's travel account for O'Brien to make the trip to San Francisco, and with the recent budget tightening, there was nothing left. It would have to come out of his pocket. "I'll have it for you tomorrow."

#

O'Brien felt like punching a hole in the wall. He'd just learned from the Akron Police there was no trace of drugs in Robles's van and there weren't any files, either. That wasn't the worse part. Lightfoot Bonding had bailed out Robles at the request of Ham Pogue of Jones Knight Law firm in Cleveland. When he'd called them, he hadn't got the time of day from the asshole lawyer. Now he had no idea where the spic bastard had gone. That meant he'd have to be damn careful when he busted into the home of Robles's brother, the snotty professor who'd hung up on him.

Well, he thought, *first find out when he's home. A few phone calls and some surveillance. Rookie shit, but I've gotta do it. For a lousy five hundred bucks. I'm gonna put the screws to Hodges for more money. This is too much like real work.*

#

O'Brien sweated through a warm day in a van parked behind the Twin Lakes tavern. He watched the house belonging to Robles's through binoculars but saw no activity. There had been no answer to his phone calls. He knew that was no assurance someone wasn't home, especially like that weirdo professor.

When night fell, he pulled on his gloves and started out. He checked to make sure he had a blackjack in his back pocket. He worked his way through a series of back yards to get to the house. It was silent and dark. He took a deep breath and went to work on the lock on the back door. After three minutes that seemed like several hours, he eased the door open, stopped and listened.

Except for the hum of a refrigerator, it was quiet.

O'Brien slowly and quietly toured the house to be sure no one was there, sleeping or otherwise. The house was empty. He also found two rooms with filing cabinets: one in the basement and one next to the front hallway.

It took over an hour to go through the files in the basement storage room. He found nothing that seemed even remotely connected with STR. Most of the stuff was in a foreign language. He carefully replaced everything to its previous position. It was now eleven o'clock.

In the study, he drew the curtains and went to work. The files contained material related to Kent State University, plus Hector Robles's personal records. After forty minutes, he realized there weren't any STR files. As he tidied up, he thought about where else they could be. *Guest room?*

Upstairs, he went through drawers of clothing, the closets, and even went up into the attic. Nothing. *Where the hell had that little shit hid them?* By now, O'Brien had begun to hate Daniel Robles, for not only had he destroyed his profitable business, because he should've found those files by now. It was one-thirty in the morning. He hoped the police hadn't noticed his van parked in the parking lot of the Twin Lakes' tavern. Time to go before it closed. He had the urge to burn the place down, but knew that would just draw attention to Robles, and that wasn't going to make the files appear.

Chapter 41

May 26, 1970.

On the drive from Cleveland to Akron down Route
Eight, Daniel told Nancy what happened since he'd left
California. The traffic on the divided highway was light and
they made good time heading south. "I need those files from
STR," he said. "There's the original ultrasonic test scan on
the walls of the superheater of number three boiler in a
memo to Hodges. I put the scan in a safe place, along with
the memo." The divided highway merged into a four-lane
road.

"How important is it?"

"It showed the wall of the superheater was thinner
than the recommended minimum and should've been taken
out of service. Apparently, Hodges ignored or concealed that
fact. Unfortunately, the superheater exploded, killing four
workers. From what the police said, STR is blaming me for
negligence in the accident. They say I recommended an
unsafe procedure. And as engineer-in-charge, they're saying
the accident is my responsibility."

"Will these files prove you warned STR?"

"Yes." Daniel glanced at the sign advising they were
entering Cuyahoga Falls.

"Why not tell the police where they are?"

Daniel took a deep breath. "The head of STR's
security is a former cop. I'm afraid to take the chance the
police would turn the files over to him. My experience with
the police so far hasn't been good."

"Where are the files?"

"Inside STR." Daniel slowed the van as they crossed
Graham Road. They passed the Cathedral of Tomorrow with
its tall, grey tower that he'd often thought was phallic in
form. He also thought it was a symbol of what had been done
to the congregation who had tithed heavily to pay for its

construction. Traffic became heavy once they got into business district of Cuyahoga Falls.

"D'you think he found the originals?" Nancy said. "Those files might have been destroyed." She braced her hands against the dashboard as Daniel braked hard to avoid a car that turned on to State Road without stopping.

"Idiot," Daniel said. "I don't think so. I hid them inside a set of operating manuals that haven't been touched in years." He glanced at Nancy and smiled. "I stuffed them inside a pocket that had lots of other notes. Someone will have to know exactly where they are to find them and know what they are to recognize them."

"How're you going to get them?" Nancy felt a rising sense of excitement. She knew he couldn't just knock on STR's door and ask for them.

Daniel took a deep breath. "I don't know, but I have to get them." He flicked on the turn signal and slowed. He turned into the almost empty parking lot of the Moonlite Motel. It had a large sign promising 'giant king-sized beds' for only fifteen ninety-nine a night. To the left of the motel was a strip of stores, several with 'for rent' signs in their windows. On the right was a Mo-Jo's restaurant whose neon sign intermittently flashed 'Food'. It had seen better days.

Nancy's eyebrows rose as the van bumped across the pothole-populated lot to a parking space adjacent to the motel office. She had agreed earlier that going back to his brother's home might not be a good idea under the circumstances.

The Moonlite Motel looked like an early version of a Holiday Inn with an open central court. Its three stories had rust-stained white railings lining the balconies that provided access to the rooms. The front office had a tiny glassed-in cubicle with a dusty plastic palm in the corner and a battered blond wood counter. The motel showed years of deferred maintenance.

As they entered the office, a balding middle-aged man lifted his gaze from a TV. His expression didn't change.

Both the man and the motel looked shabby.

"Two rooms for tonight," Nancy said. "Adjoining, please."

"Two rooms?" The desk clerk eyebrows rose slightly as though it were an aberration for a couple to want separate rooms. He reached for an additional registration form.

"Yes, please."

The clerk said nothing as he went through the registration procedure. His expression didn't change when she asked if she could pay cash, in advance. The clerk's reaction to a couple checking-in during the middle of the day was almost boredom. "That'll be thirty-two dollars and sixteen cents, tax included. You're in rooms one-ten and one-eleven. Check out is eleven a.m." He handed her two keys with large plastic fobs. "Park in the rear." He sat down and resumed watching the TV.

#

Nancy picked at her food. *Mo-Jo's cuisine left a lot to be desired*, she thought; *less grease and fresh vegetables would be an improvement*. Besides, she found it difficult to think about food. She had the feeling her life was about to change. It was an unsettling thought.

"Are you finished?" Daniel's plate was clean.

"Yes." Nancy felt a rising sense of excitement, for they'd avoided talking about their plans for the evening. She wondered what would happen with Daniel close, in bed... *Stop it*, she thought, *you're imagining things*. She reached for the check.

As she walked back the motel, she asked, "Your room or mine?" She felt her cheeks warm as she thought about what those words implied. She glanced at Daniel, but his expression remained neutral as she added, "So we can make plans."

"Doesn't matter." A trace of a frown appeared. "My room's fine." He opened the door and stood back for her to enter.

Nancy felt a rush of excitement. It had been a long

time since she'd entered a hotel or motel room with a man, especially one to whom she felt a strong attraction. *Get yourself under control*, she thought, *don't make a fool of yourself.*

She excused herself to use the bathroom and when she returned, Daniel was sitting on the king-sized bed that was a featured attraction of the Moonlight Motel. The comforter on the bed had a ubiquitous early American pattern often used by the hospitality industry. Its color and design camouflaged stains and dirt quite well.

"There's only one way to get the files," Nancy said. "We have to go inside STR and get them."

Daniel's eyebrows rose. "You mean I should break in and take them? Just like that?"

"No, we should break in and retrieve evidence that proves you're innocent of negligence that killed four men." Nancy knew she was taking a bold step with her words.

"I don't know about that." Daniel pursed his lips and frowned.

Nancy sat on the bed next to Daniel. She took his hand and pulled it to her lips. "Look, Daniel, I came all the way from California to help and help I will. Even if it means this."

He stared at her for a moment and then shrugged. "Let me think about it--"

"No," Nancy said. "Let's put a plan together and do it. Get your map and show me the factory's location."

Daniel got his bag and rummaged for a moment before pulling out a dog-eared map for the city of Akron, which he spread out on top of the bed. "STR covers about ten city blocks." He pointed at the map. "However, we're only interested in this building, off Market Street, here, on Schirmerling Avenue." It was a tiny rectangle adjacent to a larger block on the map. "There's a gap in the fence near this corner, which should be a good way to go in unseen." He pointed. "This is the boiler house. We'd better do a drive-by to confirm they haven't put a guard at the entrance here."

"Are there people in the boiler house?" Nancy wanted to be sure they considered every potential problem.

Daniel looked up with a trace of a smile on his face. "Yes, there are three operators and a foreman each shift. However, around shift change, the shift going off-duty usually showers before heading home." He wrinkled his nose. "A union-negotiated working-condition benefit," he said. "They're only supposed to take ten minutes, but most usually knock off work twenty minutes before shift change. I've never seen anyone in the boiler house during that time. The next shift arrives about five minutes after the hour."

"How long would we have?"

"Fifteen minutes for sure, starting at eleven-forty-five."

"A little inside knowledge?" Nancy nodded. *Yes*, she thought, *Things like this could make a difference as to the success of our mission.*

"Yes. I've worked every shift in that building. I know their routine." He rubbed his chin and frowned. "We may want to observe for one evening," he said. "They may have changed the schedule after the explosion. It would be better to be sure, rather than get caught inside."

"We sure don't want to get caught."

"You're not going in with me," Daniel said quickly. "This is my problem, and I've got to solve it--"

"I'm going with you," Nancy said. "We're in this together. I said I'm going with you, and I am." She felt herself frowning. *Why did I say that*? She thought. *Why do I want to be with him all of the time?*

Daniel took a deep breath. "What we're doing is illegal in itself. If we get caught and I have no intention of getting caught, but should it happen, STR will not be amused, neither will the police--"

"I understand. Now, details. What kind of clothing d'you plan to wear?" Nancy figured successful burglars wore dark clothing.

"What I've got on," Daniel began as he looked down

at his blue oxford cloth shirt and tan chinos. Both were worse for wear from time spent in the prison and they needed laundering.

"No," Nancy said firmly. "Let's do some shopping. I think you'd look good in black." She reached out and grasped his hand. "Let's go."

Chapter 42

At the nearby shopping center, which had a Sears, Roebuck store, Nancy found the clothing she deemed necessary. She had also insisted he get clothes to replace those he'd worn in prison, which, in her opinion, were not worth saving. Shopping always gave her a lift and added to her sense of excitement.

Back at the motel, Nancy handed him the package of clothing. "Let me see how you look dressed for the job. I'll be back in a minute to show you what I'm going to wear."

She went through the door to the adjoining room. She peeled off her clothing, removing her bra and underwear. *Why did I do that?* She realized in an instant what she was about to do. She pulled the black sweater over her head and slipped into the slacks. She felt her nipples tingle and harden. She opened the door.

Daniel had just put on his navy-blue cotton slacks and straightened up. He was bare-chested. His face reddened and he froze. He licked his lips.

Nancy moved quickly to him and raised her hand to his chest. "Daniel..." She found her hand moving over his chest, rising to his neck and behind his head. She pulled him to her, closed her eyes and kissed him. She felt his arms surround her, pulling her close to him. The kiss seemed to go on forever. Finally, she moved her head, putting her lips next to his ear. "I've wanted to do this for a long time."

"Nancy, I don't know how I've kept my hands off you--"

"Then don't try," Nancy said. She ran her hands over his back. She felt his hands slip under her sweater and rise up the full length of her back. His hands found their way to the front. At that instant, she wanted him to touch her, all over. She stepped back and pulled off the sweater in one quick movement, then slid out of her slacks.

#

Daniel woke from a most amazing dream in which he'd made love to Nancy. The thought of it aroused him, and restlessly, he began to roll over.

"Uh?" Nancy said. Her hands reached for him and found him.

It wasn't a dream, he realized, as his lips found hers. That afternoon they'd made love twice. The first time had been explosive and fast. The second time, intense and satisfying, they lingered long over arousal before joining in an exhausting test of endurance. No wonder he thought it was a dream. Afterward, they'd talked and talked, as if a verbal dam had released. Daniel had the revelation he could have a partner with whom talking was another pleasure. Eventually, they'd dozed off.

"Are you up for more?" Nancy said with a chuckle as her hand found him.

He felt an instant response.

"Hmm, maybe," she said. She reached under the covers. "It seems like it." She pushed him over onto his back. "Let me see."

Daniel closed his eyes as he felt her climb on top of him. Her lips found his and her hard, erect nipples touched his chest. He bent forward and took the nipple of her right breast into his mouth and began to suck and nibble.

Nancy took a sharp breath.

Daniel moved to give her left breast equal treatment. He felt her hand guide him as she moved her hips into position over his. Her nipple popped out as she moved more upright. Her eyes were closed as he felt her guide him into her. She began to move, slowly. Her mouth opened as she began to breathe deeply.

She kept adjusting her position until he was completely lost within her. He closed his eyes and concentrated on the sensation as she moved faster and faster. Pleasure swept over him as she tightened convulsively around him and gasped loudly. He felt the pin-prick of concentrated pleasure explode into an all-consuming wave.

They lay still and silent for several minutes.

"This is nice, but not really comfortable," Nancy said. She rolled off Daniel and adjusted her position alongside him. She pulled the covers up.

Daniel felt her slide onto his shoulder. He covered her hand and smiled. He felt wonderful.

Passion spent, they slept.

Chapter 43

May 27, 1970.

Daniel woke to the sound of a shower. The alarm clock by the side of the bed showed nine-thirty. He saw light creeping in around the edges of the drawn curtain. For a moment, he thought he had slept through the night. He sat up quickly and realized the light came from the parking lot outside.

Nancy stepped from the bathroom, rubbing her hair with a towel. Beads of water glistened on her bare skin.

Every muscle rippled as she moved, even in her long, slender legs. *She must work out regularly*, he thought. Her small breasts had prominent dark nipples and her stomach was completely flat. He felt an immediate rush of arousal. "Come here," he said.

"You're awake? Good." Nancy bent over and kissed him.

As his hands reached for her, she said, "No, not now. We have work to do. Remember?" She backed away and picked up her clothing from where she'd dropped them alongside the bed.

Daniel found it hard to take his eyes off her. He felt enormously lucky to be with her, for not only had she come to his rescue, but their relationship was even better than his wildest fantasies. She was right, he had to get those files if he wanted to clear his name of criminal negligence.

"Okay," he said. "I better take a cold shower."

Nancy smiled, the corners of her mouth turning down. "That will have to do, but for now, first things first."

After a quick shower, Daniel put on a pair of dark blue work pants and a navy blue sweatshirt over a black polo shirt. He also put a pair of black leather driving gloves in his back pocket.

Nancy wore slacks and a black wool sweater. She

pulled her long hair into a ponytail, which she tucked under a billed cap.

"Ready?" he said.

Nancy nodded and took a deep breath. "Let's go."

#

They drove down High Street in the center of Akron, keeping pace with the light traffic found late at night during the middle of the week. Daniel turned east on East Market Street until they reached Schirmerling Avenue. "This is it." He turned south. "A few more blocks and we'll be there."

"What next?" Nancy had a frown as she glanced back and forth at the road ahead.

He took a quick look at her. "Twice around the block, so to speak. I want to make sure things look the same as before." He slowed the van as they drew near the three-story brick factory buildings that made up the Schirmerling Tire and Rubber Company.

Light rain had begun to fall and light from the overhead mercury vapor lamps glistened off the empty street. Daniel could smell the familiar tang of chemicals used for curing rubber. Long streamers of steam swirled from vent pipes on the factory where tires were made.

Rows of cars filled the parking lot across the street from the plant. He knew there was no parking on the street, but he also knew the parking lot operators were lazy and only periodically checked upon their patrons, most of whom paid by the month. He'd take a chance and park in the lot opposite the boiler house entrance.

On the first pass, he confirmed the guard shack at the street entrance to the boiler house was unlit and empty as usual. STR had stopped staffing the guard shack as a cost-cutting measure at the beginning of the year. The gate was wide open, but he had no intention of going in that way. Near the corner of the boiler house was the loose section of chain link fence the operators had used to sneak out mid-shift when the guard shack was manned. He'd intended to put a work order in to get it repaired, but had been fired before doing so. He was glad it had been low on his list of priorities, for what served the operators well on getting out, would work just as well for him going in. The fence still was loose.

"I don't see any changes," Daniel said. "What time is it?"

Nancy leaned forward and a light flared briefly. "It's eleven-thirty-two."

"Okay. The workers will head to the showers about twenty to twelve. I'm going to kill ten minutes, then we do it. Let me know when five minutes have passed, so I can start heading back on in." He glanced in the rearview mirror and turned off Schirmerling Avenue.

Nancy nodded. "All right."

He drove west into a residential area. He knew the streets were laid out in a block pattern in this part of town.

An eternity later, she said, "Five minutes."

Daniel retraced his course on parallel streets maintaining the same steady pace. They arrived in what felt like a much shorter time on Schirmerling Avenue. He carefully turned into the parking lot and slowly cruised toward the back section. As expected, there were a few vacant slots. Someone was always off, either sick or for some other reason and everyone wanted to park at the front. He still had a sticker on the back of his rearview mirror from a parking lot. Sure, it was out of date, but they all looked the same at a distance, especially so at night.

"Walk like you belong here," Daniel said. "Not fast, not slow." He put on a baseball cap. He wished that he'd brought a jacket. This won't take long. I can put up with this. The temperature had dropped, even though the rain had eased to a drizzle.

"This way." Daniel pointed north along Schirmerling Avenue. They walked parallel to the boiler house until they reached its end where they stopped. He glanced in both directions. The street was empty. No cars, no one on foot. He grabbed a section of chain link fence and pulled it up. "In here." He opened wide enough for them to slip through.

He led the way around to the back of the boiler house to an emergency exit he knew the operators used. He remembered the operators had disabled the alarm system so their exit wouldn't be noticed. At the door, he listened carefully.

All he could hear was busy sounds of the factory in the distance. No voices, no footsteps.

He grasped the door handle and pulled. The door opened smoothly. He heard something click. He strained to remember if he'd heard that before. He couldn't recall. He paused and glanced down the brightly lit corridor inside. It was empty, just as he expected. It was now or never. "Okay, we're in. Let's go."

Chapter 44

May 27, 1970.

Blodgett yawned. It was another hour and fifteen minutes until his shift ended at one a.m. Yeah, he knew the reason plant security had different hours from the workers was to provide an overlap at shift change. He just wondered why it couldn't be one hour before the workers' shift ended, rather than one hour later. Then he'd be able to spend more time with his family.

He yawned again. He'd finished the crossword puzzle and knew better than to have another cup of coffee. He wanted to get up early and have breakfast with his kids. Things had finally settled down in the STR plant security headquarters after the boiler explosion. *Maybe I can just rest my eyes for a moment, he thought. Nothing much happening tonight.*

A flicker of something caught his attention. He glanced over the monitoring board. A flashing red light showed an emergency exit had been opened. *Aw, it's just the one at the back of the boiler house*, he thought. The operators used it from time to time to sneak out. *They probably forgot we repaired the alarm.* He reached for the reset button and then paused. *Wait a minute,* he thought. *It was too close to shift change. They only used it if they were going over to Barneys for a beer, which was usually mid-shift.* He remembered Captain O'Brien's instructions—at any sign of a break in, he was to be called immediately.

Blodgett smiled. It would be fun rousting O'Brien at midnight with a problem. He reached for the phone.

#

"Yeah? O'Brien." The phone had awakened him. He'd fallen asleep in the armchair in front of the TV. "A break in? Where? The boiler house? Okay, I'm on my way."

He splashed cold water on his face, then grabbed a

jacket from the hook by the door and headed for his car. He loosened the gun in his shoulder holster. He wanted to be ready. It was less than five minutes from his apartment in Akron to STR, and with light traffic, it could take even less time.

As he drove to the plant through the deserted streets, O'Brien thought about his search for the missing files. He had come to realize Robles might have hidden them somewhere within STR. The boiler house made perfect sense. He had a hunch this break-in just might be Robles. He touched his gun again. He had an urge to use it.

Before I do anything, he thought. *I'll force Robles to tell me where he hid those stupid files. Then I'll take care of the little prick. If it is him and he's in the boiler house, I'll do the same thing to him that I did with Rogan. That'll teach the spic bastard to fuck with me and my meth lab.*

#

"What've you got, Blodgett?" O'Brien eyed the corpulent guard and thought. *He needs to eat less and work out more.*

"The rear emergency exit of the boiler house, exiting on--"

"Yeah, yeah, I know the one you're talking about. Did you see anyone?"

Blodgett frowned and pursed his lips. "Well, I couldn't leave my station--"

O'Brien began tapping a pencil against the desk. He could feel a frown forming. *Time to get rid of this jerk. Not only is he fat and out of condition, but he's also stupid.* "When did it happen?"

"It was at eleven forty-four P.M., which was--"

"Okay. Listen up," O'Brien said. "I want you to padlock all emergency exits of the boiler house on the outside, then get back here to cover the shift change. I'm going in after the perp. I'll chase him out of there." It had been nine minutes since the alarm had triggered.

"Er, padlocking them? Isn't that against the law?"

213

Blodgett frowned and stroked his chin.

"It's only to make sure I've chased the perp out of there." *For sure I'm gonna replace him,* he thought. *Not only is he dumb, he wants to play lawyer with me.* "You can remove them later."

Blodgett's frown deepened. "Shouldn't we call the police?"

O'Brien shook his head. "Naw, I don't think it's necessary. I've handled stuff like this before when I was on the Philly police force. Piece of cake." He wanted the guard to think he had no intention of apprehending the intruder. "Besides, if the cops are involved, then there'll be a bunch of paper work. Probably won't get out of here until late, maybe not even until tomorrow morning." He pretended to yawn. "I'd like to get back to bed tonight." He knew that Blodgett left exactly on time every night and had asked several times for the shift times to be changed so he could get home earlier.

Blodgett nodded. "Okay. I gotcha." He rose and went to a cabinet and retrieved a box of padlocks.

"Good," O'Brien said. "Get moving. I'll take the inside, you do the outside."

#

O'Brien decided he'd better move fast to make sure Robles didn't try to leave with the operators coming out of the boiler house at shift change. He had no intention of chasing him away. He wanted a permanent solution.

He waited at the side of the front steps to the boiler house, leaning against the dingy brickwork of its entrance. Four men headed out of the boiler house, which he figured must be the evening shift. They would head to the locker rooms to get showered and changed. That meant there wouldn't be anyone in the boiler house for at least ten minutes, which should be enough to do what he had to do.

A steam whistle sounded in the distance. It was midnight. Ignoring the workers streaming out of the factory, he kept his focus on those who came out of the boiler house locker room. Four men carrying lunch buckets clattered down its steps and headed for the gate on Schirmerling Avenue. Robles wasn't among them.

Good, O'Brien thought, touching the butt of his gun. *Now the fun begins.* He turned and walked slowly up the steps into the boiler house. Once inside the door, he took out his gun, a Smith & Wesson thirty-eight police special and held it loosely, his hand hanging down his side. *Okay, time to do it.*

#

Daniel closed the thick three-ring binder. On the grey metal desk before him lay three memos and a long strip of paper that he'd just removed from a pocket inside the binder. He looked up at Nancy. "They're all here. These are the originals." He slipped them inside a sturdy manila inter-office mail envelope and tied it shut.

"That's it?"

"This'll prove I warned STR's management--"

"Shouldn't we get out of here?" Nancy glanced over her shoulder. Every sound was strange, different than anything she had ever experienced. She could feel her heart pounding away. She wanted out of this building. It smelled awful and sounded like the entrance to hell. Sooty grime covered the peeling once-green walls and dingy yellow paint that marked the pathway over the chipped concrete floors.

Daniel rose. "Okay, let's go." He cracked open the door and peered around the jamb. "Oh, no," he said. "Someone's coming. We've got to run for it." He grabbed her hand and pulled her into the corridor, and they sprinted toward the end.

Behind them a man's voice yelled, "Stop!"

As they ducked through the door, a shot rang out.

Chapter 45

"In here, quick," Daniel said, breathing hard. He slammed the door shut just as the gun fired. The bullet struck the door with a loud clang. They sprinted down the corridor back the way they'd come in. "The emergency exit's just around the corner." At the door, he pushed on the handle several times, but nothing moved. "What the hell? They're supposed to open from the inside. Always."

Nancy saw a deep frown crease his forehead. The knot in her stomach tightened. "Something's wrong. Let's go, that way." He pointed to the right and began running.

Nancy lengthened her stride. Even though she ran regularly, she had to hustle to keep up with Daniel.

They reached main section of the boiler house with a ceiling three floors high. Large pipes descended from the wall to tanks and equipment with gauges. The hissing sounds of steam and the rumbling sounds of machinery were much louder. A wide steel stairway at one side of the room rose to the floor above.

"Up there." Daniel pointed and ran.

Nancy followed him up the stairs to a steel platform that ran the width of the room. They went through a large metal sliding door on rusty casters, which had a metal bar jammed into the steel grating to hold it open. They stepped into a room that reminded Nancy of a cavern. Dusty light bulbs on thin cords hung nakedly from the ceiling at widely separated intervals. Thick rectangular steel pillars rose from the floor. An overhead maze of thick pipes clung to the ceiling. Along the walls, pipes descended to rows of valves with gauges. Cobwebs festooned the ceiling and walls. The rumble of machinery and roar of the furnace filled the room, along with the hiss of steam in the pipes. It was hot.

"Where are we?" Nancy put her mouth to his ear and repeated the question. The hissing of steam almost drowned out all other sounds.

"We're in the manifold room, under the

superheaters."

"What does that mean?" Nancy had no idea what he was talking about.

"It's, never mind. There's an emergency exit at the back of this room," he yelled into her ear. "It lets out on to a walkway that goes to the main plant. We can get to the street that way. C'mon, let's go." He touched her shoulder and pointed. He walked slowly, picking his way through the room's clutter.

The floor was covered with dust and Nancy deduced the room was little used except for storage. The room contained boxes and strange looking equipment, some with wires hanging loose, others with disconnected pipes lay scattered everywhere. It was like a maze, a surrealistic jungle of dead technology.

"Damn." She tripped on something that she hadn't seen in the dim light. She fell and slammed into the hard floor. She coughed and spat out dust she'd inhaled.

Daniel bent over her. "Did you hurt yourself?"

"I think I'm okay." Nancy looked at her hands, which had taken the brunt of her fall. They were sore, but there was no broken skin. She took his hand and began to clamber to her feet. As she did, she saw movement out of the corner of her eye. "Look." She froze and pointed.

Silhouetted in the doorway was a man with a pistol in his hand, backlit by the bright lights of the main hall. He stood motionless while his head made an arc. He took a step into the room and stopped.

"Wait until he looks away," Daniel said. "Then follow me. We're going over there." He gestured to a dark section of the room that had a dimly glowing exit sign suspended in mid-air. "Ready? Let's go." He moved quickly behind a metal column and stopped.

Nancy joined him. "Now what?"

"The same thing again. Wait until he looks away." Daniel peered around the column. "Let's go."

They sprinted toward the sign. Daniel slammed into

the door's emergency opening bar. It clanged loudly but didn't move. "Ouch. This one's locked, too. What the hell's going on? These are supposed to be kept unlocked."

Nancy could see that his face seemed paler than before. "What're we going to do?"

"I don't know. There's no other way out."

She realized they were trapped. She looked back toward the entrance, but could no longer see the man. For a moment, she felt a surge of hope. Maybe he left, she thought. A flicker of movement caught her attention. It was the man, who'd stepped away from the entrance. He was coming toward them.

#

O'Brien caught his breath. *Who the hell is with Robles? Doesn't matter much, both will fit into the furnace.* He was sure they'd gone into the manifold room. The place was poorly lit, which made it a good place to hide. He moved away from the entrance when he saw his shadow before him, realizing he was backlit by the bright lights in the mezzanine of the main hall. As his eyes became accustomed to the dark, the emergency exit sign stood out.

Yeah, he thought, *that's where they'll head, if they're not already there. They'll expect it's open.* He looked slightly away from the sign, knowing that peripheral dark vision was better than a direct stare. Beneath the sign he saw something move. Since it was shift change, he knew it could only be Robles and his buddy. Still, he realized he had to finish this off quickly, for the third shift workers usually came on the job ten minutes or so after shift change. *I'm gonna kill the bastards.*

He raised his gun and fired.

For a moment, the flash of the gun destroyed his night vision. *Did I hit him?* he wondered. It seemed ages before his night vision returned. As the shapes in the room became clear again, the shapes beneath the sign were no longer there. *Next time, I'll blink as I shoot.*

O'Brien saw heavy metal beam supports, each

stretching from floor to ceiling, lined up in four rows. He began to move left, along the wall of the room to get a better view behind the beams so he could keep his gun hand to the outside, ready to fire. The furnace noise seemed even louder.

O'Brien moved carefully, watching. Behind him, pipes ran along the wall to an opening near the ceiling where they bent and went through the wall on their way to the tire factory. On the opposite wall, some forty feet away, were multiple valves and gauges, which had something to do with controlling steam distribution. He tripped but retained his balance. He hadn't seen several lengths of piping on the floor, apparently left over from a repair job.

He looked up and saw two figures move from behind a metal column toward the entrance. He raised his pistol and took careful aim at the lead figure. As he fired, he blinked.

He opened his eyes. They had disappeared.

Chapter 46

The gun boomed, loud, even over the noise of the furnace.

Daniel staggered and slumped against the steel column.

"Daniel?" Nancy touched his shoulder. She ran her hand down his back. "Daniel, are you all right?" Her hand felt wet. It was sticky and dark. It took a second to register that it was blood. For an instance, she thought that she hadn't noticed that she'd cut her hand earlier.

Daniel coughed and leaned his head against the column. His face was contorted with pain.

"Daniel," she said. "What happened?"

"I've been shot, in my back—my chest." He coughed again. A trickle of blood appeared at the corner of his mouth. "You've got to get out of here." He dropped to his knees and looked at her. "Crawl," he said. "He can't see us behind these boxes." Daniel pointed to where a line of boxes and equipment extending almost to the entrance. Moving forward on his hands and knees, he coughed again, splattering brilliant splotches of blood on the floor. Crawling, swaying from side to side as he moved, stopping with each advance of his hands, head slumped down. He leaned against a metal beam and dropped the manila envelope as he again struggled forward.

Nancy picked up the envelope that contained the files and stuffed it inside the front of her slacks. She began to crawl after him. "Wait," she said. But he kept moving.

Daniel's crawl became slower and slower. He stopped when he reached the last metal column, the one nearest to the entrance. They were less than twenty feet from the metal door that led to the mezzanine. He beckoned to Nancy. "Get out of here, now."

"I'm not leaving you and that's final."

"He'll shoot you, like he shot me."

"Daniel, let me help you get out of here."

"Go." Daniel's voice was weak.

"No, I'm staying with you, no matter what."

"Oh, God. You need a diversion." His voice was raspy and faint. "Open that valve." He pointed.

Nancy looked and saw a jumble of pipes, wheels and levers. "Which one?" She felt helpless, not knowing what he wanted her to do.

"Help me," Daniel said, "help me over there." Again he pointed. The valves were ten feet away, out in the open.

Nancy bit her lip and stood. She moved behind him, putting her arms beneath his and pulled.

Daniel groaned. "Oh, that hurt."

"I'm sorry." Nancy began to lower him to the floor.

"Don't stop. Keep moving. It's our only chance." Daniel coughed. Red froth bubbled from his lips. His face was ashen, making the blood and smudges of dust on his face stand out in stark contrast.

Nancy pulled him to the valves.

Daniel looked up. "That one." He pointed to a long, red-painted, horizontal lever. "Move me over there, out of the way; then push the lever until it's straight down. Stay the hell out of the steam jet. Do not stand in direct line of the valve."

As Nancy bent over to grasp Daniel, she heard the boom of another gunshot. Simultaneously, metal sparks flew with a loud clang from the pipe leading into the valve next to her head. "Damn you!" Nancy yelled.

"The valve," Daniel said with a gasp. "Valve, open the valve." His head lolled to one side and his pupils rolled out of sight as he slumped over.

"Daniel," Nancy screamed. "Daniel."

Another shot rang out, and a bullet ricocheted off a nearby metal support beam.

Nancy glanced back.

The man was walking toward them. He held the gun in both hands, out in front, pointing it at them. He stopped and began to aim. He was thirty feet away.

Nancy turned and grasped the lever and pushed. It began to move, and her hand slipped off it. She rolled back from the exertion. The gun boomed, louder this time.

Something hot stung her cheek.

She grabbed the lever, now marred with a star-shaped scar of fresh metal in its red handle. She gritted her teeth and pushed the lever. It moved and swung through a ninety-degree arc.

The lever actuated a ball valve, which rotated and opened the main steam line to the tap. Steam, superheated to six hundred degrees at two-hundred-and-fifty pounds pressure flowed from the four-inch diameter steam tap. Fully opened, the steam screamed out at a ferocious rate.

A high-pitched screech filled Nancy's universe. She felt a rush of air and a wave of heat.

Outside the manifold room, a bell began to clamor loudly.

Nancy glanced up, but saw nothing. She looked toward the man.

Ten feet away a huge white plume of steam appeared, to slice horizontally across the full width of the room to where the man had been. He had disappeared. A roiling mass of steam expanded throughout the room, which steadily got darker as steam filled it. The room was becoming hotter and hotter.

Nancy put her arms under Daniel and dragged him in the direction of the exit of the manifold room and the ringing bell. Visibility dropped to the point where she couldn't see more than a foot or two through the luminous fog. Water dripped steadily from condensing steam. The floor was slick from the lubricated dust. She bumped into the valves. "God damn it!" She stopped for a moment. *That has to be the wall,* she thought. *I've got to keep moving.*

Pulling Daniel became Nancy's sole focus. She dragged him a foot at a time. She found it hard to breath, for the steam vapor choked off her lungs. Cool air wafted against her, and she felt a thread of hope. She resumed dragging him in the direction of the cool draft. She began to swear again as her arms and legs grew evermore heavy from the effort. Soaked with sweat, her grip kept slipping. Out of breath, she could only move him a foot or so at a time. A puff of cold air cleared the steam for a second. She saw the doorway.

Nancy began praying and found the energy to move Daniel the last few feet, through the exit and over its threshold, out onto the grated metal platform of the mezzanine. Clouds of steam poured out of the room. Cold air flowed in along the floor.

Breathing heavily, Nancy laid Daniel down and collapsed over him. She caught her breath and knew that she didn't have the strength to take him any farther. She feared the man was just behind her. Steam continued to billow out of the exit, and the bell overhead continued its infernal clamor.

The door, she thought. *I have to close the door*. She grabbed the metal bar that held the door open and tugged. She couldn't move it. She felt panic rising and kicked the bar. It didn't move.

Nancy sat on the floor and braced her back against the doorjamb. She put both feet against the bar and pushed. It moved, and as it did, so did the door. She grabbed the bar and pulled it out of the door. The door began to move, slowly and ponderously. She crawled out of its way. The door rolled shut with a loud clang.

Nancy jammed the bar through a caster on the base of the door. She kneeled over Daniel and put her ear to his chest. She could hear his heart just barely beating. "Oh, Daniel, please hang on." She glanced up and saw a phone on the wall. She staggered to her feet and grabbed it and dialed zero. She could hear the phone ring and ring and ring. "C'mon, pick up, please."

There was no answer.

Chapter 47

"Hey, what're you doing here?" a loud voice called.

Nancy turned, startled. "I'm trying to get help." She held up the phone.

"You're not supposed to be here," said a portly middle-aged man wearing a blue coverall who was climbing up the stairs from the ground floor. A younger, red-haired man in similar attire followed. "We've got a bad steam leak somewhere. High pressure steam is dangerous." The older man continued to climb up the metal stairs. As his head rose above the level of the second floor, he stopped, and his eyes widened. "What's going on, here?" His eyes fixed upon Daniel. He resumed his climb.

"He's been shot." Nancy pointed to the phone. "I've been trying to get help, but no one answers the phone. Please, please call an ambulance. He's lost a lot of blood. He's unconscious. He needs medical help right away."

The portly man in the coverall inserted a key into a box on the wall, and the alarm bell stopped ringing. He pulled a walkie-talkie from his belt and twisted a button. "Plant security, come in." He put the radio to his ear.

The walkie-talkie squawked something that Nancy couldn't understand. The man spoke into the walkie-talkie. "Call the police and Akron Superior Hospital. A man has been shot at the boiler house. He's hurt bad. Hurry."

The walkie-talkie squawked again.

"Look, if you don't call, then I will. You don't have to clear everything with your boss." The portly man clicked off the walkie-talkie. "Asshole, he said he has to clear it with his boss first," he muttered and shook his head. "Lady, lemme at the phone, willya?"

Nancy stepped away from the wall. She watched the man dial nine, then wait a moment before dialing zero. "Yeah, this is an emergency. A man has been shot and is in critical condition. My name is Crowley, I'm at the Schirmerling Tire and Rubber Company, in the boiler house on Schirmerling Avenue... Okay, you know where it is. Police and ambulance, right away. Tell em to hurry; the guy's lost a lot of blood. Yeah, he's unconscious. No, he don't look good at all. Okay, thanks." He hung up the phone and opened his mouth to speak, then stopped.

"Why's that door closed?" The man pointed at the sliding door to the manifold room. Steam wisped around the edges of the door. The sound of escaping steam had subsided.

"I closed it," Nancy said. "The man with the gun is in there, the one that shot my friend."

"Shit," the man said. "That's where the leak is and there're superheated steam lines in there."

Another coverall-clad man climbed the stairs, puffing and panting, carrying a box of tools. He was heavy with grizzled gray hair showing beneath his metal hardhat. "What's going on, Crowley?" His eyes widened when he saw Daniel, as though he'd seen someone familiar. "Is that Robles, the guy that used to be our engineer?"

Nancy looked up at the man. They'd find out soon enough who it was. "Yes, it is." She looked back down at Daniel, wishing that she could help him. "Shouldn't we take him downstairs?" she asked.

"Lady, I don't want to move him in case I make things worse for him. Wait for the ambulance guys, they'll have a stretcher. Better that way." The grizzled haired man frowned. "It isn't safe here, in fact, it's dangerous. We just had a steam accident. I don't want anything like that to happen again. So, I'm going to have to ask you to go downstairs and leave the building--"

"I want to stay with him."

"Lady, four people died when number three blew up. There's always a chance this leak is from a similar problem," the grizzle-haired man said. He seemed to be in charge. "I don't want to take any chances." He turned to the red-haired man. "Jimmy, go get the first aid kit, from downstairs. The big one."

As Jimmy went down the stairs two steps at a time, Nancy saw a uniformed man pass him on the way up. *Police,* she thought. *That was quick.*

"Jeez, here comes the toy cop," the grizzle-haired man said. "Plant security." He turned to Crowley. "Did you call him first? Gonna be a problem if you didn't."

"Yeah, I called." Crowley shook his head. "He said he had to clear all communications with the police or outside agencies with Captain O'Brien, who, apparently, is currently unavailable. That's when I used an outside line to get help."

"What's going on here?" the security guard said. His nametag said Sergeant Blodgett. His eyes swiveled down at the supine figure of Daniel on the floor. "Who's that?" he began, and then swallowed hard. "Is that blood?"

"That's why we need an ambulance," Crowley said.

Blodgett looked around and then focused on Nancy. "Who're you? What're you doing here?"

"Blodgett, get her out of here," the grizzle-haired man said, frowning at the guard. "We don't know what caused the steam leak. It may be the same thing as number three. And, supposedly, there's someone still in the manifold room. Understand? We already called for an ambulance and the cops. They'll be here soon."

Blodgett swallowed hard again. "Yeah, right. Miss, come with me, right now." He pointed toward the stairs.

"I don't want to leave him," Nancy said.

"Miss," the grizzle-haired man said. "We're not going anywhere until the medics get here, okay? It'll be safer for you outside. I don't think you know how dangerous it is here right now." The serious frown on the man's face deepened.

Dangerous? Nancy thought. *What if that man with the gun comes out here?* "He's badly hurt, I want to make sure he's treated right."

"Lady, if you don't move it right now, I'm gonna have to use force." Blodgett put his hand on his nightstick. He licked his lips, as though he was about to sit down to a good meal.

Nancy turned to the grizzle-haired man, "Please look after him, won't you?"

The man nodded. "I'll do my best." He pointed at Daniel. "I know who he is. I'll make sure he's treated right. You can count on it."

Nancy followed the security guard down the stairs. He directed her out to the street, past the wire fence and the chain link gate. He ordered to her stay there and left, mumbling something about returning to the crime scene.

Alone on the sidewalk, in a light drizzle, Nancy waited for the ambulance.

Chapter 48

Nancy wrapped her arms around herself and shivered. *Where are the police? It seemed like ages since those men in blue coveralls dialed for help. I can't believe they made me leave. They told me it was dangerous. Dangerous? They have no idea.* Another shiver ran up her spine and it wasn't from the cold. The manila envelope that was tucked inside the front of her slacks pinched her damp flesh. *I've got to keep it safe. It's what we came for.* She adjusted its position.

A siren screamed in the distance and her vision sharpened.

In the drifting drizzle, haloes of harsh, blue light formed rainbows around mercury street lamps. Old newspapers and weeds littered the cracked sidewalks. Hulking factory buildings of Schirmerling Tire and Rubber Company lined the glistening street. Steam swirled around the factory that was busy with the sounds of industry. Nancy could smell the acrid aroma of chemicals and the sulfur stink of curing rubber that left a bitter taste in her mouth.

She stepped to the curb as a police car, siren wailing and red lights flashing, turned onto the street. *Come on*, she thought, *hurry, Daniel's been shot*. Just the thought of his being hurt made her heart lurch. *Dear God, please don't let him die!*

She stepped onto the street and waved.

An Akron city police car stopped in front of her. The officer inside talked briefly into a microphone before getting out.

"What's the problem, lady?" The short, heavy-set police officer adjusted his peaked hat and put his hand on his gun. He sounded hostile. A second police car pulled up.

"Daniel's inside," she said, "he's been shot--"

"Where's the shooter, ma'am?" The policeman's hand tightened on the handle of his gun.

"Inside the boiler house. I locked him in." Her voice quivered. "Daniel's unconscious, bleeding. He needs help right away." She saw again the image of Daniel covered with blood. "I tried to get him out, but I couldn't carry him down the stairs." The lump in her throat threatened to choke her voice.

"Where is he, ma'am?" A second police officer, tall and gawky with a noticeable overbite, joined the first officer. Even though he carried a shotgun, his voice was softer, even gentle. "Who is he? What's your relationship to him?"

An ambulance rolled to a halt, siren fading.

"He's in there." Nancy pointed to the boiler house. "On the second floor, at the top of the stairs. There are some workers with him. His name is Daniel Robles. He's a close friend."

The two officers glanced at each other and nodded. They went to the partially opened chain-link gate and pushed it open wide. They guided the ambulance past the ramshackle guard hut toward the boiler house.

An unmarked car with a flashing red light on its dashboard pulled through the gate entrance. Two men got out, and one hurried through the gate.

Nancy started to follow the police officer when a hand tapped her shoulder. "You can't go in there, ma'am," a voice said.

"Why not?" She turned to see a police officer. "My friend's in there; he's badly hurt."

"Ma'am, a shooting makes it a crime scene. You can't go there. Stay here." The officer's mouth had the tight, hard expression of controlled neutrality. He shook his head. "Let us do our job, okay?"

A cold shiver swept through her. It wasn't just from being wet in the cool night air; it was also the frustration of not knowing--fearing that Daniel might be dead. She wrestled with her feelings and caught her breath. "My," she started to say. My *what?* she thought. *My friend? My lover? Now he may be dead.* "My friend is in there. I've got to see him." The lump in her throat grew larger. "I was there when he got shot."

"I see," the officer said. "Ma'am, please sit in the back of this car." He directed her to the unmarked police car and opened its rear door.

"I've got to--" she began.

"Ma'am, sit in the back of the car." The officer extended his arm. "I'm not going to ask you again. You said a crime has been committed. You seem to know something about it. You're a witness. Therefore, you have to wait until we can take your statement. Understand?" The officer's voice was louder, harder. His chin jutted out, as though daring the world to take a poke at it.

Weariness and depression swept over her. She bit her lower lip. The officer put his hand on her head and guided her into the back of the car. She could smell second-hand cigarette smoke and a hint of vomit mingling with sweaty odors reminiscent of a locker room. There were splits and cigarette burns in the gray plastic that covered the back seat. A crushed paper cup and a crumpled fast-food wrapper lay on the floor.

The door squealed shut with a metallic clang.

There were no door handles or window winders inside, and a wire screen divided the front seat from the rear. She couldn't get out unless someone opened the door. She squirmed, uncomfortable. She realized she was a prisoner.

#

Nancy had no idea how long it was before two teams of men hurried out of the boiler house carrying stretchers. It seemed to take forever. As they slid them into the ambulance, she tried to see who was on them but couldn't tell. Moments later, the vehicle left with its siren screaming and red lights flashing.

A slim man with graying hair in a grubby tan raincoat opened the front passenger door and slid in. He turned toward her and looked through the steel mesh. His face, long and thin, was accentuated by long sideburns, and his eyes carried a wealth of worry and weariness.

"Ma'am, I'm Detective Grueden with the Akron police." He pulled back his coat to reveal a badge pinned to the top pocket of a gray suit that had seen better days. "Officer Kincaid says that you know something about this." He jerked his thumb in the direction of the boiler house.

"Yes," Nancy said. "How's Daniel? Is he all right?"

Grueden sniffed. "One's shot, and the other's been, well, cooked. They're both alive, just barely. They're on their way to the hospital. What d'you know about this?"

The police radio squawked and words came out in the strange code of numbers and letters that only police and emergency workers seem to understand. Nancy caught the words, "One's D.O.A. We couldn't save him." She felt her throat constrict, and a giant lock clamped down on her chest.

"Ten-four," Grueden said into the microphone.

She forced out the words. "Who died? Was it Daniel?" The vice gripping her heart tightened.

Grueden shrugged and shook his head. "I dunno. They didn't say. I'll get their identities later. Meanwhile, it's in your best interest to tell me what you know about this."

Nancy leaned forward and put her head in her hands. "I was there when it happened. I saw the man shoot Daniel." The constriction in her throat grew enormous, choking off her words. She tried to maintain control as tears filled her eyes.

The seat squeaked loudly as the heavyset policeman eased in behind the wheel. "What's going on, sir?"

"Let's go downtown," Grueden said. "We've got at least one fatality, possibly a homicide and this lady's a material witness." He turned to face forward and waved his hand as though encouraging the driver to get moving.

"How about the crime scene?"

"Forensics is coming." Grueden shrugged. "They won't find much. It's been steam cleaned."

Chapter 49

Fears about Daniel overwhelmed Nancy and she couldn't stop the tears. The detective, Grueden, stopped asking questions and remained silent. The remainder of the trip to the police station was a kaleidoscope of city lights and pothole-filled streets. She had no idea where they were until they pulled up to a grimy, three-story building with a gray stone façade. The officers hustled her inside. After a lengthy trip down brightly lit corridors that echoed every footstep, they put her into a small room. It held a small wooden table and two chairs. A raft of fluorescent lights hung over the table.

After a short wait alone, Grueden returned with two Styrofoam cups of coffee and gave one to her. "It's all I could find this time of night." He shrugged and retrieved envelopes of sugar and creamer from his coat pocket.

"D'you feel up to telling me what happened?"

Nancy realized that Grueden wasn't hostile; he was just doing his job. She bit her lower lip. "I guess so."

\#

"Did you find out what happened to Daniel?" Nancy said. Amid her fear, she felt a weariness unlike anything she'd previously encountered. Grueden questioned her for two hours, going over her story of the events at STR's boiler house again and again. From the onset, she decided to tell the police the truth as to what had happened and why, except she didn't tell them about finding the memos and ultrasonic test data about boiler number three superheater. It was still in the manila envelope tucked inside the front of her slacks. She had no intention of giving it up, for she was sure that would clear Daniel, but she wanted to talk to a lawyer first.

"I'll see if there's any news from the hospital." Grueden stood up and left the room. It was almost four a.m.

Nancy laid her head in her arms, but couldn't sleep. The images of Daniel's pale face, the blood and the terrible sounds of that horrible place filled her mind.

The door creaked open. It was Gruden.

Grueden sat down in the chair opposite to her. His long face seemed almost gray and the fluorescent lights exacerbated the bags under his eyes. "Daniel Robles is out of surgery. They've removed the bullet, but there was a lot of damage," he said. "The other man, O'Brien, is dead. The steam got to him. We found his gun. Forensics will check the bullet to see if it matches the gun."

Nancy sat upright. "Daniel's alive?" A wave of hope surged through her. "How is he?"

Grueden took a deep breath and looked down. "He's not in good shape. The surgeons aren't saying much about him. He's got a hole in his right lung. He lost a lot of blood."

"Oh, no." Nancy covered her eyes. *Dear God, please save Daniel's life.* She offered up a silent prayer, hoping against hope.

Grueden cleared his throat. "He's unconscious. It doesn't look good. They've got him in recovery, on life support. I've put an officer outside his room." He rose to his feet. "Ma'am, I'm sorry." He went to the door and stopped. "Look, I've got to charge you with unlawful entry, so you'll have to post a bond. It's not a big deal."

Nancy looked up. She saw the look on the detective's face and realized that he'd offered the closest thing to sympathy of anyone this evening. "Can I go to the hospital now?"

Grueden frowned briefly. "First, there're some papers you have to sign at the front desk; then you can go." He turned as if to go, then stopped. "You don't have a car." It was more of a question than a statement.

"No," she said. "Daniel has the van's keys. It's still in the parking lot at STR." Having to get around Akron, a city that she knew nothing about, was a reality that she hadn't yet faced. "Can you give me a lift to the hospital?"

"I'll have a patrolman take you there after you're done at the front desk. I'm not supposed to do this, but I'll have the van towed over to the hospital instead of the pound.

If you can get the keys, you can pick it up there."

#

"Mr. Hamilton Pogue." Nancy leaned against the phone cubicle. She felt ethereal, almost disconnected, for it was already nine a.m. It had been a night without any sleep. The lobby of Akron Superior Hospital had pale yellow walls and checkerboard patterned tiles on the floor that all hospitals seemed to have. A vase of drooping flowers decorated the reception desk. There was the usual smell of disinfectant and stale food. She waited as the operator at Jones Knight law firm routed her telephone call. "Ham?"

Nancy recounted what had happened and the need for legal assistance. "I have no idea why that man shot Daniel. He also shot at me several times."

Ham's voice sounded faint and fuzzy over the phone. "What happened to the man? Did the police arrest him?"

Nancy grimaced. "He's dead. He got..." she hesitated. "Parboiled by steam."

"Parboiled?" Ham's voice rose an octave. "You'd better explain everything. Wait, better yet, come to my office so we can go over it."

"I can't do that. I'm staying here at the hospital until I know about Daniel. They've just transferred him to the intensive care unit. He's still on life support." She took a breath. "Can you come here? I need advice on some other issues. It appears that the management of STR tried to frame Daniel for the boiler explosion there. We have evidence they forged documents to make him appear guilty."

"Evidence? What kind of evidence?"

"Daniel sent memos to management warning them the boiler needed repair. This is the boiler that blew up and killed four men. Apparently, Daniel included test information that proved the boiler was defective. However, somebody in management destroyed the memos and put fake memos in the files to make it look like Daniel was negligent. Last night, right before Daniel got shot, he recovered the memos and the original test data that proves he warned management about the boilers. I have those memos with me."

"Really?" Ham said. "In that case, I'll be there as soon as I can. I know how to deal with something like that."

Chapter 50

June 16, 1970.

"Daniel." Nancy had a gritty feeling that came from taking the overnight flight from San Francisco to Cleveland. She had returned to California to take care of her family's business once she was sure Daniel would recover. Almost three weeks had passed before she got a call telling her Daniel would be discharged. Upon hearing the news, she had booked a flight right away.

Daniel looked up and a smile blossomed across his face. "Nancy, so good to see you." He was sitting on the edge of the hospital bed, dressed in blue striped pajamas. His face was gaunt and pale. There was only one bed in the room, which overlooked the tree-filled Cuyahoga River valley. The window was open, and the sound of birds filtered in past the swaying curtains. A vase of multi-colored flowers perched on the window ledge. He stood and raised his arms toward her.

"How do you feel?" Nancy said after she kissed him. She wanted to squeeze him, but resisted the urge. The surgeon had told her that O'Brien's bullet was the type that expanded and had torn a hole in Daniel's right lung. Two ribs had been broken, and he had a golf ball-sized scar on his chest.

"Much better, thank you. They're letting me out tomorrow." He smiled widely. "When did you get in?" They both sat on the edge of the bed.

She scrunched up her face. "This morning, on the red-eye." She took his hand and pulled it up to her face, kissing it. "I've got some interesting news for you. You know those files we got from STR?" She raised her eyebrows.

Daniel frowned. "I thought I'd lost them in the manifold room." The police said the steam had destroyed all the evidence, effectively cleaning all surfaces. "They said the steam had turned all the cardboard boxes and paper into pulp."

"No, I had them. I didn't tell the police." She tried to suppress a smile. "Ham Pogue believes you've got grounds to sue STR because of what Hodges and O'Brien did to you. Ham has already opened negotiations with STR."

"I didn't know anything about this." Daniel's eyebrows came together in the beginning of a frown. "Why didn't you tell me?"

"Since you were so ill, I took the liberty to lay the groundwork for you," Nancy said. "You've got to retain Ham so he can represent you. He's been looking into this at my request. He believes you have good grounds for a lawsuit." She leaned forward and kissed him. "I've really missed you. I was worried sick."

"Nancy, I don't know how to thank you." He took her hands and pulled her close to him. "You bailed me out, you saved my life and you're still looking after me." He closed his eyes and nuzzled her hair. "I don't ever want to lose you."

"Don't worry, you won't." Nancy stroked his hair and then pulled his head onto her chest. "I've missed you. I keep thinking about our being together. We've got to make up for all that lost time."

"If you'll let me, I'll do my very best to make it up to you." Daniel pulled Nancy's hands to his lips. "I love you, Nancy Chanson, more than I've ever loved anyone."

#

"I'm not disturbing anything, am I?" Detective Grueden stood in the doorway, a crumpled trace of a smile on his face. His hair needed combing and his jacket was rumpled. "I was in the area and decided to stop by." His smile widened. "I want to tell you what we learned. Can I come in?"

Daniel nodded. He still felt a little leery about the police, for they'd questioned him several times at length over his entry into STR and what he knew about the meth lab he'd found. At first the police had seemed hostile, but later, he found them almost neutral. They hadn't answered any of his questions about what was going on, and Hector hadn't learned anything either.

"All charges have been dropped. STR decided it was in their best interests to abandon the unlawful entry charge." Grueden slipped into a chair and leaned back. "We think we know what happened. However, proving it is another story. Also, the San Francisco police finally lifted a partial fingerprint from the drug paraphernalia in your apartment there. It's a match with O'Brien's. So you're cleared on that count.

"We found evidence in O'Brien's apartment that leads us to believe he was the one manufacturing the illegal drugs. You discovered his lab. That explains him copping an attitude."

"Attitude?" Daniel said. "That monster tried to kill me."

"We also found items belonging to Rogan, the guy from STR research, which make us think O'Brien had something to do with Rogan's disappearance. But, we have no indication as to Rogan's whereabouts."

Daniel shrugged. "I never met Rogan. I don't even know what he looked like."

"As for the boiler explosion, I've heard the state investigators found your files very interesting. A guy by the name of Hodges apparently forged memos to cover his ass. Seems he knew all along about the condition of the boiler." Grueden's eyebrows rose briefly. "That makes him and STR criminally negligent. The local DA is licking his chops over this one."

"Where does this leave me?" Daniel said.

Grueden rose to his feet. "We keep tripping over your attorney, Pogue, who's been taking depositions from our people and other witnesses. I get the feeling he's going after STR big time. I hope he makes them pay. They hired O'Brien, who was a dirty cop when he was on the force.

Apparently he had quite a history in the Philadelphia police department, where he was a detective. We don't like dirty cops and O'Brien was a real scumbag."

"That's what I was telling you about earlier," Nancy said.

Grueden rose and stopped in the doorway and looked at Daniel. "Next time, give us a chance before you go breaking in someplace to clear your name, okay? Less chance of picking up a chunk of hot lead. Just wanted to let you know we don't have any interest in you anymore. Stop by the station, and we'll take care of the paperwork. See you around." He nodded and left.

Daniel turned to Nancy. "Now what?"

"Tomorrow, you're getting on a plane to California. You're coming home with me, where I'm going to make sure you recover properly." Nancy leaned forward and kissed him.

Epilogue

October 24, 1970.

Daniel slowed to a walk, his chest sore from the run. He was recovering from the injury steadily, but its damage would be with him for the rest of his life.

Ordered rows of vines stretched away from the road to distant hills, golden and sere in the early morning light. He turned down Dealy Lane, toward the white, vine-covered buildings of the Chanson Winery. They were now a familiar sight to him; they had been his home for the last four months while he'd recovered his health and strength. It was a place where he felt comfortable, secure, and wanted. Even though he lived in the small apartment above the cooperage barn, separate from Nancy, there was no one else. They'd already made plans to marry in January. For an instant, he thought of Carol and her self-centered ways. *I'm happy. I only hope she is.*

He'd put everything in place to start the grape vine pruning disposal business for Chanson. This winter Chanson's workers would start shredding the trimmings from the grape vines. When spring arrived, they'd get grass clippings from the local golf courses. They'd mix them with the shredded vines, which would raise the nitrogen-to-carbon ratio. He figured it would take a year for the mixture to decompose and change into compost. Several landscaping firms had expressed an interest in using the compost. It would be much cheaper than the bagged compost that came from Milwaukee, which they used to make topsoil that landscapers used to grow high quality turf.

Daniel thought of it as being a way to pay Nancy and her family for their support while he was broke. In addition, it gave him a sense of participation and belonging.

Ham Pogue had negotiated a settlement from STR that had netted Daniel three hundred and sixty thousand dollars, which eliminated any financial concerns for his immediate future. Sooner or later, he knew he would invest the money, probably in a business because he wanted to get back to work. He had no desire to live off Nancy's income or Chanson winery, even though Phillipe, her father had assured him he was welcome to stay as long as Nancy wanted him around.

Already, he had seen opportunities to apply engineering methodology to winemaking, techniques to improve the efficiencies without compromising quality. This year's crush had been exceptionally good. He had worked with Phillipe so Chanson's entire harvest could be made into their wine, rather than selling off a portion due to processing constraints. That had pleased Phillipe. Other winemakers had already inquired how they'd done it. Daniel had come to realize he liked the whole atmosphere of living in this wine-producing culture. He planned to stay.

#

Carol Meadows stared at herself in the mirror. *I'd better get some new clothes. These are getting too tight.* She rationalized her weight gain as being normal. Many of her lesbian friends felt that the male stereotype of female beauty was wrong. Many felt the Earth Mother image was a more enduring standard of beauty. *What was the word they used? Zaftig?* She liked it because it sounded exotic.

She'd found the Earth Mother image appealed to her, for she did like to eat and dieting was such a bore. Even though Frieda maintained a constant weight, it didn't seem to bother her that Carol had put on a few pounds. In fact, Frieda seemed to like the fact Carol's breasts had gone from a B to a C cup.

I'd better get a move on. We're having a get together with a group of couples at a cute Italian restaurant over in the Portero district. She liked that part of San Francisco, for it had recently become popular with the gay community. It felt like home.

#

Barry Mansky tried to force a smile, but failed as he

shook hands with Harvey Rock. It was the final meeting and the execution of the complex agreement where Bonrock Rubber would acquire Schirmerling in lieu of a bankruptcy filing. Mansky's stock options were now worthless and his severance package had been nullified. He was essentially broke. Tomorrow, he would file for personal bankruptcy due to the lawsuits filed against him. In the back of his mind, he knew he was partly responsible. However, it had been the actions of that asshole, Hodges, which had completely destroyed the company.

"Congratulations," Mansky said. "I'm sure that you'll find Schirmerling to be a fine addition to Bonrock."

Harvey Rock sniffed as though something smelled rotten. "Right. We'll certainly deploy those assets in a rational fashion, raising cash where possible."

Mansky knew that meant Bonrock would hold a fire sale on those parts of Schirmerling that didn't immediately fit their plans. Rock was well known for his ruthless management style.

#

Hodges ignored the stream of chatter and concentrated on the task at hand. He still found it hard to believe how fast everything had turned to shit. First O'Brien turned up dead and the news media treated Robles like some kind of hero. Then the state investigators got Robles's memos and test data on Boiler Number 3. He winced as he remembered Mansky's rage at learning this, how Mansky blamed him for bringing down STR. The state investigators passed their findings to the State Attorney General who brought charges of criminal negligence against both STR and Hodges. He'd just got out of prison, the worst six months of his life, where he'd seen things done he never dreamt people would do to each other.

"Hurry up, Benny," a voice called. "We need another batch. Check your attitude, man, you gotta be a part of the team."

It pissed him off these young kids called him Benny.

 Somehow, they'd learned his name and refused to address him properly or with the respect he thought was his due. *Benny*, he thought, *another insult*. He knew he had better flip these burgers and send them on their way. At his age, with his record, it was the only job that he could get.

#

Detective Grueden closed the file. *I'm never going to solve the Rogan case. There's no body.* However, he was sure O'Brien was responsible for Rogan's disappearance. Proving it was another thing.

Yeah, O'Brien was really in the center of that mess over at STR. He was still disgusted about what he'd found out about O'Brien's background in Philadelphia. O'Brien's finances and gambling habit pointed to another income well beyond his salary, and he certainly didn't work a second job. The traces of methamphetamine in O'Brien's apartment convinced him O'Brien had been involved with Rogan, for it was identical to the methamphetamine found in Rogan's apartment. Yet O'Brien was no longer around to confess. So, maybe justice had been served by that blast of... Grueden looked down at the report - superheated steam.

The End

About the Author:

M.B. Wood, a native of England, began writing in college. Like many of us, the demands of life, completing his education, paying the bills, starting a career, overran his writing ambitions.

As luck would have it, while completing a dry economic series for publication, his muse for fiction returned. This spawned 11 Novels to date, with more in the works.

His series of novels SUPERHEAT, HUNTED, BLOWOUT and TRASH are in the mainstream fiction category.

Wood's writings come from actual life experiences trekking through Australia, South Asia and in the Middle East, something which most of us could not do today, or even in years past.

There's something that focuses the mind when you're brought awake by the muzzle of a soldier's assault rifle up your nostril and a stern looking train conductor demanding your train ticket.

Indeed, when close to death with amoebic dysentery in the high Himalayas, appreciation for life grows strong. It leads to good writing eventually and a good life (married for forty-two years and three cats).

Wood's interests are quite varied. Trained as a Chemist, holding an advanced degree in Economics, he retired from a steady practice as a Registered Professional Engineer. Whether enjoying the thrill of the hunt from high atop a deer stand in Ohio, driving a racecar or in the open skies as a private pilot, he's constantly taking in new experiences to add into his next work.

Rocky River, Ohio, just west of Cleveland is home to Wood. For more information, please find his website http://www.malcolm-wood.com